THE PHILIPPINE PACT

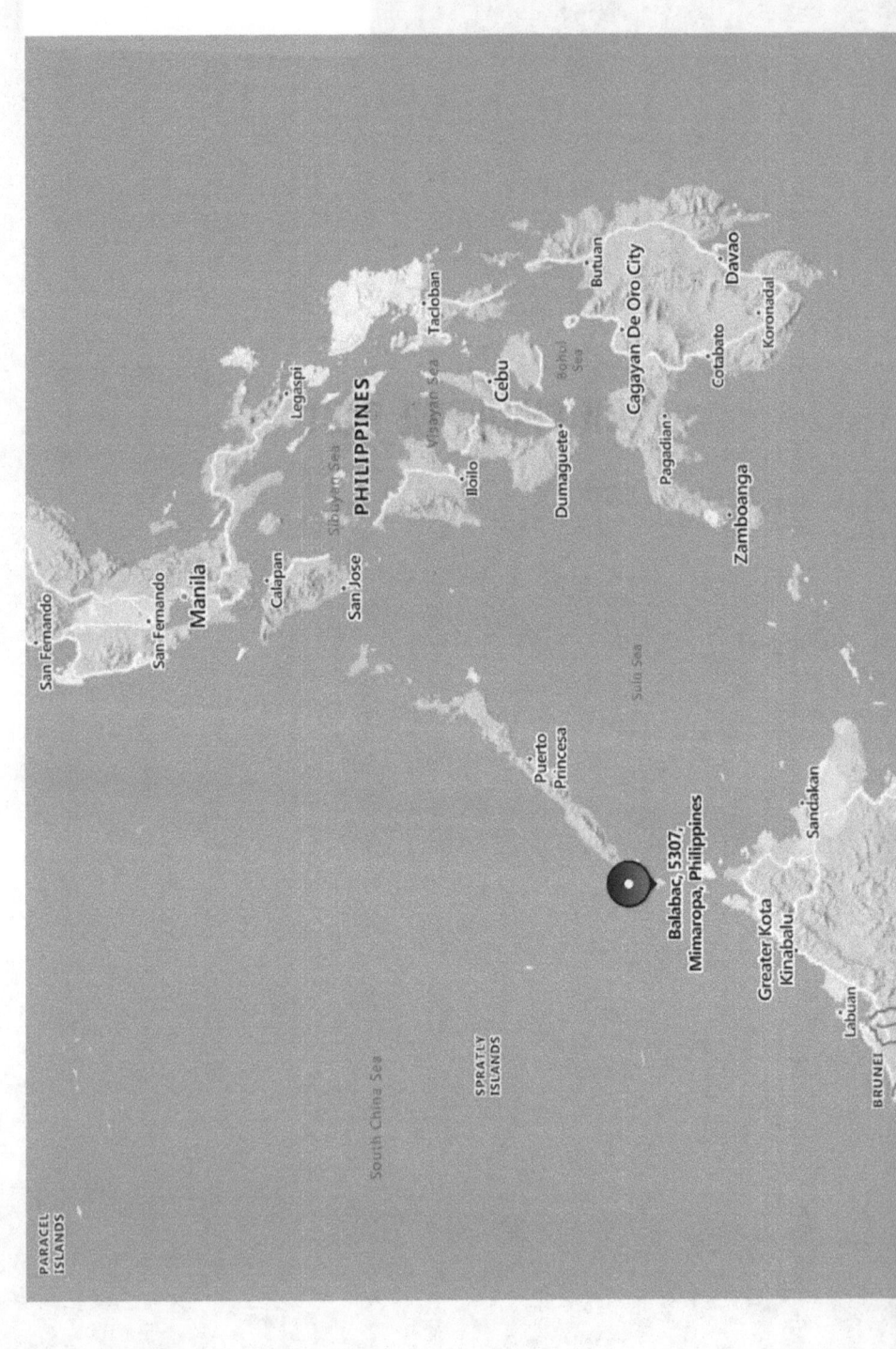

THE PHILIPPINE
PACT

A CONNOR STARK NOVEL

CLAUDE BERUBE

MILFORD
HOUSE

an imprint of Sunbury Press, Inc.
Mechanicsburg, PA USA

MILFORD HOUSE

an imprint of Sunbury Press, Inc.
Mechanicsburg, PA USA

For information about special discounts for bulk purchases, please contact Sunbury Press Orders Dept. at (855) 338-8359 or orders@sunburypress.com.

To request one of our authors for speaking engagements or book signings, please contact Sunbury Press Publicity Dept. at publicity@sunburypress.com.

FIRST MILFORD HOUSE PRESS EDITION: April 2023

Set in Adobe Garamond Pro | Interior design by Crystal Devine | Cover by Tobi Afran | Edited by Sarah Peachey.

Publisher's Cataloging-in-Publication Data
Names: Berube, Claude, author.
Title: The Philippine Pact : a Connor Stark novel / Claude Berube.
Description: First trade paperback edition. | Mechanicsburg, PA : Milford House Press, 2023.
Summary: Connor Stark's Highland Maritime Defense private security company is training elements of the Philippine Navy on a remote island when terrorists join China to establish a foothold in the Western Pacific. Only Stark's team stands in their way.
Identifiers: ISBN : 978-1-62006-490-0 (paperback) | 979-8-88819-102-6 (ePub).
Subjects: FICTION / Thrillers / Military | FICTION / Thrillers / Terrorism | FICTION / Thrillers / Political.

Product of the United States of America
0 1 1 2 3 5 8 13 21 34 55

Continue the Enlightenment!

For Command Master Chief Richard Curtis, USN (Ret)

Lahat ng gubat ay may ahas.

Every jungle has a snake.

—Filipino proverb

The Israeli-built twin-engine G280 Gulfstream jet cruised at a comfortable altitude of thirty thousand feet at a speed of 520 miles per hour. No reasonable creature comfort had been spared for this jet. The previous president wanted comfort and the staff knew that for him, it meant luxury, no matter the cost. She glanced out the right-side window as they passed over the archipelago she governed. Panay was behind them as they cruised over the Visayan Sea.

Each of the ten passenger seats was filled with her closest staff as well as the secretary of national defense, the chairman of the Joint Chiefs, and the chief of the navy. The president rose and placed one hand on her seat, pointing to her aide with the other.

"Water," she said curtly.

The aide quickly got a cold bottle from the flight attendant as the jet hit some turbulence. He lost his balance and dropped the bottle as it rolled under the last seats to the rear of the cabin. The president, still securely holding the seat, rolled her eyes.

"Get another bottle," she ordered.

The senior officers suppressed a chuckle. They knew that to do otherwise would incur a curt, sharp rebuke like the ones that had made her famous in the country, especially among the media. The people loved her for it. They found it an honest sign of leadership, and they thought the media deserved it. They were less enamored of the vice president, a quiet, minor politician.

The heavily insulated cabin with an internal noise-canceling system made it easy to hear anyone nearby. The passengers could see but not hear the two FA-50 Fighting Eagle jets from the Philippine Air Force providing escort for the Gulfstream for the first leg of the two-hour trip. The jets didn't have the legs to make it from Luzon to Mindanao. Two different Air Force teams were needed for the eight-hundred-mile journey. Visible now were the jets that had assumed duties for the second leg.

The president snapped her fingers at the aide's hand, which now held the day's schedule. She returned to her seat and swiveled it toward the aisle as the passengers did the same to face each other. The senior officers, aides, and press secretary shuffled their briefing papers.

"Start," the president said to the scheduler as she sipped some water.

"We land in Davao City. You'll be greeted by a local delegation headed by the mayor."

"He's an asshole," the president muttered under her breath. The scheduler continued, pretending she hadn't heard the comment. Aides tended to do that a lot with the president.

"Your limousine and protective detail have been prepositioned at the airport. After you shake the mayor's hand, you'll be driving directly to Headquarters Naval Forces Eastern Mindanao to address navy personnel there. Your speech is here."

The president lifted her chin to read the speech better. At first, she eschewed reading glasses as a sign of physical weakness but realized they conveyed an air of intelligence. Her lifted chin gave her an affected, imperious look. She was fine with her people viewing her as a benevolent empress.

"Admiral, will any foreign representatives be there?"

"Yes, Madam President," he said, double-checking his notes. "The naval attachés from the United States, Canada, United Kingdom, the Republic of Korea, Japan, and Taiwan. The speech will mention cooperative engagements, including the ongoing multinational exercise."

"Do you foresee any issues, Admiral?"

"We received a formal protest from the Chinese defense attaché."

"Fuck them," she said. "And fuck their new islands," she said of the former coral reefs China had covered with concrete and upon which they built military bases.

"We can't hold them off, Madam President," interjected the secretary of national defense.

"That's why we need the other countries. Every day China takes more and more. If the Americans had had any balls a few years ago, they could have helped us prevent those islands from being built and militarized. It stops here."

"Multinational exercises don't always translate into political will," the chairman of the Joint Chiefs added.

"No. But they're a start. Even if the Americans don't help in the end, we have to build up an anti-China partnership with Japan, Korea, and Taiwan. Anything else?"

"The headquarters you are touring is at Naval Station Felix Apolinario," the admiral said. "Three weeks ago, we briefed you on the history of attacks in Mindanao."

"I want to know why you haven't been able to stop the attacks since then," she said. "This speech has me congratulating the station's personnel. What am I congratulating them for if you're not stopping those attacks?" She slapped the speech against the arm rest.

"One challenge for us is that we still don't know who they are, Madam President," the admiral replied. "We don't know if they're Jamaah Islamiya, the Moro Islamic Liberation Front, Abu Sayyaf, or the New People's Army."

"Not the New People's Army," the chairman interjected. "We haven't heard anything from them in a year. It's like they've disappeared or been absorbed into other groups."

"Still," the admiral continued, "those we have killed have no identifying information. Those we tried to capture killed themselves. They don't have any patterns to their attacks."

"The definition of insanity is to repeatedly attempt the same thing with the same failed results. What can we do differently in Mindanao?" she asked, not for the first time. If she had learned one thing as president, her generals and admirals were conservative, risk-averse, and short-sighted.

"Our junior officers have been training with the private security company you ordered us to work with. We would prefer instead to work with our formal naval partners," the admiral said, uncharacteristically challenging the president's idea. He had the least to lose by refuting her. The admiral was just a few months away from retiring.

"We leverage anywhere with anyone to achieve our goals, Admiral. Remember that or perhaps old thinking should be retired even sooner," she snapped. The admiral bowed his head in silent submission.

"Are we fucking clear, people? We use whatever we have to protect our interests," she barked.

"Madam President, there's a call for you," the aide said. "It wasn't on the schedule."

"Who is it?"

"It's the gentleman from Hong Kong. But he didn't call on the plane's line. He called my phone. I've never given him my personal number."

"Give it to me," she said, stretching out her arm for the phone.

"Yes?"

"You haven't stopped. We told you to stop opposing us. Do you understand that?" said the cold voice.

"Who the hell do you think you are?"

"I'm the person who is stopping you." The line went dead. The president noticed the chairman squint at something out the window. She turned in time to see one of her escort jets explode. The Gulfstream lurched to the left in response.

She never saw the second AIM-9 Sidewinder missile launch from the remaining escort. It hit one of the engines, disintegrating it and half the tail. The president's aide, flight attendant, and three others were immediately sucked out. The president managed to grab the handle of the seat in front of her as the jet went into a tailspin, throwing her senior military leaders around as another lost his own grip and joined the other passengers in the sky outside. The chairman wailed for his wife and children while the others were silent, both from the confusion of how the attack happened to the realization that their own deaths were imminent. The president heard one of the pilots screaming into the radio about the attack. There was no response.

The president just held on and closed her eyes. She cursed her killers, then remembered the highlights of her life.

"It was a hell of a ride. Fuck 'em," she said aloud shortly before the fuselage crashed into the sea.

CHAPTER 1

SULU SEA

"She's riding as smooth as ever, boss," the big, red-headed engineer said.

The two men were topside just outside the off-center pilothouse of the twin-hulled ship. There was nothing but blue water in their three-hundred-sixty-degree view. Local fishing vessels dotted the scene. A few freighters and tankers in the distance were transiting east to west, west to east, and one was heading north. The only other unusual ship was two miles off the port quarter. Both ships were nearly identical.

"She's looking good, too," the engineer remarked. "Wish you'd taken command of her instead?"

Connor Stark looked wistfully at the latest addition to his company. *Minerva*, like her older sister-ship *Syren*, was a small-waterplane-area twin-hull (SWATH), 1,600-ton aluminum ship powered by two LM2500 gas turbines. The interior could house shipping containers individualized as extra crew berthing, medical bays, or any other mission-specific module they needed.

"No. She's got a great skipper, Jay," Stark replied.

They had slipped out from near Davao City in the early morning hours while it was still dark. They had already transited the passage between Zamboanga province and Basilan Island, the last land masses before their ultimate destination. Stark tapped on the open window of the pilothouse. His executive officer put up three fingers, then made two zero signs with her thumb and forefinger. She made a fist, then opened it up to two fingers. She used both hands for two and five fingers.

"Course three-zero-zero, twenty-seven knots," he said more for his own benefit than Jay's.

"What's your worry level, boss? Zero, no worries, or ten, 'oh shit, oh shit'?"

Stark paused momentarily. "I think we're always safe at five—no situation is ever as perfect as you want, and level five has you ready just in case anything goes down."

"Is that why you're out here?"

"Out where?"

"Topside instead of the pilothouse."

"Why do you say that?"

"Being in there won't help except to change speed or course. You've been going back and forth between the extra watchstanders on deck," Jay observed as he motioned to the four crewmembers posted on each corner of the two-hundred-sixty-foot vessel. Those were only the watchstanders. Four more were at the posts on the port and starboard guns. He knew *Minerva*'s captain had similarly positioned some of her crew.

"The traffic is comparatively light right now, but without our radars and radios, we just need to be extra vigilant. I don't need either of our ships hitting or getting hit by another vessel."

"Do we really have to do this?"

"Yes, we do. I know it's just an exercise, but we're not in a friendly region," Stark said.

"Are we ever?"

"Point taken."

"The new paint jobs aren't enough?" Jay asked.

Connor looked over at *Minerva* again. Had there been even the slightest fog or difference in light, she'd have been difficult to see. Both ships had a new dazzle-camouflage paint scheme of blues, grays, and blacks, abandoning the old gray hull paint. But they also had another advantage—or disadvantage if one was conning the ship.

"We had to go to EMCON." Emissions Control. That meant no communications, no radar, no electronics were to be used. That also meant navigating by sight only.

"It's one thing only to see those ships by sight, Connor. It's another level of dangerous for them not to see us."

"You were the one that put together the new paint project, Jay. Keep coming up with those brilliant ideas and I may just keep you employed for a few more weeks," he said, winking at the taller and broader man.

Connor had first met Jay Warren when they worked on *Syren* when it was simply known by the Navy as FSF-1 *Sea Fighter*, an experimental ship. Connor had been its first CO as a young lieutenant commander. Jay was one of the scientists and engineers assigned to it by the Office of Naval Research. Stark never would have guessed that within a short time, he'd be drummed out of the Navy and Jay would lose his job as a Navy civilian or that both would return to this ship as the flagship of Stark's company.

"After that mission in Sri Lanka, boss, I thought we needed something a little more defensive. If you hadn't made that deal with Ambassador Sumner and gotten all that money, I never could have had what I needed to develop it."

"I told you we don't talk about that, but yeah, that money's paid for a lot—the paint, building *Minerva*, and paying off the mortgage for Maggie's bar back home." He didn't mention helping Gunny Willis's family with their own home and a fund for his kids as well as the other crew he'd lost in Sri Lanka and Yemen.

"I'm still not a fan of shaving off a knot or two from our top speed, Jay," he said as they began to walk around the deck.

"It couldn't be helped. You add that much paint to a frame and it's going to add weight and reduce speed. Some of the airlines minimize their paint patterns for the opposite reason. Less paint means less weight and better fuel efficiency."

Radar-absorbent paint wasn't unheard of but it was expensive. And, as they knew, it had drawbacks. Still, Jay had convinced Stark of the benefits.

"Your contacts in Israel helped a lot," Jay noted to Stark.

"Help is easy when you pay for something or trade." Stark almost regretted giving the Israelis some of the electromagnetic pulse source elements from the Sri Lanka mission. But in return, the Israelis provided paint that had nanoparticles. Stark didn't understand the science behind it, but watching Jay bounce up and down when he first heard he might get it meant it was the right thing to do. If the Israelis did use it, America's national security advisor would know exactly who gave it to them.

"You need coffee," Jay said. "I know you want to stay up here. I'll get some for both of us and we can chat some more about Dragonfly."

Jay went below as Stark turned in a circle, again watching the horizon. Added eyes never hurt good seamanship. A few Filipino officers and sailors were topside now, admiring the waters of their home country. This assignment was a proof of concept for their government in many ways. Looking ahead to where Palawan would be over the horizon, Stark revised his assessment of caution from a five to a seven.

SOUTH CHINA SEA

Sergei Stepanovich Makarov threw his head back as he emptied the one glass he entitled himself to after tonight's mission. He chuckled lightly at the thought of the stereotypical vodka-drinking Russian male. But it was true. He had watched it since he'd been a child growing up outside Donetsk. Statistics didn't lie. Russia had a high death rate among men due to alcohol consumption. But that statistic didn't stop them from drinking and dying. Makarov drank, but at least he had enough self-control to prevent it from overtaking his body. He needed what quickly aging body he had to make money in this environment.

He had been hydrating since returning to the small cabin. He shuffled across the passageway to the head and relieved himself. He tried to flush the toilet, yellowed by time and dried urine, but the chain broke. He shifted to the equally disgusting sink. The faucet sputtered brownish water before a clearer flow rinsed his hands of the soap. He pushed the door open, though it was already partially open since the bottom hinge was gone and the wooden door hung on precariously to the frame. Even at the end of the Soviet Union, when he was a young naval officer, the ships weren't this bad. This, however, was pretty standard for every fishing vessel from this region of the world.

He had once read a *New York Times* series called "The Outlaw Ocean" by a reporter who went to such ships. The reporter covered how the world's marine protein was caught on rusty, dilapidated fishing vessels by crews from developing and third-world countries who might not see their home again for years. They were essentially modern slaves housed in the worst of conditions by shady companies at best and criminal elements at worst. High-end shoppers buying fish at upscale markets in Washington, DC, had no idea in what conditions that fish was caught. If they did, they might drink vodka like Russians to rid themselves of the taste and the thought of how that seafood was stored on a rusty ship like this. Fortunately, there were no Whole Foods in Russia. At least not yet.

The first time he had seen a large body of water was during a school trip to Odessa and Sevastopol. There he saw the Soviet Black Sea Fleet when it could still challenge the United States. Then he saw the guided missile cruiser *Slava*. Her design was dominated by the eight Bazalt anti-ship missile launchers on each side of the superstructure. That looked like a warship, unlike the photos he had seen of America's then-new *Ticonderoga*-class cruisers. He wanted to serve the Soviet Union. He wanted to serve on *Slava*. He wanted to take that ship into battle with the Americans and sweep them from the seas. He got his first two wishes.

Makarov continued with the new Russian Navy for as long as he could after the fall of the Soviet Union, but with little money for ship deployments, he accepted an offer to wear the black beret of the Russian Spetsnaz special operations naval force. After a few years, even that was unsatisfactory, and he sought opportunities outside Russia.

A Chinese company saw the value of an experienced naval and maritime officer. Makarov took over its small maritime operations branch and expanded it. The money was good. The mission was as good as he could get. But as with everything, there was always a price.

Makarov headed below to the engine room, unusually quiet since they were simply drifting. The Malaysian chief engineer, his coveralls and hands perpetually covered in dirt and grease, painstakingly went through the list of parts they'd need to replace next time they could get resupplied by one of his ships. Makarov just wished the crew could fix the toilet.

He spent the next two hours inspecting each compartment on the ship. Few met any standards at all, but they didn't have to. It was a fishing vessel with no fish, nor would it be again.

He checked his watch as he entered his last stop—the bridge. A crewman was at the helm almost unnecessarily. There were no nearby ships and, without the engine on, the wheel could only make the tiller respond to the gentle current. Makarov motioned for the crewman to leave. After he secured the hatch behind him, Makarov plopped himself onto the captain's chair, its black vinyl cover torn in several places, exposing the cheap foam.

"How much longer do we have to wait here, Sergei," asked one of the two figures. Crossing her arms, she stood on one foot with her other resting on the bulkhead. Her brown roots were quickly overtaking her bleached-blond hair, the tragedy of being far from port and some of life's luxuries.

"Be patient for once, Toni. The other boat will meet us here. Are you packed?"

"I never unpacked. I haven't even taken a shower. There's no air conditioning, there isn't a breeze outside, and this ship smells like shit," she complained. "And you've seen this crew. Hell, it's like they haven't even seen a woman before." No, but it had been months or years since they had. To be fair, she rarely complained, but then again, she was used to living in better conditions. He didn't feel sorry for this American. Still, it was helpful to understand she had a breaking point. She was not invulnerable. But it took a few years of working with her to see her crack her manufactured façade, even for a few moments.

He looked at the other person on the bridge, who rarely even spoke. Jianyu Qin had been part of Makarov's team for longer than had Toni. Qin was his gunman. One of the best snipers in China, as he had proven yet again that night. Their employer once told Makarov that Qin honed his skill behind the lines with the Fedayeen Saddam in Iraq and the Taliban in Afghanistan, racking up almost as many kills as Chris Kyle, the famed American sniper. But no one would hear about Qin, much less make a movie about his life. Qin was precise and cold and very, very private. Makarov remembered how cool he was when Qin took a shot that took off half a Somali's head as the man was being taken by an American agent.

"What about you? Do you want to take a shower?" Makarov asked. Qin shook his head.

The sea was calm, devoid of currents and waves, just the sparkle as sunlight hit the water, like a million dancing fireflies. Makarov mentally counted the return on this job. He couldn't do this forever. He didn't want to. He just needed enough to ensure a comfortable life in Russia, so he could retire and maybe just run a simple boat running supplies to the oil rigs in the Black Sea.

PARIS

The City of Light was best in the off-season. Tourists infested the city in the early summer. The Americans were the worst. Always taking photos of everything, clamoring and pushing their way through crowds, and being loud. God, were they loud. Tonight, however, Paris belonged to its residents and a smattering of Europeans who deemed Paris less of a holiday destination that was as close to a regular religious pilgrimage as these secularists could experience.

Damien Golzari took a drag on his cigarette, the cancer stick that had finally done in his father. He only smoked in Paris. It was an exhibition of self-discipline or the fact that this was one of the few places he could succumb to petty sins. He finished off a glass of expensive wine, but not so expensive that the waiter would think him wealthy, which he was because of the money his family and their security had transferred out of Iran before the Ayatollah and his followers could get the money, or them. Some of the money went to quick real estate transactions, like the third-floor, three-bedroom condo he now called home on the corner of Quai d'Orleans and Rue le Regrattier just two blocks away.

He nodded to the waiter for the *billet* and paid cash. He rarely used credit or debit cards, preferring to stay off the grid as much as feasible in the twenty-first century. The outdoor portion of the café was a third full. His table was against the wall, as far from the street as possible. His formal training and his experiences in the world's most dangerous places had made him constantly over-vigilant. His only problem was that it sometimes made him too reactive. Years before, when a dish was dropped in a Bogota restaurant, he reflexively reached for his holster. He practiced less visible caution. Maybe such alertness was warranted here. In the previous hour, no less than three teams of soldiers passed by the street. Increased terrorist incidents and threats had resulted in the increased presence and use of force.

Golzari exited the café and walked across the street to the Pont Saint-Louis that crossed from Île Saint-Louis to Île de la Cité. The gothic cathedral of Notre Dame, still braced by scaffolding and supporting beams from the roof fire that nearly destroyed it, dominated the view even at night. There was no darkness in the City of Light.

Some people walked slowly across the bridge while most sat on the stone, listening to the evening's entertainment. A piano had been rolled out from one of the cafés so more people could enjoy the music. Emile played a lively, upbeat piece and smiled while making eye contact with everyone he could. Connection with a happy audience meant a few euros in the upturned hat near the piano. Emile shifted effortlessly from Billy Joel's fast-paced "The Entertainer" to Ray Charles's "Hit the Road Jack." Golzari sat midway between two lamp posts, as distanced as possible from the others beguiled by the music and the least lit.

At the end of his playlist, Emile caught Golzari's eye and nodded to him to take over. Golzari rarely played in public. He didn't like to call attention to himself. But it was late, he had had a couple of drinks, and it was Paris without tourists, just locals and local carefree visitors.

He lit a fresh cigarette, pushed up the sleeves of his black turtleneck, and walked across the pavement to the piano. People applauded Emile as he rose to take a bow. Most put more money in the hat that he passed around. Then he patted Golzari on the shoulder, passing the torch of entertainment.

The crowd went silent as some continued on to their next destination, uninterested in the unknown and untested new pianist, but a few of the locals had seen him before. Golzari went through his mental rolodex of songs, then decided to add a jazz flavor to an old Belgian composer's music. The first was a gentle play on "Les Taureaux." The crowd was pleased. A few placed euros on top of the piano. One young woman in her early twenties approached him and asked in broken French if he might welcome her vocal accompaniment. Golzari shrugged his shoulders in a non-verbal way that conveyed, "why not?" Her accent suggested she was a native British speaker.

"*Quand on n'a que l'amours?*" she asked. He acceded to the request and played "If We Only Have Love," the second Brel song of the evening.

She was a passable alto and sang it gently. The crowd approved of this duo. They continued on with "Marieke" and an appropriately playful "Les Taureaux," where she added a little acting, cajoling the crowd by pretending she had bull's horns, charging them one moment, then turning into a bullfighter using their cape in their death dance.

Golzari liked her style and the way her voice exuded more confidence with each new interpretation. He decided to challenge her and quietly said the only word he'd thus far spoken: "Amsterdam."

She was momentarily startled. Clearly she had some training; otherwise, she wouldn't have comprehended Jacques Brel had composed for a baritone like himself. She had a twinkle in her eye and said, "*On commence.*" *We start.* Golzari was glad she accepted the challenge.

"*Tres lentement,*" she added. *Very slowly.*

Her low-toned introduction was sung in clear but accented French, better to appeal to the crowd. Golzari heard the attempt to sound like Edith Piaf by starting gently like a dollop of honey dripping off a gritty spoon. The song was told in the voice of a lost soul in the port of Amsterdam where sailors sang of the dreams that they had.

Golzari appreciated her interpretation of the song. David Bowie's cover version had massacred it, making it sound more akin to Bowie's duet with Bing Crosby of the Christmas song "Little Drummer Boy." *Pah rum pa pa pum*, Golzari thought, trying not to disturb the flow of the song.

The stanzas kept returning to the port of Amsterdam where sailors ate fish and drank beer, their pants bursting as they did what sailors do in every port. The sailors drank to the whores of Amsterdam.

Her tone escalated in its smokiness but not to the near belting required when Brel himself sang it. The street was quiet so they could hear her better. Her eyes were closed as she steadied herself on the upright piano and the song "Amsterdam." Absent was the anger and contempt Brel poured into it. Her interpretation was practically sultry. Brel would not have approved, but he was long dead. The crowd enjoyed it, and Golzari found himself accepting having a vocalist accompany his normally solitary work.

He always preferred to work alone, although his previous work with Connor Stark in Yemen and Sri Lanka saw benefits in cooperating. They were different, but as Ambassador Sumner observed, their skills complemented one another and that had saved them twice. It was also the reason he was now in Paris and unemployed.

Golzari pushed away the bench and lit another cigarette, ignoring the scattering of applause from around the bridge and the closest café. The young woman playfully curtsied while placing her forefinger on her chin, then turned to her pianist.

"*Bonsoir, je m'appelle Alexandra.*"

"Not bad," he responded.

She was slightly taken aback that he wasn't responding in French.

"Thanks for joining me," he said, wiping the piano keys with a handkerchief. "You're from the Midlands?"

"Um, yes. My accent?"

He nodded. Golzari had a hint of British himself from his years of education at Cheltenham.

He pushed down his sleeves and headed across the bridge toward Île de la Cité.

"Wait, you forgot the . . ."

"The donations are yours," he said, turning his head back briefly. "I just play for the talent."

With that, he disappeared into the night.

CHAPTER 2

One of *Minerva*'s rigid-hulled inflatable boats (RHIBs) approached the *Syren*'s stern as the two large ships remained anchored in the lee of Bancalan Island. In addition to the coxswain driving the craft were two others clad in the gray coverall uniforms of Highland Maritime, Stark's security firm. One was a male in his mid-twenties, looking more weathered than the fresh, baby-faced recent Naval Academy graduate Stark had met years ago. The other, by coincidence, was also an Academy grad but far more familiar to Stark. A blond ponytail and wiry strands hung under the company's charcoal gray ball cap. Behind her Maui Jim's sunglasses, she looked directly at Stark and gave a quick, informal salute. He returned the courtesy.

The boat tied up and the two deftly hopped out.

"Permission to come aboard, Captain," she said as she reached a hand to Stark.

"Permission granted, Captain," he said, handing her a coffee tumbler with the *Syren*'s name and logo.

"Thanks, cousin," she said, removing her glasses.

"How's your new executive officer working out, Jaime?" he asked with a smile and a thumb at the younger man.

"I think I'll keep him around for a while," she said.

"Good morning, sir," Bobby Fisk said eagerly.

"Good to see you. You two still have no regrets about joining us?" Stark asked as the three made their way forward.

"My only regret, sir," ignoring their forced resignation from the Navy, "is that we're out of the Navy and Admiral Rossberg is still in it," Fisk replied, not without some bitterness. But it was a shared bitterness between the three, all having been the recipients of the Rossberg experience.

"Come on, the team's waiting," Stark said.

Twenty seconds later they were in *Syren*'s operations office—one of the twenty-foot metal containers normally used for shipping but could be modified for other uses, such as berthing, offices, or, in Warren's case, a research lab. Waiting for the arrival of *Minerva*'s leadership were *Syren*'s XO Olivia Harrison, Warren, the ship's security chief, and two Philippine Navy officers. Jaime Johnson and Fisk assumed two spots against the bulkhead. Bobby pulled out a pen and notepad from his left sleeve pocket.

"Good morning, team," Stark began, taking his place in front of the easel.

"As of today, we've completed three of the five training and exercise support modules under our contract with the Philippine Navy. We'll be maintaining radio silence and reducing emissions for the remainder of this module. Our current status is that we have ten officers and enlisted from the Philippine Navy on each of our ships. Commander Castillo here, their senior surface warfare officer for this exercise, has operational authority.

"During the second portion of the exercise, we employed and trained on the Crow's Nest. We had great comments from Commander Castillo on how it can be incorporated on their ships and how we can modify it. Thanks to our resident evil scientist, Jay, those improvements have already been incorporated."

"Sir, how soon can *Minerva*'s Crow's Nest get the same modifications?" Fisk asked.

Crow's Nest was a tethered drone system that enabled a drone to remain aloft for more than a week and with a greater payload than most drones. The eighth-of-an-inch tether included copper and fiber-optic cables to feed its energy need and have a direct link to the sensors. This allowed data to be transferred by wire rather than emissions that were detectable.

"Jay?"

"Oh, jeez, I dunno. What have you got for me?" Warren asked. He had a reputation in the company for shameless bartering rather than obeying an order from his chain of command, or rather the guy and company that hired him and could fire him. Fisk leaned over and whispered something to Jaime Johnson. She nodded immediately.

"Cornish pasty and a six-pack of red ale from a brewery," Fisk offered.

"What? Yeah, yeah, that's good, that's good. You'll have the specs for your folks by the time you leave here."

"Is this really how things get done?" Commander Castillo asked.

"It's cheaper, faster, and easier than working through a Naval Sea Systems Command," Stark replied.

"Yes, we have the same challenge," Castillo replied with a knowing smile and wink.

"Okay, *Syren* will get underway with *Minerva* taking station one nautical mile off our port quarter again. We transit to Balabac Island. All four RHIBs will deploy with passengers from the Philippine Navy and the pre-assigned Highland Maritime crew. Once Commander Castillo, the others, and I are ashore, Captain Johnson and *Minerva* will assume command and transit over the horizon."

"If we're at EMCON, how can we communicate with the teams ashore, sir?" Fisk asked.

"We'll only communicate at night. We'll either be at the designated points or not. Send back *Syren* close enough as the relay ship. Have your watchstanders keep an eye on all three sites at midnight each night. The teams will have the appropriate flashlights for Morse code."

"How close will we need to get to see the lights?" *Minerva*'s XO asked.

"We've tested them for 1.2 nautical miles on a clear night. Check with the team's weatherman. They have a conversion table," Stark said.

"Aye, sir."

"Look, this is a training exercise. If this was like our hot experiences elsewhere, the teams might not make it back to the comms sites ashore the first night," Stark added. He was intentionally circumspect about the "elsewhere," but he knew Jaime and Bobby understood that to mean their previous incidents off Yemen and Sri Lanka.

"At this point I'd like to ask the PN's intel officer, Lieutenant Christina Santos, to brief us."

The young Filipina officer rose from her seat. She stood ramrod straight, making her five-foot-four height appear much taller. She exuded disciplined training and confidence. She flipped the first page of the large paper pad on the easel to expose a map of the area.

"The exercise will occur on Balabac Island, the southernmost Philippine Island," she began, pointing at each place as she briefed. "We will remain on its east coast, well away from the North Balabac Strait between Balabac Island and the northern territory of Malaysia because of the high traffic in that shipping lane.

"The RHIBs will land their teams here, at the beach just south of Indalawan Point on the east coast of Balabac. The RHIBs will then return to the ships. The teams will proceed via this valley that cuts across the island, east to west. Team Four will proceed three kilometers to north by northwest of the landing site to Balabac Peak, located at 7°55'13" North and 117°2'35" East. Its elevation is 1,800 feet. The team will assume station there. Teams One, Two, and Three will proceed due west to Rabor and the naval base currently under construction, which will serve as the enemy force for this exercise.

"The objective is to reach within one hundred yards of the base's perimeter. It is heavily forested beyond that. Once a team has reached point, you will sound a provided horn at the agreed-to hour and minute, signaling to the base that you have achieved your goal. All teams will then enter the base and meet outside the boathouse for further instruction from the base commander. Are there any questions?"

There were none.

"Thank you," she said politely, returning to her seat.

"Thank you, Lieutenant," Stark said. "You have your read-aheads to consult. The last phase of this entire episode will be dicey. We're going to use what we practiced earlier this month and conduct real-time maritime security patrols on the west coast of Palawan to deter illegal fishing in Philippine territorial waters. But first things first, let's get this done. Dismissed."

While the others left, Jaime paused.

"You okay?" he asked his cousin.

"Yeah. I was more comfortable with the firepower of my destroyer, but I made the right decision to step aside and out of the Navy—again. And back with the company—again."

"It's okay. Our 'navy' doesn't have someone like Admiral Rossberg. We'll be just fine," Stark said.

PARIS

Golzari always felt more comfortable in cities at night. There were fewer people, fewer distractions so he could focus on anything out of the ordinary. There was the darkness, the shadows where he could obscure himself if he needed to follow anyone or hide if anyone was after him. It was one of the many traits he had picked up from his father's personal security. His father had been a general during the Iranian Revolution, forcing the family to leave. His personal security was SAVAK—Shah Pahlavi's ruthless but effective secret police. Golzari never admitted to anyone that he learned more from them than when he went through the police academy or the Federal Law Enforcement Training Center when he became a Diplomatic Security Service agent. They wouldn't have understood or agreed with the methods he had sometimes used himself.

He had passed Notre Dame ten blocks back and took position along a stone-walled building typical of every Beaux-Arts architectural structure in this area of Paris. Nearby, the old stone had holes in them, left over from the Second World War when French partisans were put up against the walls by Nazis and executed.

He kept away from the closest streetlight and nudged himself into an old arch to further minimize the risk of anyone seeing him from more than a few feet away. He had watched the restaurant across the street for the past two nights since he had eaten there. It was a less-than-satisfactory meal. It was not one of the finer dining establishments that Golzari was accustomed to and frequented in whatever city he was in. This was a place that catered to tourists, primarily Americans. Few had an appreciation for real French cuisine, and they were notoriously cheap, ate quickly, and were overly demanding of the staff. That's why a restaurant like this survived. It made affordable food that could be prepared and served to increase the volume of diners.

Congratulations, Golzari thought as he recalled the years of service to America. *You ate in Paris.* The only reason he himself had eaten at the restaurant was to confirm a suspicion.

Golzari had also realized that where there was inexpensive food, there was inexpensive labor. When he had gone from his table to the restroom, he glanced in the circular window of the door leading to the kitchen. A chef scrambled, a waiter placed an order, and on the far side a much shorter, rail-thin, black-haired person washed dishes with their back to Golzari. The short hair exposed a mocha-toned neck. It was only for a split second, but his SAVAK-trained mind didn't require much to absorb as many details as possible.

The restaurant had been closed for an hour and there was no foot traffic, only an occasional passing car. The waiter and chef he'd seen in the kitchen exited along with the maître d' and the waitress. They paused and chatted for a few minutes, the chef and waitress sharing a light for cigarettes. They waved to each other, then left in separate directions.

The lights went off inside the restaurant, then the light on the outside above the name. A man in his thirties emerged holding the hand of a young girl. Given the dark hair and height, it was the dishwasher. The man looked both ways, then across the street in Golzari's general direction. Golzari froze, careful that even the slightest movement in the dark arch would betray his presence. It was why he had worn the black turtleneck and black pants. Anything that would help him silently observe and follow.

The young girl looked worn and cast her head down. The man said something inaudible, but it was a clear admonition as he waved his finger at her. The frail thing was perhaps ten years old. She appeared to say something. The man slapped her across the head, then looked around again. Golzari resisted his urge to race across the street immediately, but his training kept him in observation mode. The man pulled the girl as he began to walk. Golzari waited until they were a block ahead, then followed. She never looked up, even to where she was being led.

Twenty minutes later they arrived at a four-story building on a narrow side street. It had a glass front on the ground floor. The faded letters revealed it to have been a tailor shop at one time. The windows were sealed. The man pulled out a key, unlocked the door, then dragged the girl inside. No light came on until a minute later when a dim one outlined another sealed and darkened window. Golzari remained at the closest corner where he could observe the building and those adjacent to it. It reeked like New York City here, with piles of week-old trash on the sidewalks.

He waited ten minutes on the silent street. He double-backed to the last turn and made his way to the alley behind the buildings, careful not to crush a discarded can or plastic bottle under his footsteps. He stopped at the four-story building. The rear door boarded up. Only one way in or out on the ground floor and not a good sign. Looking up, he saw a fire escape and a metal ladder. Avoiding the chance that the ladder would make too much noise, he found a large wooden pallet nearby and moved it under the fire escape. Reaching up, he could barely get his fingers to grip the metal mesh of the first landing. Pulling himself up by his fingers, then hands, then arms and a leg were difficult, but not more so than the rock climbing he'd done in the Colorado Rockies and other mountain ranges.

Golzari made it to the third floor, still as silent as a cat. He checked his surroundings again. No lights or sounds in the alley or the other buildings. The four windows were covered with paper from the inside, but one was cracked open a half inch. It was enough. He pulled out his phone as well as a coiled, flexible wire. It was a fiberscope used by police. He unrolled it and connected it to the phone. The other end had a camera, similar to an arthroscope. There was just enough room—about ten millimeters—to insert the fiberscope under the window slowly so as not to make a noise, then he went to the side, moving the paper slightly. The camera scanned the room, dimly lit at the far end, but what he saw was enough. Strewn about the floor were ten small mattresses, each with a sleeping child.

BALABAC ISLAND, PHILIPPINES

Stark's was the first of the four RHIBs to come ashore. Each RHIB deposited a team of five—two teams from *Minerva* and two from *Syren*. Stark and Commander Castillo each led a team, as did Bobby Fisk and *Minerva*'s head of security, Sivan Abraham. The teams were comprised of Highland Maritime personnel in their gray coveralls and Philippine Navy personnel in their gray and black Camopat pattern camouflage uniforms. All were armed, although since this was a training exercise, they carried minimal ammunition in their backpacks. The teams unloaded the RHIBs with food, water, medical kits, and other supplies for their three-day training.

It was high tide and the lengthy beach had only twenty yards depth of sand between the water and dense flora. Had this been an actual operation, Stark would have come in at night since the trees and leaves were perfect cover for an enemy lying in wait. Still, it was a training exercise. He called out to two of the Highland security personnel.

"I want each of you to take two PN sailors. Lars, head south on the beach one hundred yards, go into the jungle fifty yards, then double back. Forney, you take your guys north and do the same. Let's make sure our Blue Team opponents didn't get smart or lucky with our Red Team plan and set up folks against us here." The two experienced Highland Maritime security personnel complied.

Stark then called the team leads and Santos to a spot away from the boats and activity.

"Lieutenant Santos, may I have the map?" he said, resting on a knee as the others did the same.

"Yes, sir," she said, pulling out and unfolding a four-foot-by-four-foot map and laying it on the sand. "This is a topographical map of the island with all the roads and known footpaths and trails. Most of the population was relocated to Palawan two years ago when the new naval base was announced. There's a town of farmers and fishermen remaining on the northeast side with some port facilities but well outside the parameters of this exercise. The town is called Población I."

"Any chance they'll wander around here?" Fisk asked.

"No. They understand that most of the island is now restricted for naval activities and exercises," she said matter-of-factly. "The local community tries to minimize their contact with the country as a whole and focuses on local trade with nearby islands. Team Four, under Abraham, will find a trail three hundred yards north of us that guides them to their objective."

"Thank you, Santos," Stark began. "Teams One, Two, and Three will remain together and head due west from here until we reach this road."

"It's not a paved road, sir," Santos remarked. "It's mostly dirt but our navy's civil engineers keep it clear of debris."

"Then we'll stay on it for a few kilometers until we reach this point," he said, pointing to a few kilometers east of the base. "Team Three—Bobby—will then proceed to a point due south of the base here and remain under cover. Team Two—Commander Castillo—your team will proceed to this point due north of the base. I'll take Team One to this point to the eastern entrance of the base. Commander, anything you want to tell us about it?"

"The base is surrounded by twelve-foot-high fences with concertina wire at the top. The only vehicular entrance is on the north side. The base has about one hundred personnel plus crew assigned to the three cutters currently based here. I was only here once at the beginning of construction. They had dredged the basin and there was a long breakwater planned but they hadn't started it. It's a small base, very condensed. There is a headquarters building, a barracks, a boathouse, and a dozen other buildings for storage, medical, and whatever else, I am not sure."

"Copy that, Commander," Stark said. "You have three hours to arrive on your stations. Our objective is not to be caught or sighted. The base thinks it's being attacked from the sea, which is why we landed on the east side of the island. At the designated time, each team will sound its horn, indicating to the base that it is formally under attack. If the base sights you first, they'll sound their horn. At the conclusion of this portion of the training exercise, their commanding officer will come out to greet us and take us to the base for a debrief and a barbecue. Okay, let's pack up our supplies and move out."

With that, the RHIBs returned to their ships. When Teams One through Three reached their first waypoint, they separated.

"You going to be okay, Bobby?" Stark asked the young former Navy officer.

"Beautiful day, a walk in the woods with my friends. How does it get better than this?"

The young man had grown a lot since Stark had first met him years ago on the bridge of the Navy cruiser USS *Bennington*. Bobby Fisk had seen more action off Somalia and Sri Lanka than most Navy officers—outside of SEALs—since Vietnam had experienced in a lifetime.

"You get caught and you're paying for it, got it?"

"Got it, sir. Two bottles of Highland Park for you and Captain Johnson," Fisk replied. "What do I get if I don't get caught?"

"You get to keep your job. . . ." Stark said with a smile. "Good luck."

"Same to you, sir."

Stark's team paralleled the road about ten yards in. It was much slower going, but since the other two teams had to arc to the north and south, he could avoid the delay. Less than a kilometer from his objective, he double-checked the map and compass. He turned to Santos.

"Know anything about this elevation to the east?" he asked.

"Nothing more than the map shows, sir. It has an elevation of one hundred fifty feet. I don't know if it's been cleared. But it would make a better spot for observation than if we went to the planned site."

"I agree. Let's do that."

The jungle had less growth here, making their trek easier. They arrived at the hill, with Stark and Santos lying prone with their binoculars. Stark scanned the base.

The north gate was easy to see. No guards were apparent. He turned to the base buildings. All were of new construction but nothing out of the ordinary. There were several trucks and two Humvees. One slightly larger ship—an *Armidale*-class Australian patrol vessel—was alongside a pier. It was a quiet base. So quiet he hadn't seen any PN forces yet. *They must be lying in wait for us in the buildings*, he thought. *Unless they're all in the jungle*. Had the base realized his teams would approach from across the island?

He checked his watch. His team was twenty-five minutes from the point where they'd blare their signal horn.

Beyond the breakwater was a large fishing vessel bobbing in the open sea about half a nautical mile offshore.

"Santos, are this island's fishermen allowed to be so close to the base?"

"No, sir," she replied, training her binoculars on the boat. Stark did the same.

Several men were on the vessel's open stern. Three, in the digital cammies of the Philippine Navy, were kneeling with their hands tied behind their backs. Several men with guns were standing in front of them. One appeared to be shouting. The man brought up a pistol.

"Jeezus, no," Stark said aloud, then regretfully watched as a pink mist suddenly exited the back of the kneeling man's head. Then the gunman did it again to the next one, and again.

"Santos, this is no longer a training exercise. Have the team load their weapons."

C H A P T E R 3

CAMP DAVID, MARYLAND

Caroline Jaha Sumner—CJ to nearly everyone except her mother—was roused from a deep sleep by her assistant. Her first reaction was to check the sixth analog clock on the far wall, if two feet from the bed could be called far in this tiny bedroom. Each clock had a different time for Beijing, Washington, London, Moscow, Tehran, and Calcutta. The previous national security advisor to the President of the United States preferred digital. CJ was more comfortable with analog and how the black hands and white faces reminded her of piano keys. She'd been asleep for about two hours. Just three hours ago, she was playing Rachmaninoff on the Steinway Model D in the living room of Aspen Lodge for the president, chief of staff, and secretary of state. The last time she had played the piece was as a rare duet with her former personal security officer from the Diplomatic Security Service.

If there were any myths about the creature comforts of Camp David, they were quickly dispelled by guests staying in the older guest cottages built during Franklin Roosevelt's presidency. Some cottages had been renovated better than others. It was known as Shangri-La then. Unable to use the presidential yacht, Roosevelt transferred its Navy crew to the Maryland retreat, thus establishing it as a Navy command. At least that's what Sumner remembered from her orientation about its history the first time she visited Camp David.

"Sorry to wake you, Madam Ambassador. They need you," she said as she provided a folder to her superior before exiting.

Sumner slipped out of her nightgown and grabbed her blue jeans, a light sweater, and sneakers and read through the classified brief. The assistant and her military aide escorted her outside and down the path to Aspen Lodge. A guard opened the front door. The first thing she saw was the painting of the sailing frigate USS *Constitution*, the country's oldest commissioned warship. She could smell coffee wafting from the left hallway toward the kitchen. She led the aides in the opposite direction from the kitchen, then a quick left into the main living room with the grand piano. Another left found them at the large dining room table that doubled as a conference room. The sword Congress presented to Commodore Stephen Decatur was mounted on the wall directly behind her seat.

The secretary of state was next to her. Along the wall were aides. The far wall had a widescreen with a map of the Philippines on it. All rose as the president made his way from his bedroom to the table, steadied by a cane. President Dunner had aged, Sumner thought, well beyond the standard accelerated maturing that was the physical toll on any president. She was also responsible for him being where he was right now. Years before and well behind the scenes, she had given President Hamilton Becker an ultimatum, forcing him to step aside and endorse the elder statesman Dunner as their party's nominee. He had won a full term, but it was taking more of a toll on him, at least physically. His strength was in his measured wisdom and his decency, so uncommon in modern politics. Dunner was never a politician. He'd come up through the diplomatic ranks.

When he sat, everyone followed suit.

"I regret we had to wake you so soon after a wonderful evening," he started. "It won't be the last time we enjoy some time together."

Sumner appreciated the monthly weekends at Camp David. Dunner had no close family, having lost his son and wife. CJ had become like a daughter to him.

"Commander, would you kindly start," he asked the briefer at the end of the table. Even in an unknown crisis, Dunner was measured but sincerely polite. She'd seen other politicians who were notorious for yelling and throwing items, like coffee mugs.

"Mr. President, the Philippines have come under a massive attack. It has affected nearly every island, from Mindanao in the south, to Palawan in the west, to Luzon in the north as well as their leadership. The cyberattack has affected their entire infrastructure—banks, power stations, the cellular phone network, the internet, television and radio stations, hospitals, traffic lights, ports, and others. Very little information is coming out of the country. Our embassy has transmitted minimal information because of the shutdown and the chaos that's emerging. Very few networks have been restored.

"We have indications that President Quinta may have been killed. We know that her plane departed Manila with several senior military officers aboard. It was supposed to arrive in Davao City in Mindanao. The Philippine government lost track of her plane over the Visayan Sea north of Cebu Island. We re-tasked satellites and swept the area. Based on where we believe the plane was at its last location, there was metal debris in the water."

"Did she have an escort who could have reported anything?" the president asked.

"Yes, Mr. President. She had two fighters escorting her. Neither returned to their base. We were able to track one that headed due south for another thirty minutes until that one was lost to radar as well."

"Speculation?"

"Best guess, Mr. President, based on the information available, is that one of the escort fighters shot down President Quinta's plane and the second escort. Given that it occurred so close to the cyberattack, it was likely coordinated. Only a handful of countries—Russia, China, Iran, and North Korea—have the ability to conduct a nationwide cyberattack. We do not believe Iran, North Korea, or Russia had the intent to conduct it. If it is China, we aren't ready to speculate on a reason to undermine the government."

"Was the cyberattack a singular event, or is it continuing?"

"There have been no known attacks since the initial event, Mr. President."

"Anything else?"

"Sir, the intelligence community needs more time to collect information."

"Very well, thank you."

"Mr. President," Sumner added, "we do have a large-scale naval exercise currently being conducted in the general region. Between the US and its partners, more than fifty ships are en route to Vietnamese waters to coordinate with the host country."

Dunner nodded and lightly tapped his cane as he collected his thoughts. "Ladies and gentlemen, I have three requests. First, I want updates every two hours on the situation, especially with regard to President Quinta. I need confirmation that she has been killed, and I want to know who was behind it, whether this was an external attack or an internal coup.

"Second, I'd like a rough plan in place by noon on what we can do to help the Philippines. Once we know who's in charge—excuse me, depending on who's in charge—I want something we can offer in terms of medical assistance and supplies.

"Third," Dunner again paused for a few seconds, "that large-scale naval exercise will proceed as planned. We must demonstrate to the region that the US can lead a naval armada if necessary and that we work closely with our partners. If this was an attempt by another country to undermine the Philippines, I'd like to have a show of force in the region. If it's an internal coup against a partner like President Quinta, I want to have our ships there for the same reason. Thank you very much, Commander. To all of you, return to your guest cottages and try to get some sleep. I'd like everyone well rested."

The president was being his thoughtful self, she knew, even though he realized they'd all go to work immediately on his behalf and that of the latest potential international crisis.

PARIS

He could see ten children on the mattresses, lightly covered with sheets. The black-and-white video couldn't distinguish dirty from clean sheets, but Golzari suspected that with the trash evident around the room, their laundry wasn't being done with any regularity. This building was a residence—if it could be called that—of human chattel. It was, in effect, modern slavery. People would be enticed from their home countries, mostly developing countries, to work in cities where they were promised higher income.

Golzari had only seen the conditions of human trafficking twice before. The first was with his brief job with the Boston Police Department. Back then, he and his partner assisted with the then-Immigration and Naturalization Service's raid on an apartment building in Dorchester. Forty wretched souls were kept in a similarly sealed four-story complex. The second was during an assignment to Indonesia when he was with the Diplomatic Security Service. He was on a break from the security detail, walking toward a café when a young African woman ran past him in cheap, tattered clothes and bare feet, chased by a man who towered over her as he grabbed her just a few feet away. He began to drag her back when she looked up at Golzari with pleading brown eyes and said something in her native language, then managed to gasp out in English, "help." Golzari, with the assistance of local police, saved her. He never found out what happened after that.

Are there more in one of the other rooms, he asked himself. All the windows were covered. The building only had one entrance that wasn't sealed. The neighborhood was borderline sketchy for Paris. And he was alone on a fire escape three stories high. The longer he stayed there, the greater the chance he'd be seen by any trafficker or people in the other buildings. He had few options.

He could simply break the window and enter the room. This would be foolhardy, he knew. He didn't know how many traffickers were in the building or what weapons they had. He did carry a lightweight Smith & Wesson currently secured on the inside of his left leg in a Kramer leather pocket holster. The snub-nosed .38 Special only held five rounds compared to some of the other ten-round concealed guns, but if shit went down and he needed something out of the holster, he preferred a make and model least likely to get snagged when he pulled it out. He once spent an entire day with several models in this holster, timing how long it took him to remove it from various positions—standing, kneeling, prone, on his back—and did it at least fifty times each to get a proper quantitative measure of what worked best. He preferred this holster to the ankle holster with the calf strap. If he was standing, he could lift his leg slightly, grab the butt of the revolver, then sort of kick down and—voilà—revolver in hand.

The downside is that the gun only held five rounds. It wouldn't help in a firefight, even if he had been one of the best shooters in federal law enforcement, but he'd need something like this to defend himself briefly before extracting himself. Under other conditions, he'd have a second pistol in his shoulder holster. Since he was lightly clothed, he couldn't have concealed it.

Breaking in wouldn't only warn the trafficker or traffickers. Every child would be awakened. They'd already been frightened by their captors. Having an armed man burst through a window at night would further scare them and lead to screaming and chaos. He didn't need chaos in this—he needed to be in ultimate control of the situation.

His second option would be to continue observing the building and its operations. He had already established a few patterns, such as the time of night the man and girl would exit the restaurant. If there were this many children, it meant more traffickers or captors to manage them. The lucky ones—if they could be called that—worked in restaurants and local, secret sweat shops. The unlucky ones were offered as sex slaves to the highest-paying clients. It was a dirty business with the filthiest elements of humanity. They were businessmen and politicians, lawyers and government employees. It didn't matter to them. They always thought they were immune, that they would never get caught. Most of the time, they were right.

The third option would be to leave now and report it to his contacts at the Sûreté—the Paris police. He had worked with some of them in his previous position. Now, as a local resident, he had done some work for them on the side. Golzari was an expert in terrorism. He had been around the world protecting America's top diplomats or protecting foreign diplomats while they visited the United States. He had been in some of the best and worst places in the world, knew several languages. He knew how to keep his work quiet. Paris was arguably the most beautiful city in the world, but like every city, it had a deep, dark criminal underbelly of domestic and international networks. The Sûreté needed a few people like him outside the system whom no one knew and could report to them. In turn, he managed to keep a few weapons in his apartment and be given some leeway with his operations in the months he had been here.

Of course, this option had a potential downside. He knew where these children were. If he reported it to the Sûreté, in another hour, they might all be gone. Still, it was a chance he'd have to take since the other options just weren't viable.

He felt a raindrop on his black hair that had started to grow gray, then another and then more. He slowly and gently removed the fiber-scope so as not to wake any of the children. When it was fully extracted, he rolled it and put it in his pocket. The rain quickly became heavy. Golzari took a quick look at the other buildings one last time. There was no movement in any of the windows. He descended one flight on the fire escape, then gripped the first bar of the retractable ladder as he swung his leg around. The bars were now wet with the evening rain. As he grabbed a rung with his other hand, a light came on in the next building over, momentarily distracting him. His grip slipped from the wet rung, and he desperately flung his other arm in an attempt to grasp anything else. He cursed at himself for not having anticipated the weather or having slip-resistant climbing gloves. It didn't matter as six feet and one hundred eighty pounds of Damien Golzari dropped ten feet.

BALABAC NAVAL BASE, PHILIPPINES

Lieutenant Santos followed Stark's direction to have the team load their weapons, helping one of the younger Filipino sailors who was clearly too nervous to remember his training. Stark couldn't blame him. If you saw something unexpected and traumatic and thought too long about it, even a couple of seconds, your mind would prevent you from properly reacting. He had witnessed it before. He had experienced it as a junior Navy officer himself.

"What the hell happened? Where are all the personnel assigned to the base?" he asked aloud. He took more time to assess the base itself and brought his binoculars up. Earlier he had wiped off sweat from his forehead because of what Fisk had called a simple walk in the woods. Now, he was sweating because he had four teams near a naval base where sailors were being executed at sea.

From Stark's prone position on the hill, he had a clear view of the entire base as he turned his head from left to right. The small base had a simple layout, forming a square about four hundred yards by four hundred yards. Beyond that, the jungle had been cleared out to one hundred yards. The middle of the western side of the base was the ship's basin, one hundred fifty yards long. On the north end of the basin were two piers. The Australian vessel was pier-side. There was no sign of the others. The east side had finger piers for several smaller whalers that were still there. A quay built up of boulders was on the ocean side with a wide opening on the southwest side of the basin to allow ships to enter or depart.

The north side of the base had the main gate and guard shacks in the middle. Inside and to the west of the gate were two large Quonset huts, while a third was on the inside and east. Directly before his line of sight of the basin was the car pool with the trucks and Humvees and another structure. On the south side of the base were two rows of three Quonset huts—two were under construction. Beyond them, to the southwest side of the base, was another larger structure closer to the basin with a crane nearby and a ramp. Based on his experiences with other facilities, he guessed that was the boat repair facility.

In the middle and close to the basin was what looked like an air traffic control tower about fifty feet high with a narrow shaft wide enough to support the main deck four flights up. It had a door on the ground level on the east side. Several large antennas made the tower even taller.

He took a closer look at the tower windows. He could see two people moving inside. It also had railings around the control area with a narrow deck around it. He could see no other people. If there were people in the tower, what was being reported to other PN units? Had anyone been warned? He was in the blind. None of his teams had radios on which to listen to potential communications per the conditions of the contracted training. All he had was the Mark I Mod I eyeball and his ears to listen for any clues.

"Dammit," he whispered. He checked his watch. It was now twenty-three minutes to the assigned time when Teams One, Two, and Three were to have sounded their horns. Unless the other teams were already on site, they wouldn't know about the executions on the fishing vessel, which was now underway in a north-by-northwesterly direction.

"Dammit," he said again more loudly. He pointed to two of the team members. "You two make your way through that jungle as fast as you can. You," he pointed to one, "get to the site for Team Two on the north side and you go to Team Three's site to the south. Warn them that something's gone wrong at the base. Lighten your load. Just take your weapons." The two did as they were told, dropping their food and other gear.

"Santos, from what you know of the base, is that tower the only place with communications?" Stark asked.

"No, sir, the building to the northeast is the headquarters, but you can see there are no antennas. Since they haven't completed building the base, the priority was getting the tower fully operational. The only communications would be there," she said calmly and quietly.

They were now down to a three-person team. He directed them to keep their eyes on the ocean while he focused on the base itself for any activity while monitoring the departing fishing vessel. Based on the size of the ship and the wake, he estimated it was making fifteen knots. Normally that was fast for a ship like that, but not so if the killers were trying to get away—or trying to get to something.

Twenty minutes until H-hour, he thought. In that time, the ship in this calm water would be six or seven nautical miles further from them. So, a total of six and a half to seven and a half nautical miles from the shore and a little further from Teams Two and Three. A horn might be heard at that distance, but then again, that vessel had a big diesel engine. You had to have people topside for them to hear you over it, especially if it had been cranked up to full speed. Maybe. But the vessel's pilot house would hear someone calling them on the radio.

Stark watched to the north and then south rallying points. Still no sign of them, although they'd still be behind the trees and bushes if they were there. He had no other method of signaling them. His kit did have a mirror, but all he could have done was direct sunlight to the teams.

He didn't have the background to send a message with it. He knew Fisk could read and send Morse code. He hadn't thought to ask Castillo. All he could do was rely on the runners he had sent two minutes after he realized something was wrong. Two minutes was a lifetime.

He checked his watch. Thirty seconds to H-hour. He had to squint now to see the vessel with its stern to him. The people in the control tower were now seated, speaking to each other. Ten seconds. H-hour.

Team Three's horn blared loudly for five long seconds.

CHAPTER 4

"Two minutes, two effing minutes," Stark chided himself at the thought that he should have acted more quickly.

The two control tower personnel were now on the open deck. Both had binoculars trained on the north perimeter where Team Three had blared their horn.

"Sir," Santos said, keeping the binoculars on the north while one hand reached out instinctively to Stark. "Team Two is emerging from the jungle."

He turned to see the same thing. Commander Castillo and his team were now in the open, oblivious to what had changed. Twenty yards into the open, the Team One member Stark had dispatched to warn Team Two emerged as well, running directly to Castillo. Castillo turned, listened, then stopped his team.

Stark dropped his binoculars and grabbed the closest FNC rifle the departed team members had discarded. It was one of the Belgian-made assault rifles from Fabrique Nationale Carabine that Highland Maritime preferred to use. It had an effective range of up to four hundred yards. Half of the naval base was within that range. If the control tower was inside that range, he might be able to do it.

The Navy hadn't taught him to shoot. Every time he picked up a rifle, his life experiences returned to him in a fleeting second like choppy old film reel. He had learned growing up on the Stark farm in New Hampshire, competing at local and then national events as he broadened his training to be a competitive athlete. He had won the bronze in the Olympics Pentathlon shortly after graduating from college and before being assigned to his first ship. The Navy had green-lighted him to compete in the next Olympics, but Stark was derailed following the terrorist attack on the Naples café where he and others were only looking for a decent meal while on liberty from the ship. He quickly put those memories aside and compartmentalized them lest he fell victim to them again.

He estimated the range again and quickly resighted the rifle. Stark clearly saw both men through the scope. They were now shouting something. One turned to head back into the control tower as the first man kept his eyes to the north.

Stark focused on the first man. He was only a step away from the interior. He had dark, short hair and high cheekbones and no facial hair. He wore jungle fatigues, the same forest camouflage pattern the US Army and Navy wore twenty years before. His sleeves were rolled up to the biceps. The scope's crosshairs were trained on the man's temple. Stark took a deep breath and, as he exhaled, pulled the trigger. The shot was just off as the man reeled back and brought his hands up to his neck. Stark hadn't had time for a clean shot. He had a second more the next shot, this time taking off the top of the man's skull. He then turned it to the second man, who was looking in Stark's direction. Stark put a bullet in his chest and another before he swayed to the side and over the railing. Whether or not the man was still alive from the two bullets, he likely wasn't when he hit the concrete fifty feet below.

"More soldiers," Santos remarked, still with coolness in her voice. "Seven just came out of the far northeast hut. All of them are armed. They are running toward the north gate." This was the closest to Castillo's team, who were now all prone, loading their own rifles.

Stark pointed the rifle at the emerging soldiers, but he didn't have a clear shot. Those he could see were taking cover and looking at the hill from which Stark had fired his shots.

"You two fall back," he said. There was little cover on the hill except for low brush, nothing for him to get behind. He had no idea how competent those soldiers were, but they outgunned him. The odds were not in his favor for long. Once Santos and the other team member were away, he expended the rest of his clip and slowly crawled backward, picking up a couple more clips from the packs. He heard their gunfire start, as well as a couple of runs that hit nearby. By the time a concentration of fire started hitting the position Stark had pulled back from, he was on the far side of the hill with the two other Team One members.

"Are you two okay?" he asked of the two remaining members in his direct charge. They nodded.

"Who are they?" Santos asked as the sound of continued rounds suggested the soldiers hadn't moved from the base.

"I don't know, Lieutenant. But they're not PN. The two I took out in the control tower weren't wearing your uniforms. They were woodland cammies, not the gray and black Camopat digital. What's the situation with local terrorist groups?"

"Here? It wouldn't make sense. Most of the terrorist groups are located on Jolo, Basilan, and other islands to the east. There have been no reports otherwise here. Maybe it's Jemaah Islamiyah. They're in the Philippines but also Malaysia, Brunei, and Indonesia. But they've never attacked a military target. Like most terrorist groups, they prefer unarmed civilian targets."

The gunfire slowed, then stopped.

"Stay here. I'm going to have another look," Stark said.

He crawled back thirty yards to the top of the hill, bemoaning an old knee wound and realizing that the years had not made this job easier. Maggie would have agreed and usually did to try to keep him in Port St. George. She also usually failed to convince him.

Without the binoculars, he could see soldiers getting into three Humvees. They rolled out the main gate and made a sharp right, speeding toward Team One's direction. Once the third vehicle was out of the compound, Team Two and then Three opened fire. Bobby's Team Three had taken a position closer to the water and southwest corner to reduce the risk of crossfire. The first to go were the Humvee tires. One engine block was hit, immediately spewing smoke. The third was relentlessly hit until one or more shots hit the gas tank, blowing it up. Soldiers escaped from the lead vehicle only to be cut down by Team Three.

Stark took the binoculars and scanned the scene. The seven terrorists or soldiers—whatever they were—were dead or at least unresponsive. There was no more activity at the base. He eyed the horizon. The fishing vessel was well away, oblivious to what the Highland Maritime and PN teams had done.

PARIS

As he slipped from the ladder, knowing there was nothing left for him to reach out to, Golzari prepared himself for the impact. It wasn't his first rodeo. He had had minor accidents rock climbing. It was nearly impossible not to. It didn't matter if you had a minor fall. It mattered if you were able to recover and learn from it. His cat-like reflexes didn't prevent him from landing with a thud, but it was softer and quieter than most anyone else would have achieved. Had it not been for the grunt he couldn't suppress and that empty plastic soda bottle his torso crushed, he'd have avoided exposing himself. He hoped he hadn't been prodded by any needles cast aside in this dark alley by local drug users. Looking up, he saw no sign of a light or swaying curtain that anyone had heard or seen him. Golzari quickly made his way back to the street, but he could take no chances.

If someone had heard something, he wouldn't have time to notify the Sûreté since he never carried a phone. Those could be tracked. He only had some facts to go with. There were children asleep in one room. There was one known man in the building. All the windows were sealed. And there was only one unobstructed entrance. Golzari had a gun with five bullets concealed on his inner left leg. The only things he had left on his person were a Swiss Army knife, the fiberscope, a small digital camera, a wallet with ten thousand euros. He always carried what he deemed "walking around" money.

There were also the assumptions. There was probably more than one man in the building. They could be armed. There were probably more children than those he saw. And he couldn't guarantee the children wouldn't be spirited off in his absence if he went for the Sûreté or returned to monitor the situation again the next day.

The immutable factor was that those children were essentially held hostage. And every hour they were in that building, they were denied their freedom. They were at risk. Action wasn't an option—it was warranted.

Golzari brushed himself off and tucked his shirt into his pants. He took the fiberscope and found a discarded plastic bag near a trash bin. *That wouldn't do*, he thought. *Too traceable*. If anyone in the trafficking building found it, it would indicate that someone in the area was being monitored. He surveilled the area and saw the closest sewer grate. He dropped the fiberscope in and now, as best prepared as he could, approached the building's front door. A doorbell with a camera was to the right.

He knocked lightly on the door, looked into the camera, and raised both hands to show he had nothing in them.

"Yes?" a disembodied voice answered in French.

"I've been sent by my employer to facilitate a transaction. He is well known. He wishes to remain anonymous," Golzari replied in a calm, matter-of-fact manner. He lowered his right arm and pulled out his money to show them.

There were now two options on how this would play out. Either they would ignore him or answer the door. Low-level functionaries of trafficking networks weren't rich, but they were careful. The sight of money would lure them in, but they'd be wary. They wouldn't ignore him.

The door opened as the man from the restaurant emerged. There was nothing in his hands. That probably meant someone else was the heavy just inside. Someone who was a cheap hire with a weapon. The man looked across the street and both ways. There was no one else. He motioned to Golzari to enter.

The first floor was lit. To his right was a large living room with a sofa, two chairs, and two men standing next to them. Both had short hair and shorter beards. One had a thick metal pipe in his hand, the other held a machete. *Smart*, he thought. *No guns*. If they allowed him in and started shooting, it was the surest way to wake the children and the neighbors and call their attention to the Sûreté. Based on Golzari's extensive travels through Africa and the Middle East, he suspected the men were from Algiers or Tunis. It would make sense. There had been a large wave of immigrants to France, some of whom were causing minor disturbances while others were attracted to more destructive and explosive activities.

"I'm armed," Golzari said to the two men. "I have one pistol. Let's not call outside attention to our conversation, shall we?" The men nodded knowingly. Clearly Golzari, who was also Middle Eastern, was of their own ilk. The restaurant man, possibly a second-generation immigrant based on his accent, motioned to Golzari to have a seat. Golzari pulled a pair of latex gloves from his back pocket, ensuring he'd leave no fingerprints.

BALABAC NAVAL BASE

Stark directed his two remaining team members to pick up the packs and follow him as he kept his weapon trained on the Humvees below. He could hear nothing. Even the local animals had been silenced by the deafening sound of gunfire. It was as if nature held its breath.

Castillo's Team Two was the first to approach the Humvees, then joined by Stark. Castillo made the universal sign of death, a finger across his neck, to wordlessly tell Stark all seven were dead. Stark saw Fisk's Team Three cautiously making their way along the eastern perimeter of the base, a few guns trained on the interior in case there were more attackers. Stark waved to Bobby and pointed to regroup at the north gate.

Stark went from vehicle to vehicle and body to body. All of them were in the same forest green cammies. All appeared to be Filipinos, but he couldn't really distinguish much between Filipinos, Malaysians, Indonesians, or other regional nationalities. Maybe it was the explosion or the gunfire, but some of the uniforms seemed wildly out of proportion. Of the seven dead, three were women. It was not unheard of for women to be part of terrorist organizations—if this was indeed the case here—but it was rare.

A few minutes later, the fifteen team members—less Team Four back at Balabac Peak—were together again in a place where, just a few hours ago, they thought they'd share a meal and cool drinks with their training colleagues at the base. Now there was no sign of the latter, except for the few Stark had seen executed on the fishing vessel that was now out of sight. Fisk looked at him, not unlike he had seen him do years ago on the bridge of USS *Bennington*. His eyes said, "what now?"

"Commander Castillo, your base has been attacked. As this is no longer a training event, command of the teams falls to you," Stark said, taking a drink from his camelback. The burden had fallen on a career ship driver, just as Stark had been before he became painfully experienced with incidents like this.

"We secure the base," Castillo said confidently. "Everyone, remember your training with Highland Maritime. Team Two, you will take position on the northeast corner of the basin and watch for any remaining attackers. Team Three and One, we search the base, one building at a time."

Stark pulled Castillo aside out of earshot and asked if he could send two runners back to Team Four since they might not be aware of the threat and to get them here.

Castillo simply said, "yes, yes, of course," acknowledging he had failed to think of this himself. Then Stark spoke to two of his own men.

"Get to the control tower, check the two I . . . I shot, and see if there's any information you can find. Shout down if you find anything, but I want you to stay up there to keep an eye on things." The duo pivoted and jogged to the tower.

They began with the first three buildings inside the north perimeter. The first thing they saw were the bodies of PN officers and sailors in their blue digital cammies stained dark by their blood, killed in their offices or approaching the exits. The northwest buildings had little other than dead bodies. Stark led a team into the northeast headquarters Quonset hut.

Desks and papers were scattered. File cabinets were toppled. Extra uniforms were strewn about. A PN lieutenant commander was tied to his chair, his chin on his chest, one hole in his temple. His blood was splattered on the wall covering posted memos on a corkboard and a photo of him with a woman and two small children.

"I knew him. He was the executive officer here," Castillo said. "My wife and I introduced him to Estella. His son was born the same year as mine."

"I'm sorry." That's all Stark could muster in what was a giant death zone. "How many officers and sailors were stationed here?" he asked.

"One hundred twenty," Castillo said as he sifted through some papers on the XO's desk, not in a manner of looking for anything in particular, just in trying to do something to keep his mind off the mass murder.

The Philippine Navy, by order of President Quinta, hired Stark's Highland Maritime Defense to train their personnel in a variety of modules—maritime security, littoral operations and insertions, open-source intelligence gathering, use of sensors and other equipment, and foreign materiel acquisition and exploitation. The last one had, coincidentally, been one of the goals of this particular module on Balabac Island.

Foreign Materiel Acquisition and Exploitation (FMA/FME) was conducted by a few governments, whether under formal or informal conditions. The goal was simple and had been used throughout history—find out about the enemy by getting what they have, analyzing it, finding out how it works, and developing a countermeasure if appropriate. Stark would brief clients, like the PN, using historical examples, such as two from the Second World War. In 1943, a team from the Office of Strategic Services found Italian naval weapons during Mission Macgregor. The other was Project Simmons, in which the Allies obtained information on radio-controlled bombs. The man behind both and more missions was Lieutenant Commander John Shaheen, US Navy Reserve. Stark had the fortune of meeting Shaheen in his later years through one of Stark's mentors, Admiral Denby Cole, shortly before an incident in Canada which had led to Stark's court-martial.

Stark and Castillo looked around some more, and then they made their way to the northeast corner of the basin, where they listened and observed. There were more indications of the bloodshed, reports of more bodies and where they were located. There was no sign of any terrorists, insurgents, or whatever they were.

"One hundred twenty personnel here?" Stark asked Castillo. "Does that include the ship's company?"

"Yes. Why?"

"Two cutters are gone. Those are fifteen people each. That one isn't one of yours. That's an Australian *Armidale*-class. It has a crew complement of about twenty-five. Based on the number of bodies reporting back to us, everyone—the base and the ships' companies—is accounted for. At first, I thought the two cutters might have already been underway for the exercise we had planned. That means they were taken by the same people on that fishing vessel," Stark explained.

"They didn't take the other ship," Castillo observed. "It's not ours anyway. It's just on a one-year loan from Australia. We are testing it as a possible replacement for our own older ships."

"Maybe they didn't have enough people to crew all three ships?" Stark offered. "Right now, I think we need to figure out how they attacked the base and when rather than who it was," Stark suggested.

"Agreed," Castillo said, taking one of the uniform blouses off the floor and covering the head and torso of his dead fellow officer to keep the flies away.

CHAPTER 5

"How did you find us here? You should have gone to the other place," he said softly.

"My employer specifically directed me not to," Golzari casually lied. "He is very well connected. He prefers to go direct to market to choose his luxuries rather than what is being sold retail. He prefers gold directly from the mine rather than what has already been melted and shaped by intermediaries." Golzari had to suck in what he was saying. He had been undercover before and knew he had to set his own principles aside and assume a role, regardless of how unsavory. Though attentive to the men in the room, he kept his senses aware of any other sounds that might be clues to the current situation.

"Ah, yes, I understand. What do you propose?" he asked eagerly.

"That depends. How much stock do you currently have?"

"Here? Thirty-seven. All ages. A few in their twenties."

Golzari suppressed any emotion.

"My employer has many residences around the world, several . . . companies . . . and a special island," Golzari said. "He has a need to populate those places with as many resources as possible. He is prepared to pay accordingly."

Golzari could sense the man's appreciation for the change in fortune. Normally his clientele would probably have been men seeking temporary "company" or someone with the money to spirit away a few captives. Not like this. Golzari had effectively offered him enough compensation to satisfy his own comfort for years. The man was a lower intermediary. When the trafficked children arrived in France, they'd be brought to a place like this. Some would remain. A few at a time would be sent up the next ladder in the chain. The man had already suggested there was someplace like it. Perhaps it was a higher-end mansion or hotel.

The children had to arrive somehow. For so many, they wouldn't be transported by plane. That posed too much risk. Trains and buses were unlikely in this case. The young girl looked Asian. If that were the case, then the traffickers would use a ship. With all the containers on one vessel alone, it was only possible to inspect a small percentage. The likelihood of one container among literally thousands being inspected at a major port like Rotterdam or Le Havre was minuscule. The containers would be transported by truck—again uninspected—to the cities.

"First," the man said cautiously, "how do we know you aren't the police?"

"Because if I had known about this building, I wouldn't have come alone. This place would have been stormed."

"Perhaps."

"Perhaps I should take my employer's business elsewhere," he added curtly. "We could go the companies out of Le Havre and get an even better price off the docks." Golzari took a chance, but since Le Havre was France's largest and closest port, it was worth a shot.

The man nodded. "I know you could, but there would be difficulties there for you that you don't have here. You would have to know the right inspection agents and trucking companies. We already have that in our organization."

"How fresh is this group?"

"Their ship arrived in France seven weeks ago."

"Good," Golzari nodded. Out of the corner of his eye, he could see the heavies grow bored with the deal. "Do you have any more arriving?"

"Yes. Soon. The past six months were the most we've ever processed. Our source seems to have had a good opportunity and seized it. It was unusual but now a wonderful opportunity for your employer."

"Certainly. Where are they from?"

"I'm never told exactly. Somewhere in the Philippines." The man blurted it out the way an impatient person was. Golzari knew what caused it. The man had been working all day and night at the restaurant. He didn't live here for social calls at the end of a workday. He was here to process people. It was time.

"The price?" Golzari asked.

The man wrote a figure on a piece of paper, probably so that the heavies—who were misnamed since their frames were slighter than Golzari's—wouldn't know how much they were being underpaid for their services. He slid it across a table to Golzari, who picked it up, leaned back, and crossed his left leg over his right.

"That is acceptable. You will tell me how to wire the money and transfer them to appropriate vehicles." The man was relieved. It was late and had been a long day. But a very profitable one. Perhaps it was because it was so late that he hadn't been more cautious with the visitor.

"My employer would be very displeased if he sent money and you were unable to deliver," Golzari added in a heavier, threatening tone.

"Ha," the man laughed. "That is not a concern. It is not good business to fail to deliver such a high quantity." The heavies chuckled too and rested their weapons, sensing the deal had been made. There had been no other discernable sounds in the building during the conversation. Golzari brought the outside of his left leg a few inches across the top of his right thigh, just enough time to reach for his Smith & Wesson, point it at them, and get to a standing position.

"Stop!" he said sharply.

The two heavies put their weapons down. They didn't make enough money to risk losing their lives. Golzari had seen back-seaters like this throughout his career.

"Now, you first—go in that corner very slowly. Take a seat on the floor and face the wall." He instructed the other two to do the same, one at a time. The room was clear except for the furniture the four men had conversed on and a few lamps. He had nothing to tie the men up. He really couldn't shoot them. And he had no method to call the Sûreté, at least from here. The longer he waited on a course of action, the more likely he'd be discovered.

He had had a career in law enforcement, first briefly with the Boston Police Department and then for two decades with Diplomatic Security. He valued the order those jobs brought out of the chaos. He was out of the system and in a chaotic world. He once criticized Connor Stark for being an uncivilized mercenary and impugned him for doing things that weren't in accordance with the law. What was it Stark had once told him? That there was a difference between the law and justice.

In some of his previous few missions, Golzari started down that slippery slope. Now he was in one of the worst buildings imaginable with the worst of humanity in the corner. There were only a few hours left until daylight, and he needed more information before he slipped out. For now, he kept the gun trained on the silent traffickers, who were breathing harder as he approached. He picked up the metal pipe, slipped his gun in the ankle holster, and firmly gripped the piece with both hands, reminding himself that sometimes the law could dispense justice and sometimes law needed a hand. Or a metal pipe.

BALABAC NAVAL BASE

The group gathered at the northeast corner of the basin, awaiting further reports. Bobby jogged over to Stark and Castillo, his dark gray ball cap slipping off. He left it on the ground for now. A younger Fisk, the one fresh out of the Academy, would have instinctively turned around to pick it up rather than be uncovered. Stark realized Fisk had his priorities, and a simple covering for a company uniform meant little if time and information were essential. Stark had seen promise in the surviving junior officer from USS *Bennington* and again when Fisk served under Jaime on USS *Charles Stewart*. It was why, when they were both required to leave the service, Stark hired Fisk. When Highland Maritime built *Minerva*, Stark had no question about making Fisk the executive officer. Stark had no regrets and was, in fact, quite proud of the young man. Maybe if Stark had had his own son . . . he stopped and compartmentalized again. Sentimentality in the midst of a situation just as this had no place. Back in the Quonset hut, he had seen that moment of compassion shown by Commander Castillo when he covered his friend. Would Stark have done the same?

That was the question, at least for a millisecond, Stark asked himself. He had been through too much in his life—his former career, his current work, the death, the betrayal by some he thought were friends. The losses that kept mounting in his life, some caused by others and some he had caused himself. In the end, it didn't matter. They were still losses, absences, things that caused emptiness, or he imagined what it would be like if one lost a limb. The knowledge of it was still there. The need for something so natural was gone. One would also miss the limb. But one would do what humans do best, adapt to the condition. So it had been with Stark. His adjustment was filling the holes with work, specifically the security work at which his firm had been so successful, if by successful one meant employed and fulfilling the missions or contracts assigned to it. If success meant always doing something by the letter of the law or ethics, then the waters became murky.

If it wasn't for solitude and security of Port St. George, Stark would not have regained at least some of the character he had built in his early life. That Maine village was where his company was based. It was where he ate, drank, and slept. It's where Maggie owned her bar. And if it had not been for Maggie, Stark would have never started to recover from that dark hole. She had strength without arrogance, nobility without aristocratic birth, compassion without weakness, beauty without cosmetics, intelligence without advanced formal education—or the same education that had bred a nation of leaders that had failed the nation in two recent wars. She was his lifeline, even though he sometimes pushed it aside to swim out further in shark-infested waters. A therapist might have called this self-destructive behavior. Stark didn't want to swim with the sharks, sometimes he just had to so that someone else wouldn't. She understood that. Maybe that's why she'd chide him before he left for each assignment and immediately upon his return. But whenever he left, she was there to watch him, and she was there when he returned.

A millisecond later, he snapped back to the here and now, at this silenced, deadly naval base, as only now could local animals be heard in the distance.

"Gentlemen," Fisk said, expelling a deep breath. "This is the logbook from the control tower."

Fisk handed over a thick, green oversized notebook to Commander Castillo. Its green cover was speckled with blood. Stark wasn't sure if that was from the PN watchstanders who had been killed or the attackers Stark had shot.

"It looks like the last entry was at sunset. One of your sailors translated it for me," Fisk said to Castillo, then turned to Stark to explain. "The base sent a radio communication to headquarters in Manila that they were going EMCON for the training exercise."

Castillo scanned it and read from it on Stark's behalf. The base reported that the remainder of the construction materials for the two final Quonset huts arrived that day, that there were 118 personnel accounted for, they were still short on a medical officer, and that two sailors were in the infirmary. The Australian ship was undergoing maintenance. One large local fishing vessel was sighted a nautical mile off the base, reporting engine problems, and requested they be towed in for repairs.

"That's it," Stark reasoned. "That's how they probably attacked the base."

"With an unarmed vessel?" Castillo asked.

"Trojan Horse, Commander. The cutter towed them in and probably didn't do an inspection since it was a Filipino vessel. By the time they got to the boat, rigged it for towing, and arrived in the basin, it would have been dark. You can have a lot of personnel on one fishing vessel down in the holds. That's when they took the base."

"Then it's just coincidence this all happened now?" Castillo inquired, putting on sunglasses from the midday sun. Or maybe it was because it was all hitting him and he didn't want to betray his emotions.

"We now have a possible when and how. Now we need a why. I suggest we go to the control tower, Commander," Stark said. The commander approved as the three of them ascended. Stark automatically did a three-hundred-sixty-degree survey, just as he'd do when he arrived on the bridge of his ship. No boats on the water. Below, the teams had taken positions looking out to the jungle. One look at the smashed radio told him they weren't going to reach headquarters. There was, however, a phone. He picked it up, but the line was dead. He assumed that if the attackers were as destructive with the Australian ship, then the closest communications systems were miles away at sea on *Syren* and *Minerva*. And he had no immediate means of speaking with them.

He looked at the basin below as Castillo tried to find anything useful. Bobby stuck by Stark's side. From here, Stark could see a few engine parts on the pier next to the Australian ship.

That's probably why the attackers didn't take that ship as well. Either they didn't have the ability or the time to put Humpty Dumpty back together.

The whalers, however, were still there.

"Bobby, get down to the whalers and see what condition they're in."

"Aye, sir," the young man replied as he scampered down the ladder.

Stark took one more look around the tower. On the outer deck, he moved the bodies of the first man he'd shot. He was lucky, if you could count killing men at a couple hundred yards lucky. It certainly hadn't been for them. He had taken too many shots and they weren't necessarily in kill zones. Of course, he had had to grab someone else's rifle and adjust as quickly as possible to get the shots out before they went back to the tower. He wasn't a sniper; he was a shooter, a former Olympic shooter of targets, not people. That had all changed. If he had taken the time to count how many times he had to shoot someone since the incident in Canada a lifetime ago, he might have come up with a number but never the faces.

He walked behind one of his watchstanders, keeping an eye on the ocean while the other focused on the landward perimeter. Stark kneeled down beside one of the men he'd shot and swatted away a fly. Neither one was old nor large. They were just kids, one of whom had turned into the control area.

The other bodies—the previous two PN tower operators—were nearby. Stark noticed a difference. The wound placements were precise. One in the forehead and the other in the temple, practically centerline for any profile. If the attack happened at night, someone had taken both of these PN sailors out with highly accurate shots. Plus, the shooter was below, probably on the fishing vessel as it entered the basin or when the attack began. That was no mean feat. In fact, it was the mark of a real professional. They had taken out the two people who could have called for help from other bases.

"Wait," Stark said aloud. "That doesn't make sense."

"What doesn't?" Castillo inquired, wiping the sweat from his brow.

"Their sniper took out the tower watchstanders who could have gotten on the radio to warn others and ask for help," Stark said, still looking at the bodies, then turning to the control room.

"So what, that's a natural reaction, right?" Castillo asked.

"Yeah, but they destroyed the radio equipment. Then why did one of the guys I shot turn back into the room? If the radio was already smashed, why would he go back inside?"

"The gunfire had already started. Maybe they were trying to protect themselves?"

"No, one of them remained on the deck as lookout. Maybe he was going to go down the ladder to help. But that doesn't resolve the other issue."

"You mean, why did they keep a small team behind?" Castillo said.

"Exactly."

"How many of the attackers were here? Nine? Two in the tower and seven in the Humvees."

"Let's assume these men—and women—are holding this base. If the Philippine government learns of it, is it enough for the attackers to hold a place this size?" Stark asked rhetorically. Castillo answered regardless.

"Either they're intended to be suicide attackers for when our forces arrive or . . . they were holding it for when the other attackers return," Castillo realized.

"But why return? And, more importantly, it gets to our original question—why attack this base in the first place? Terrorists don't normally take something and hold it. They hit it and leave. Mostly. What value does this base have?" Stark didn't like the way this was shaping up.

"Commander Castillo," he said, "I'm sorry if I must ask you this question that may be sensitive, but is there anything of value here that I should be aware of?"

Castillo didn't hesitate in replying.

"I can honestly tell you that I am not aware of anything here. It was just a new naval base, a very small one compared to the others, in order to facilitate patrols in this region. No money to speak of. No special equipment," Castillo said, frustrated at not knowing the answer rather than at Stark's asking the question.

Stark nodded, his lips tightened and his brow furrowed. There were too many unknowns. And there were problems. His teams had already expended what little ammunition they had. They didn't have a lot to start with since this was supposed to be a training mission. He doubted they had enough to ward off the attackers if they returned.

"Captain Stark," Castillo said quietly so that the watchstanders would not hear.

"Yes?"

"You have been in such incidents before, correct?"

"Yeah, a few," Stark said, knowing what was coming next.

"I realize I am the senior PN officer, but I know about ships. I don't know this situation or what questions to ask. I respectfully defer to your experience and leadership."

That had taken a lot for the Filipino commander to say. A lesser person with an ego would have either ignored what deep shit they were in or demanded they remain in command. Rossberg had been like that. And for that, most of the officers aboard *Bennington* were killed off Yemen as well as the crews of two Littoral Combat Ships off Sri Lanka in previous missions. Rossberg dismissed the suggestions, ignored the threats, and arrogantly set his rank above his capability. No, Stark respected the Filipino officer.

"Commander, we could say that, under the terms of the contract, the Filipino government representative is legally required to lead what has become an operational unit. We could say that. But I think it's better to say we have a perfectly capable officer in charge who is learning things along with everyone else." Stark paused, reflecting on his own careers.

"We're in this together, and I'm here to support you," Stark said, reaching out his hand.

The Filipino officer was relieved. He smiled and took Stark's hand in partnership. "Then let's start with what I know best. Let's get to the basin," he said confidently.

C H A P T E R   6

P A R I S

Golzari did a once-over of the room to recreate the scene and kept his latex gloves on. He searched the bodies of the trafficker and his security team. The trafficker/restaurant manager had little on him aside from cigarettes, a lighter, some money, a cell phone, and keys. That is what Golzari needed most, the keys to the building. He checked the guards. Neither moved nor would they ever again after Golzari ensured the metal pipe had done its work on their skulls. He had moved so quickly from one to the other that they were out before they could dodge whatever hell came from behind them. They hadn't had time to scream.

The guards had wallets, both with identification showing them to be residents of Paris. Both had phones, sets of keys, and drugs. Golzari compared their key chains to the trafficker's and found four identical ones. There was no need to carry more than he had to, so he inserted the keys back into the security guards' pockets and kept the trafficker's. Still hearing no movement above, he made his way to the basement door, trying one key at a time until the right one worked. The light switch was immediately to the left. He turned it on. It was unlikely anyone had been operating in the dark, but he saw some ambient light and moved in cautiously.

A few of the wood steps creaked. After each one, he'd stop to hear any movement in response. There was none. The basement had racks of food, plenty to feed the seventeen children. There were also towels and lines. He took one of the linens and ripped off a small square. Some plastic grocery bags were strewn about. He made use of one, placing the procured cell phones in them.

Along one wall were three computer terminals, a desk, and a chair. That's where the light was coming from as all were on. The first terminal was linked to the security camera at the front door where Golzari had entered. He sat on the chair and took the cloth in his hand as he opened the drawers. There was paper in one, a printer in another, and a few bottles, including isopropyl alcohol. He took that and placed it on the desk.

Golzari deftly tapped the keys as he had on the piano earlier that evening on Pont St. Louis. As a federal agent, he had taken enough training to get around most computer security. In this case, security was lax. There was no password. These security guards were local hacks. Otherwise, they would have also had a camera on the back of the building. Golzari took less than three minutes to delete any record of his approach to the building.

The other two monitors had images of the two rooms where the children were held and currently sleeping. One of the children was tossing and turning. Another few minutes and he found little else. These were only security monitors for one of the guards. There was nothing that the trafficker himself would have used.

Most of the rooms in this building were devoid of furniture, wall paintings, and knick-knacks. This wasn't a home to live in, this was a penitentiary for the enslaved. The only room that wasn't empty was on the second floor and seemed to belong to the trafficker. It had a bed, chair, large-screen television, and desk. Pornographic magazines littered the area next to the chair and desk that had a large ashtray. Like the basement, the desk had a computer terminal on it, but this one was different.

He again tapped away, circumventing the password-protected system. The trafficker's email was open. Golzari made note of anything out of the ordinary, or at least anything that might be associated with the trafficking network. The man had a name—Abdou Mansouri. He was Algerian, then. At least that was a start. Family members were emailing him from France and extended members such as cousins and uncles from Algeria. Golzari's initial assessment was right. The trafficker had either been born in France or immigrated at a young age. The fact that he had little accent supported the theory that he had been raised here.

Other emails were from friends. Still others were from companies he had ordered from. He started building a pattern around the now-deceased

Abdou Mansouri. He liked good cigarettes, hair products, turtleneck sweaters, and cheap shoes. He didn't seem to travel and was taking online business courses. Whether or not he planned to use them for improving the trafficking network or transition to a legitimate business, Golzari couldn't care less. Abdou Mansouri no longer had the opportunity to do either. Golzari had made him pay for his sins, seventeen of which were just a floor above.

The Iranian-American continued to scroll through pages of emails as well as the deleted folder until he came across one email in a draft with the name of a ship arriving in Le Havre the next day at noon. He checked his watch. He had already spent too much time here, and he knew the train from Paris to Le Havre was three hours on a good day. He'd have to drive to make it there faster, not an easy task since he'd be working off no sleep.

Golzari went through the hard drive for any folders with information about the network. His contacts at the Sûreté would have something to work with from Abdou's name. There was nothing in the drawers. He walked around the room, looking for anything. He opened the closet. The stench of nicotine wafted out. He shifted the clothes to the side, revealing some cheap wood paneling. He felt around the edges and popped it out, exposing a small nook with a fireproof box, just large enough for envelopes and 8.5x11-inch papers. He pulled the box out and set it on the desk. The key was secured to the handle with a plastic tie as if it had just been purchased. Maybe Abdou Mansouri would have learned in his online business courses not to keep the key next to a box whose contents you don't want anyone to see.

BALABAC NAVAL BASE

"It's a mess, isn't it?" Castillo asked, scratching his head. Stark shook his head, partly out of confusion, partly out of frustration.

"I guess this explains why the attackers didn't take this ship as well. What's your experience with this, Commander?"

"The parts all look new," he said as he made his way to each of the two dozen parts strewn about on the pier. "None of them are stripped and there's barely any grease. I'd say this wasn't necessary maintenance but rather they took it apart to learn about the system. It's not like they removed the shaft and prop."

"So that's one thing in our favor. The attackers didn't have the knowledge of this ship or the time needed to reassemble it. Could you?" Stark asked, wiping sweat from his brow from the midday sun.

"Could I what?" Castillo responded, now going through a nearby manual.

"Reassemble it."

"I think so. My last duty station was as a chief engineer on a minesweeper. I'd need about four of my sailors to assist me," Castillo said confidently, the first time he had done so since everything started falling to shit.

"How long do you think it would take?" Stark asked, looking at his watch again.

Castillo stood and walked around the pier looking at the pieces again and brought his hand up to rub his chin.

"Seven, maybe eight hours," he estimated. "But I need to do a better sweep of the ship itself. If the attackers destroyed the radio equipment, what if they sabotaged another system to keep it from operating?"

"I wouldn't do that if I were them," Stark commented. "Why sabotage a ship at a base your people were holding?" He took another sip from the Camelbak, conscientiously hydrating in the midday heat.

Castillo and his sailors weren't commandos. They were ship-drivers. So was Stark. The purpose of the multi-tiered training the Philippine government contracted with Highland Maritime was for scenarios of boarding other ships, small arms practice, and how to conduct basic forensics. As sailors, they'd board suspect ships or, in the case of the Philippines, possibly go ashore, given how many terrorist and insurgent groups abounded.

"Then what about the radio?" Castillo wondered, his almond eyes squinting as they turned up to the sky suddenly.

"What is it?" Stark asked, following Castillo's gaze upward.

"I . . . I don't know," Castillo said, still looking upward. "I thought I saw something. Must be the birds. I'm a little . . . jittery. Is that the right word, Captain Stark?"

"Jittery works as well as anything right now. You had a good question about the radio. But we can only solve one mystery at a time. If you've got this project, I'd like to see if we can get help."

Castillo nodded, called over a few sailors, and started directing them as Stark made his way clockwise around the basin to the southside. The large bay doors of the ship repair facility, not unlike the one he had once seen at the Naval Support Activity in Annapolis, were wide open. The lights were on, exposing a mostly empty facility. It was, of course, still new, along with most of the still-unfinished base. It didn't have that lived-in look of grease, dirt, and the sweat of hundreds of hours of labor every week. Nothing was strewn about. He stopped at the wooden finger piers at one of the three whalers tied up. A quick look on the other finger piers suggested there hadn't been more whalers that the attackers would have taken. The cleats were clean and empty of any lines normally used to secure the boats while in the basin.

"Report, Bobby," he said to the shorter, blond-haired young man who was cursing as he cut his finger on an exposed screw.

"Clean boats, sir. Except for the radios, they're operational. I checked the boathouse and there's still plenty of fuel too. I guess those bastards either didn't want or need them. By the way, I passed the armory on the way here—everything useful is gone."

"Shit—again with the radios. Castillo and I were wondering if it was the naval base personnel who took out the radios during the attack or if it was the red force," Stark said.

"But why? The base was under attack—a surprise attack if you're right. Would they have had time to wipe out the radios or even think about it? They'd have been focused on defending themselves. No, my guess is it was the attackers. But, again, why not leave the communications for their own people?" Bobby suggested.

"That would mean the attackers didn't need the radios themselves. Either they had their own comms—which they didn't have or we haven't found—or they wanted to remain at EMCON themselves no matter what."

"That doesn't sound good," Bobby said, tapping the whaler's wheel, then removing his glasses to wipe the perspiration off them.

"You okay, Bobby?" Stark asked quietly in his baritone voice.

"Aside from the fact that we killed a bunch of people who could be terrorists or a host of other bad dudes, I'm out of ammo, and I have a fucking boo-boo on my finger? Aside from that, everything's peachy, skipper," he said, showing the bloody cut on his forefinger. Fortunately, that wasn't Bobby's shooting hand, a fact Stark had learned years ago when they had stormed a ship in the Gulf of Aden. Bobby had shared that he had been the top shooter on the team at the Naval Academy. When Stark hired him and started training with him at the headquarters on the island off Port St. George, Bobby became a fierce competitor on the range and sometimes even beat the old Olympic shooter.

"Why?" Fisk asked.

"You said it yourself. We have a bad ammo situation. We can't even take anything from the guys we took out. I know Castillo wants to hold the base, but I'm not sure what we could do if they return. There's that town on the north side of the island. I'm thinking of heading up there to see if they have anything. What was the name of it?"

"Población I, Captain," Santos replied.

"I don't like that idea," Fisk said, ripping open the wrapping of a protein bar and taking a large bite out of it before grimacing. "You know, skipper, the company doesn't have to skimp on the quality of the bars," he joked.

"Thanks, I'll put that on your annual evaluation. What's wrong with the trek to the village?" Stark asked as he took in more water.

"Are you sure they haven't been attacked? It's happened before in the Philippines and Indonesia." Fisk offered a protein bar to the Filipino who politely waved it off.

"I don't know if this force had enough people or if there were multiple attacks, Bobby. Damn it, we just don't have enough information. That's why I asked if you were okay."

"You're going to tell me to take one of these whalers, fill it with fuel, and get to *Minerva* and *Syren*, aren't you," he said without missing a beat and taking another hunk out of the protein bar.

"Huh, you can read me that well already?"

"No, but Captain Johnson can. She filled me in on all your tells."

"That's going on her annual review too. . . ." he joked about his colleague and cousin. "Can you do it, Bobby?"

Stark knew what he was asking of Fisk. A small boat in the open water with no radio and needing a little luck to connect with two ships that weren't just east of the island over the horizon, they were more difficult to see because of the new camouflage.

"There were some aluminum sheets in the boat shed. Take one of them with you. That'll be a good reflective for up to twelve nautical miles in case the ships are using their radars," Stark noted, knowing that they were under direction not to. For all Stark knew, the ships thought they were still operating in a training environment.

"It's okay, I know they were under orders to remain at EMCON," Bobby said, understanding the difficult task ahead. "I think I can reach the other side of the island in an hour, then another hour straight east to find them. Based on their top speed, they should be here an hour after that."

It wasn't a needle in a haystack, but it would still take guts and skill to do what he'd just told Bobby to undertake. If anything went wrong with the engine, for example, there'd be no way for Fisk to reach the ships or the ships to know he was in trouble.

"Is your Morse code still good?"

"Aces."

"Good. In case you don't think you can make it directly to them, take the whaler to the east side of the island where we landed. Stay offshore in case there are bad guys around there. Judge the water. If the water's too rough, hold off the beach. At midnight, the ships should be in range for the light signals. Get them over here. With a little luck, you'll all be here by 0300. And tell Jay I want Crow's Nest ready."

"Aye, sir. I'd like to go this alone. One more sailor adds more weight and increased fuel cost."

"Agreed. Good luck, Bobby. And don't take any unnecessary chances," Stark said, placing a firm hand on the young officer's shoulder.

"How could I? I work for you, sir," he said with a wink as he went to prepare the eighteen-foot whaler for its mission.

SOUTH CHINA SEA

"*Ubl'udak!*" Makarov shouted to his counterpart on the large fishing vessel. The man just shrugged his shoulders and threw his arms up. He didn't understand Russian. Makarov had nearly slipped and fallen after the two boats tied up alongside each other. He stepped onto the gunwale and set his foot onto the deck, still wet with the blood of three Filipino naval officers.

"Couldn't you fucking clean this up?" he shouted again as Toni and Qin grabbed the closest stanchion. Qin deftly landed on the wet deck and accounted for the slippage, surfing it for another two feet. Toni threw her legs over the gunwale and slid down a couple of yards away from the mess.

"Welcome aboard, Sergei," the boat's master said in broken English. He was a full head shorter than Makarov and about a hundred pounds lighter. He smiled broadly, showing what yellowed teeth remained. His old brown, wrinkled face bore the scars of war and the effects of prolonged exposure to the sun. He wore the forest green camouflage uniform of the scores of other men and women on the ship. The others all wore the same patterned ballcaps with no other identifying information on the uniforms. No name or country name patches. These were not professional soldiers, but they had experienced warfare in the southern Philippine islands.

Makarov wasn't sure who he had more disdain for—this ragtag group for the ideological tools they were or himself who had taken jobs like this where he had to work with people like this on rusty, shitty fishing vessels like this. He already needed another drink at the thought of it. On the far side of the fishing vessel, he saw two patrol vessels fast approaching at a distance of about seven nautical miles. He checked his watch and made a quick mental calculation. There was time until they arrived.

The engine on the vessel he'd left cut off as the ships completed tying up after a series of rubber tenders kept the hulls from crushing each other. Dozens more soldiers emerged from it and started waving their rifles and chanting when they saw their counterparts on this boat. They broke into a song Makarov didn't understand. He went back to his happy place of counting the money he was making each day and how each brought him closer to retirement from this god-forsaken business.

"Have you heard anything on the radio?" he asked the master.

"We hear the usual traffic. The freighters and tankers passing south of Balabac Island only chat about their directions. Nobody is talking about the news. It is too soon. No one knows," he said, laughing.

"No laughing yet," Makarov admonished. "Too much can go wrong."

"What? Everything is quiet. No internet, nothing. And we just took over a naval base from the Philippine Navy! We never did that before. Listen. Listen to what victory sounds like, my Russian friend," the master said, waving his arms toward the soldiers of both boats.

"Success is when everything goes right and we finish the job," Makarov responded, pointing a finger into the chest of the shorter master, who stopped rejoicing.

"Remember who I work for," Makarov continued. "When he says we've accomplished our job, then you can sing and dance and do whatever the *ebat* you want." He turned back to his other two companions. "Did you get the bags off the boat?"

Qin nodded and showed him what he was carrying. Toni did the same and finally hopped down onto a dry area of the deck.

"You know you weren't supposed to kill them, right?" Makarov told the master.

"We were carried away by the moment. One of my men found out the base commander had once served on his island. He started questioning him about the war, the commander spit in his face and wouldn't answer his questions, and my man shot him. After that he figured the other two ought to die since they represented the Philippine government," the master said unapologetically.

Makarov knew his limits here. He, Qin, and Toni were outnumbered. Despite who was running the show and despite the fact that he was the operational commander of this assignment, he knew better than to throw the bastard overboard or the soldier who had killed the base commander. The level of chanting increased as some paced it, striking the decks like giant beating war drums. Makarov had been in places like this before, where the blood lust was so pronounced that there was no reason, no control, and any minor misstep would mean that he and his two colleagues could be shot or have their throats slit. Most of these soldiers had no respect for authority, hierarchy, or a chain of command. Most had no idea that they could accomplish anything like this without the vision and financing from someone someplace far away. They were all like this, whether they were insurgents, separatists, or terrorists. All they knew and understood was the here and now, and they didn't think there'd be any repercussions to what they did in defiance of the puppet masters. Makarov knew better. For now, he'd ignore the master's defiance. For now, Makarov just needed to succeed and retire. Toni was clearly growing uncomfortable. Even the stoic Qin made eye contact as if to say it was time that they find a more defensible position.

The two Philippine Navy patrol boats slowed in their approach, making a wide arc to their stern as one took station on the port side of the vessel and the other on the starboard side of the fishing boat Makarov had just left. He couldn't believe the cheering could erupt even more, producing a deafening sound.

"I need to see what's happening. Take us to the operations room now," he told the master, who complied with the order, opening a creaking hatch to the interior.

CHAPTER 7

PARIS

The strongbox held more evidence the Sûreté would need to fully investigate and prosecute more people associated with the dead trafficker. Golzari carefully removed the documents with the cloth and lined them up on the floor. He took the burner phone out of his pocket and began taking images of them. Lucky—there were a few names and numbers of local Parisian businesses, lists of "customers," petrol receipts on the road from Paris to Le Havre and back, and the names of ships used in the past to transport the innocent victims of this dark and despicable business. Another was a list of the security teams and their schedules. He quickly checked his watch again. The next shift would arrive in two and a half hours.

He looked back at the petrol receipts and checked the times and dates. They were all in the afternoon when Mansouri was working at the restaurant. Someone else was driving the trafficked children from Le Havre to Paris. He'd give these to Emile to track down the lorry driver or drivers.

What Golzari didn't know was where the trafficked children were from based on the paperwork. He could ask them, but without knowing what language they spoke, he might simply scare the children. He'd have to take a chance that no one else would arrive by the time he got to his contact with the Sûreté.

Golzari gathered up the papers and put them back in the strongbox and put that on the desk so that the police would find a nice, tidy package awaiting them. He stood for just a moment to recall if there was anything that might prove he was here—other than the dead bodies. Secure in the knowledge that his SAVAK trainers would not have found evidence of his presence, he made his way down the staircase. He was about to exit when he remembered the front—and only—camera. He had wiped the recording clean from when Abdou Mansouri had let him in, but it would also record him leaving, and there would be no way to wipe that afterward.

He weighed the decision, taking longer than he wanted to. Leaving any video of him departing was unacceptable. Only a few people in the Sûreté knew of Golzari's work. Other officers would ask too many questions about his dark operations on their behalf. He couldn't leave out the back since the doors and windows on this level were secured, and it would cause too much noise to open them to the alley. There was a window ajar on the third floor where he had used the fiberscope, but that also meant taking the chance of waking the children as he waded through their mini-dormitory. His only option was to return to the basement and turn off the recording. The only problem with that was it would result in more questions.

It took him far longer than he thought to creep down the creaky stairs and navigate through the security terminal. No matter how much he wiped it or prevented the video from working until after he had left the building, there would be some trace that a better Sûreté computer specialist would see. They wouldn't know it was Golzari himself, but they would know this was more than a simple hit on the trafficker and security guards. Five minutes would be enough. He set the recording to stop for five minutes to allow him to get out of the building with the phones he had secured and get word to his contact.

He went back upstairs and made his way out the front door. He heard something down the street to the right, a rustling of paper as the morning wind picked up. He went to the left and kept close to the buildings as he passed them. Within two blocks he heard steps approaching him, the pace picked up. As Golzari approached the crosswalk of the next street, he darted to the left, pressed himself to the wall, and pulled out his Swiss Army knife.

The footsteps stopped just before the corner. Golzari began backing up slowly, recalling the truism not to bring a knife to a gunfight. He made it another ten yards when an arm waived, then both arms appeared with two empty hands. The black-shirted figure slowly emerged around the corner.

"*C'est moi,*" the figure said in a loud, raspy whisper as his torso then head popped out.

Golzari breathed a sigh of relief, put the knife back in his pocket, and walked toward his contact.

"You should have stayed for the second set. Come with me," Emile said in a hushed tone.

Golzari grabbed his arm and pulled him along. The man tried to keep up with the longer-legged Golzari. They were silent for another minute until Golzari knew it was safe and out of sight of neighbors.

"How long were you following me?"

"Long enough. I was thinking of helping when I saw you fall from the fire escape, but you got up fast enough and Robert told me you preferred to work alone," he said.

"Robert isn't wrong, Emile. You need to call your colleagues. There are seventeen souls in the building," Golzari said to his contact in the Sûreté. Emile didn't miss a beat, calling them with the details Golzari provided.

"Thank you, Damien. I need to get back there. Is there anything else I need to know?"

"I took their phones just in case you couldn't get in there before the other traffickers found the bodies," he said, handing the bag to Emile. "There's a ship arriving in Le Havre today with more trafficked souls."

"We don't have jurisdiction and we can't risk notifying the port's security. We know there are leaks there. Are you going?" Emile asked as he texted back and forth with his teams en route to the trafficking house.

"I'd like to dig around," Golzari said. "I'll be back tonight. Good luck."

"I owe you, Damien."

"Standard payment, Emile. Two bottles of acceptable wine," Golzari said as he headed back to his apartment.

BALABAC NAVAL BASE

Stark watched Fisk at the Boston whaler's center console as it left the basin for the open water. The ocean was still calm, but he knew how unforgiving it could be and how, in practically an instant, the wind would pick up and the waves start kicking a small boat around. Bobby wasn't inexperienced with small boats. The training on the Highland Maritime island off the coast of Maine was a good teacher in respecting the conditions of the ocean, especially with the local lobstermen who worked with them on the side. Still, even experienced sailors could be overpowered by Mother Nature and Poseidon when they got into a fight.

Commander Castillo and his sailors were busy putting Humpty Dumpty back together again. Actually, Stark thought, it was completely unfair to suggest the Australian *Armidale*-class ship was anything but elegant, effective, and lethal, designed for offshore patrols. That was the kind of ship he wished the US Navy had invested in to expand maritime security in addition to the larger capital ships, but the entrenched, conservative thinking in the Pentagon and Naval Sea Systems Command (NAVSEA) wouldn't think of anything but carriers and destroyers for the fleet. In fact, Highland Maritime's ship *Syren* had been a discarded ship built not by NAVSEA but through an innovative experiment from the Office of Naval Research. She was born FSF-1 *Sea Fighter*, built at a tenth of the cost of the continually challenged littoral combat ships. The first four of those abortive efforts had already been decommissioned while *Syren* continued to sail. Two other Navy littoral combat ships were at the bottom of the ocean off Sri Lanka after Admiral Rossberg had failed to heed Stark's warnings during his mission there.

In just the past few hours, Stark had almost forgotten the paradise around him. The miles of near-white sandy beaches, the palm trees, and the clear, azure waters would have been a natural destination for vacationers. It was better that it was undeveloped. He had seen too many places in the world that had been spoiled by first-world desires and needs. This base was borne out of the necessity of maritime security or, rather, the insecurity posed by illegal fishing by other nations.

Stark made his way back to the headquarters hut, making sure to keep an accounting of every one of the remaining PN and Highland Maritime personnel around the base. Six were now working on the Australian boat and another two were in the tower. Five were patrolling the perimeter. Only Santos was temporarily unaccounted for until Stark walked into the Quonset hut with the dead Filipino XO's body.

Santos was sitting at the front desk at what had likely been the station for the command's yeoman. A map and ruler were set out as she looked up. She was about to stand out of respect for the older man when Stark motioned for her to remain seated. The XO's covered body was now lying flat along a wall. Santos must have moved him out of respect and yet she still showed no emotion. She just kept doing her job. Stark respected that. He had a brief flashback to a morning run on the Washington Mall when he was a military fellow in the Senate to someone else who was always so focused on the matters at hand. Santos was keeping her head about her even with what she had seen and experienced in the past couple of hours. He pulled up a seat on the other side of the desk.

"Anything interesting on the map?" he asked, removing his ballcap.

"I'm refamiliarizing myself with the region, sir. I failed to see this," she said without looking up.

"See what?"

"This attack. As the intelligence officer, I should have provided better situational awareness. I should have known of potential threats."

"Really? There was an entire base here that didn't know. We have no idea what else is going on beyond this island. Maybe other bases were attacked. Sometimes, Lieutenant Santos, we don't have all the information we need to make the best decision, so we make decisions on the information we have. Plus, we add experience and some intuition," he said in a fatherly but not condescending way. "I've been around a long time. I didn't see this either."

She looked up. He was wrong about her stoicism. A hint of a tear appeared in one of her brown eyes. "I should have known," she said firmly.

"Tell me, Lieutenant, when was the last time you had access to a classified computer terminal," Stark said calmly, reaching in one of the pockets of the beige reporter's vest he wore above his coveralls. He pulled out two of the shitty protein bars Bobby hated and offered one to her. She again politely refused.

"You've been burning calories. You'll burn more. Have one," he said as she acquiesced to the sensible suggestion. "So, when was the last time you had access."

She thought about it for a moment. "About three weeks ago, before we started this training with your company."

"If you had had access to that system since then, would you have known about this threat?"

"I don't know."

"Maybe, Lieutenant. Again, the base must not have known either, and they must have had computer access or radio reports in the past three weeks. It didn't make a difference," he said.

Santos nodded, appearing to understand. "They didn't even have un-classified access," she muttered.

"What?"

"The generators are still operational. The buildings have power. The computer has power. But there's no internet access," she had observed.

"None?"

"Their Wi-Fi hadn't been set up yet. I was reading through the XO's reports. Their only internet access was from the cables to Palawan. The XO had written . . ." she looked through the hard copy reports and found what she was looking for, "here. Here it is. He wrote that the internet went down. Based on when we think the attack happened, internet access was terminated a few hours in advance. He didn't think it was important since it's a new base and a lot of systems still weren't functioning properly."

"Do you think it was an accident?" Stark asked the young officer.

"It could be a coincidence. But the fact that the base had no communi-cations and was attacked suggests this was more extensive," she surmised.

"Do you know anything more about that cable?"

She pulled out another map of the island's infrastructure and slid her forefinger across the island to the north.

"Huh, it's the only cable off the island. That would mean if it went down for the base, the island's population wouldn't have it either," she realized.

"I think we need to make a trip to the Población I, but on the way, we can check on that cable," Stark said grimly at the thought of dividing what little forces remained available to him.

"I'd like to join you, sir. You need someone from our military—our government—to help you there."

There it is, he thought. She realized she wasn't at fault and that she wasn't quitting. One of the PN sailors knocked on the door.

"Sir, Team Four is here. They've got wounded and dead."

Stark, accompanied by Santos, yelled to Castillo as he raced to the north gate where Team Four, what was left of it, limped in. Earlier that day, Stark had divided his teams according to the training plan, sending two Highland Maritime personnel and three PN sailors on Team Four to Balabac Peak. One PN sailor clutched his bloody arm. Another growled with each step on a mangled leg, helped by leaning on a large stick he used as a crutch. The two larger Highland Maritime personnel and the two runners he'd sent were helping to carry the body of another PN sailor.

"Get them to the medical hut, Santos, and have our folks start treating the wounded as best they can. Sivan," he called to Team Four's lead. "What the hell happened?"

The tall Israeli brunette watched as the sailors under her charge were taken away to be cared for, then nodded out of respect to the PN commander joining them.

"We took position on Balabac Peak as planned for the training mission," she said. Stark could hear the controlled fury in her voice. She didn't look at Stark when he spoke with her but rather back where she had come from.

"We had set up the site and I was familiarizing the PN sailors with one of our weapons. I set two of the men on watch. That's when we were hit. They killed the sailor and hit two others. We managed to return fire. We got lucky."

"How many of them were there?" Stark asked.

"Two."

"Two?" Stark replied in disbelief. "You checked the area for more?"

"We did. Thoroughly. There was no evidence of anyone except those two."

"Did you find anything on them?"

"We checked the bodies of both shooters," she said, turning back to speak directly to her boss. "They were in forest green cammies. All they had was some water, their rifles, and some ammo. Nothing else. They could have been Filipino or Malaysian."

"None of this is making any sense," Stark said more to himself than Sivan Abraham or Santos. "If they were traveling light, without food or anything else, they didn't have to worry about supplies."

"Which means they had supplies elsewhere?"

"Right. But were they part of the base attackers or another group?" Stark posed to the other two.

"Base attackers?"

"That's when we realized something had happened here." Stark gave her the thirty-second situation report. "Thanks, Sivan. Get over to the medical hut," which Stark pointed to. "The other teams have the watch."

"Aye, Cap'n," she said, jogging off.

"Commander Castillo, we have a larger problem."

"I understand. More unknowns."

"Exactly. Were the two who shot at Team Four from the base attackers, were they prepositioned on Balabac Peak, or did they come from somewhere else?"

"We've been lucky that we outgunned them each time. Here at the base and at Balabac Peak," Santos observed.

"Very," the commander answered.

"If that's been the case, is it possible that there aren't many people in this force?" Santos said. "That would suggest more of an armed terrorist group than any other option. We can rule out a larger force from a state actor since, in a military action, they would have used overwhelming force. And there has never been a separatist movement here in Balabac."

"Tell me more about the Molbogs," Stark said to both of them.

"She's correct, Captain Stark. The Molbogs have never had a separatist inclination like other islands to the east and no history of armed groups. They've had a peaceful history here. Mostly they just prefer to be left alone as much as possible so they can farm, fish, and trade."

"Is there much interaction with them?" Stark asked.

"Maybe less than with other indigenous island populations because this is the far reach of the country. Even when we started building the base, they kept mostly to themselves, not really curious about the navy being here. They understood our ships would be here to protect their fishing industry," Castillo said.

"From illegal fishing vessels?"

"Yes. And some legal. Mostly they come from China, North Korea, Vietnam, and elsewhere."

"Commander, with your permission, once *Syren* and *Minerva* arrive, I'd like to take Lieutenant Santos with me in one of the remaining vehicles and see what we can find out in the villages to the north and east. We were going to check their communications ability with the other islands and the government."

"Do you think that's wise since Team Four was attacked?" Castillo stiffened.

"As it stands, I don't think there's a choice. We need more information about what's going on out there. If they only had two people attacking Team Four, I don't think they have an unlimited force. And if they do, well, with due respect to the lieutenant here, it will just be the two of us. The majority of our force has to remain to hold the base as best as possible," Stark said apologetically.

"Are you always this positive, Captain Stark?" Santos asked, cracking an uncharacteristic half-smile. Stark returned the comment with a grin. Despite the gravity of the situation, they both knew humor could help them push through it.

"Of course, I understand. Are you okay with this?" Castillo asked his subordinate. "You're not infantry and if you're not comfortable . . ."

"Sir, I am not comfortable, but I don't believe any of us are right now. As the intelligence officer assigned to this program with Highland Maritime Defense, I'm the most familiar with this island. This is my duty," she replied with a growing but cautious confidence.

"Very well," he said proudly of his junior colleague. Turning back to Stark, he advised, "You're more likely to find people near their port to the northeast who can speak with the lieutenant."

"Why is that?"

"Molbog is an Austronesian language. Most don't speak Tagalog like the majority of us do. I know none of my sailors are from here."

Stark took a long deep breath for the unknown ahead and was oblivious to what was above.

CHAPTER 8

This ship's interior was slightly better than the fishing vessel Makarov and his team had just left. The passageways with blue linoleum floors were well lit. The crew was more professional and uniform than the developing world citizens the fishing vessels normally relied upon. Makarov had seen the specs for this vessel a year before when it was in a Malaysian port being refitted. He directed that it be gutted of all its fishing equipment, nets, and cold storage spaces. Below the first deck, those spaces were converted to short-term transport of people. It wasn't a comfortable voyage, but it didn't need to be. It only had to house a couple of hundred people at a time on two-day trips. It had already served that purpose twice a week for the past year, and it was only one of four ships converted for that purpose. This ship, however, also served as his command post for this mission.

He ducked his head as he continued forward through the third hatch, then turned left, entering the room that had been the crew's mess in its original configuration. Now it was equipped with the best technology his company could purchase and permanently staff with three people from his company. The room was barely lit to allow its staff to monitor their screens and equipment. On the left wall, or forward bulkhead, sat the communications officer. On the right, or aft bulkhead, was the tactical officer monitoring ship movements in the regions. Straight ahead on the starboard bulkhead was his pilot, tapping away at a keyboard below large monitors. Makarov stood behind the officer and placed his hand on his shoulder as he set his backpack aside.

"Welcome back, sir," the tactical officer said, looking up at the wide-shouldered Russian. "I have everything ready. It's on the right monitor."

Sergei Makarov leaned back and crossed his arms as the video came up. At first it was grainy on a blurry screen, with blue on the left side of the screen and green on the right. As it came into focus, the blue became the coast with a basin, and the green palm trees, flora, and green grass surrounding the Balabac Naval Base. Humvees sped through the north gate.

"That was stupid," he said grimly. "They should have stayed where they were."

Small sparks appeared on the screen from the north and south perimeters of the jungle, ripping apart the Humvees and their occupants. They never had a chance in that crossfire. The pilot fast-forwarded as three teams emerged from the north, south, and east and entered the base. Makarov took mental notes of how they entered each building, the control tower, and set up their watches inside the fence line. He also noticed two figures who remained together as the others went back and forth from them. That was the command node. The other figures approached the team and then took stations elsewhere on the base.

"Freeze there," he told the pilot. "Magnify it." The pilot tapped some more keys, zooming in on the pair.

One wore the gray and black Camopat pattern uniform and the distinctive two suns on the insignia—a Philippine Navy commander. The other—the other had a dark ballcap, gray coveralls, a beige vest, and a black backpack. Because of the drone's high azimuth, the camera couldn't show much of his face.

"Continue," he said. The image zoomed out again, showing the whole base. While Makarov absorbed all the activity, he kept coming back to the two men. At one point, the man in cammies looked up, almost in the direction of the drone as the dark-capped man followed his lead.

"There. Stop there and zoom in again. Did they hear the drone?" he asked the pilot.

"Possibly, but according to the sensors, there was a shift in the wind. The man in the gray and black uniform probably heard something above, and that's why they're not looking at the drone and then they turned away after this," the young drone pilot said softly.

Regardless, the faces were clear when the camera zoomed in on them. The man in the gray coveralls had a darker ballcap with a logo that read "Highland Maritime Defense." He was in his late forties with a face that had the tell-tale signs of years on the water—the tanned skin, the deep lines. His thin lips were bordered by a few days of hair growth.

Makarov reached into his backpack and pulled out a notebook. He turned to the third page, which had three side-by-side photos of Connor Stark. On the left was an image of him as a young, smiling man in a red, white, and blue tank top with a bronze medal hanging around his neck, his arm raised in recognition of what Makarov imagined was the applause for his name and country being mentioned at the Olympics. In the middle was a formal photo taken a decade later, a serious lieutenant commander in his Navy dress blue uniform, saluting a flag officer. On the right was a more recent photo taken covertly on the Maine coast. Stark was at the helm of a motorboat, tying up to a pier where tourists were getting ready to board a ferry.

Below the photos were several pages of biographical notes about his career in the Navy, the secretive court-martial that had ended it because of some illegal activities in Canada. It had more information, such as when he was recalled to duty and took command of the USS *Bennington* off of Yemen, as well as some of his actions with Highland Maritime Defense, like the one in Sri Lanka. Makarov remembered that operation. He hadn't played a significant part since they were only supporting the revolution from the coastline. But he read through the account of how the entire operation fell apart because this man had organized a joint Navy and private security counter-operation.

Now Connor Stark was here. And so was Sergei Stepanovich Makarov.

CAMP DAVID

President Dunner heaved a heavy sigh as he sat back in the recliner near the piano and closed his eyes. His steward had just placed a fresh cup of tea next to him and dutifully exited back to the galley without saying a word. Dunner had just received the next requested brief about the situation in the Philippines. The brief lasted all of eight minutes. Information continued to be sketchy throughout the islands. Power had yet to be restored to the majority of the country. It was daylight there. The concern was what would happen at night. Would there be large-scale looting as had occurred in major US cities?

The intelligence community had only picked up sporadic details, but they did confirm that President Quinta's plane had been shot down by one of her escort planes, and there were no survivors. Dunner had met Quinta twice, once when he was secretary of state and she was a senator. The second time was a few months after he had assumed the presidency, and the two met at the White House, her first foreign trip as head of state. She was tough, no-nonsense, and although she knew how to play China and the United States off of each other, she favored the United States. China, she told him, had become the most powerful military and economic power in the world. But, she argued, it was a threat to the region, which was why Taiwan, South Korea, Japan, Vietnam, Indonesia, and Malaysia had begun an informal alliance to contain the growing power which, at one time or another in history, they had all faced. The Philippines, she knew, was the key to it all, given its geostrategic location east of the militarized islands China had constructed in the South China Sea.

The secretary of defense and secretary of state left the lodge to return to Washington to be closer to their own senior teams. The Philippines was in trouble, but it wasn't clear if it was a crisis that went beyond that country. And, in Washington, every day had at least three crises with which these two cabinet secretaries dealt. The only person to remain behind at his request was CJ Sumner. Among his senior appointed national security officials, she had the most experience in Washington, having worked as an aide for two senators, as a professional staff member on the Senate Foreign Relations Committee, and as an ambassador to Yemen when Dunner's only son had died. He remembered hearing her name when she worked for Senator Padraic O'Rourke, the longest-serving member in the Senate's history. She had staffed a meeting between them. At a later dinner, O'Rourke told him to keep his eye out for her as she had been the smartest and toughest legislative aide he'd had in his five decades as a senator. O'Rourke was right about her.

"Stop pacing and sit down, CJ," he said.

"Yes, Mr. President," she said in her soft, mellifluous voice.

"Would it help if you played something?"

She laughed. He knew that's how she could relax and let ideas come to her.

"What would I play?"

"Brahms? C.P.E. Bach? Chopin? Yes. Play his Polonaise Militaire. Please?"

"That would take too much energy right now," she responded wistfully.

"Wait until you're my age, Madam Ambassador," he said with a twinkle in his eye.

"You continue to inspire, Mr. President," she responded, her brown eyes looking at him in admiration.

"You lie about as well as anyone in Washington, CJ. But I can't think of anyone better in government. Maybe you should run in my place next year," he said seriously.

"Me?" she said in a shocked voice. "I've never run for anything. I have no constituency. And no one knows me outside of Washington. No, when you're done, I'm done. I'll find a nice teaching job and read student papers instead of intelligence briefs," she responded light-heartedly.

"They would be lucky to have you, but so would the next administration," Dunner said, opening his eyes as he reached out for his tea. The large picture window overlooking the valley showed the early signs of dusk as the black night shifted to a blue hue.

"If it's a coup, we still don't know who's behind it," she said. "Their vice president is Felipe Reyes. I've met him several times. He's not what you would call a thinker. He was always turning to his aides for facts during our discussions. He didn't seem particularly strong, which is supported by the various intel assessments and our own ambassador in Manila. He's not from one of the most powerful families, either. The consensus is that Quinta chose him since he wouldn't pose a threat to her in terms of capability or ambition."

"Do you think it's the military?" he asked, taking another sip of his tea.

"I'm not sure. We know from our embassy that she boarded the plane with the national defense secretary, their Joint Chiefs chairman, and their navy chief. That leaves the heads of their Army and Air Force. The Air Force isn't robust enough that their chief would be able to carry out a post-coup government. The Army? Maybe, but the last coup attempts were decades ago by mid-grade officers known as the Reform the Armed Forces Movement, who supported the removal of Ferdinand Marcos and then tried to oust Corazon Aquino. The government has been pretty good at identifying problems within the ranks since then."

Dunner reflected on that.

"If it is a coup attempt," she continued, "we'll know soon who's in place. Generally, whoever takes charge announces it as quickly as possible to reduce the risk of anarchy and legitimize their power. There's more," Sumner faded off.

"More bad or more good?"

"More, Mr. President. Last year when President Quinta met with you and I was with my counterpart, they expressed an interest not only in the formal mil-to-mil naval exercise but in adding a training component with other types of organizations."

"I don't think I like where this is going," Dunner said, looking her in the eye.

"Quinta was concerned with how Russia and China are evolving their hybrid warfare capabilities. She asked if I knew of a private security company that could provide additional training outside of ship operations. I suggested Highland Maritime Defense as a possibility since they're based in the US."

"Hmmm. Stark's firm?"

"Yes, Mr. President."

"I see. We were scheduled to return to Washington the day after tomorrow. Do you think we should return today instead?"

"I don't think so. It might escalate the concern for this. Everyone is reporting on the situation to you here. We'll have the others via video teleconference. And we should have your photographer take some pictures of you being briefed at the conference table. It will show that you are fully aware of the situation but that you're not losing your head when everyone else is losing theirs," she offered.

"Like the Kipling poem?"

"Yes, Mr. President, like the Kipling poem," she answered, thinking back to when Connor Stark had first used that phrase with her when he was a military fellow in her Senate office.

"Okay, CJ, let's do that," he said, closing his eyes again.

What she didn't tell him was that he needed those two more days of rest and relaxation at Camp David. The Philippine issue was only one issue, and he'd have more to tackle when he returned to Washington.

OFF BALABAC ISLAND

Within a few minutes of leaving the naval base, Bobby Fisk was already guiding his fuel-heavy whaler from its center console, one hand on the wheel and the other holding firmly onto the crossbar in case he hit something. At this speed, he knew if he hit a sandbar, coral reef, or flotsam lost by a passing ship, the small boat would experience a broken propeller or split hull. Plus, he'd probably hit it hard enough to be thrown from the craft. Even holding on to the bar was unlikely to prevent that. If he was lucky, he'd be far enough from the shore not to have to worry about the saltwater crocodiles in this region. Still, he had enough experience on small boats from Highland Maritime's facility off the Maine coast and as a small boat officer on the cruiser USS *Bennington* and destroyer USS *Charles Stewart*.

He had little time to get underway once he got his order, but he knew enough to pack the basics—water, binoculars, flashlight, a local nautical chart, the metal plate, a three-ounce air horn, and extra fuel. In addition to that, he had on him his Leatherman multi-tool and his nine-millimeter pistol with only one clip. Pushing the throttle as he did would burn a lot of fuel. A whaler this size with two small six-gallon plastic fuel tanks would burn it all in under two hours if he kept up this speed. He had thrown in two additional tanks that shifted around behind him. It was the best he had since that was all that remained in the basin. He had four hours at best to find *Minerva* and *Syren*.

He tapped the fuel gauge. It wasn't working. He checked his watch and mentally calculated when he'd have to switch the fuel line from one tank to the other and then the third. For now, he kept his eyes on the water and maintained, as Stark kept harping on, situational awareness.

He headed due south from the naval base and then casually turned the boat on an easterly course two miles from the ninety-foot-high Cape Melville lighthouse prominent on a hill. He made sure to stay well south of the point because of the shallower waters but remained out of the shipping lane between Balabac and the Malaysian islands of Balambangan and Banggi, which, according to his chart, were twenty nautical miles away and out of sight. A few ships were transiting the shipping lane. A massive blue tanker was on a leisurely eastbound passage, while two other freighters in the distance and a closer tug with a barge were on a westbound transit.

All of them had radios, but since the Highland Maritime ships were at EMCON, even if he stopped one of those ships to borrow their comms, it wouldn't do him any good. Another ship appeared on the horizon and its silhouette was familiar to him. He had seen plenty of longline fishing vessels in the Indian Ocean. Their miles-long nets scooped up any marine life they could to feed the world's growing population.

Ships are still transiting, he realized. They weren't being diverted from Balabac or the Philippines as a whole. That meant, at least, the whole world wasn't going to pieces. Standard communications and internet service were probably still available, at least beyond Balabac.

Ten minutes later he began his second turn when he saw the tiny, triangular Lumbucan Island at eleven o'clock. He made a nice, easy turn north until he was a thousand yards from the white sandy beach the boats had landed on earlier that day. He slowed the whaler to a few knots and used his binoculars to check the coast. There was nothing there. The grooves in the sand from the RHIBs—the rigid-hulled inflatable boats—were still there, as was evidence of the four teams that went ashore.

It would be dark in a few hours. If he waited until the predetermined hour based on the training exercise's parameters, one of the ships would be in range to see his flashlight. But he didn't have that time. Neither did his shipmates back at the Balabac Naval Base. He lifted each fuel tank to manually estimate how much fuel he had remaining. The first was already low. The 150-horsepower four-stroke outboard was guzzling the fuel faster than he thought. Looking in the distance around him, he prayed the sea would be as calm as it was right now, but experience told him that could change in an instant, and the further away from shore he got, the rougher the waters and the slower he'd be able to maneuver the small craft.

"This boat can hit about forty miles an hour in calm waters," he said out loud to the empty boat. "The ships were ordered to stay over the horizon until nightfall, so they're at least twelve nautical miles from here. Captain Johnson doesn't take chances. She's probably out around twenty or twenty-five nautical miles so she can't be seen by someone on a hill given the ships' high freeboard, even if the new paint jobs do make them tougher to see. The question is if she's directly out there or if she's gone north or south."

He turned off the engine, unplugged the fuel line from the first tank, attached it to the second, and hand-pumped it so there was no air in the fuel line. It was easier to do so here in case he ran into rougher waters. He returned to the center console and turned on the engine as it sputtered, giving him a momentary pause and a curse word or two.

The sky remained clear except for some stationary cirrus clouds to the north. *Nothing to worry about there*, he thought. The wind was barely detectable and another good portend for calm seas. He made the call and hit the throttle, making course 090 degrees—due east at thirty-five knots.

Forty minutes later he was at the twenty-nautical-mile point east of Balabac. This far out, the sea began to slightly heave his small craft. The ships weren't here. He cut the engine and made the switch to the third tank. The craft bobbed as he slipped on spilled fuel and fell, knocking his shooting arm against the hull. He cursed himself for being clumsy, even in this environment. He drank one of the bottles of water that he had taken since his camelback was long since empty. He removed his glasses, wiping more sweat from his brow. For some reason, he remembered being on a heaving dhow when he was on the *Bennington*'s crew and chucking his lunch as the local "fishermen" laughed at the greenhorn.

He took the binoculars and began scanning the horizon, starting southwest in a counterclockwise pattern to the northwest and back again.

He kept doing this for nearly an hour when he started to get a sickening feeling that he missed them. There were no fishing vessels, nothing out there.

Finally, he saw ships. One looked like a roll-on roll-off car carrier. It was about ten nautical miles south of him. He caught two ships to the northeast that seemed blurry. They were heading in a southwesterly direction at about ten knots. That meant toward Balabac. He put the binoculars down and started the engine, which started sputtering as it did after he changed the first tank. It kept sputtering and then stalled. He hit the button on the console again and again. Nothing, and he knew that with a sinking feeling that it wouldn't start again.

He had one shot and grabbed with one good arm and his sore arm the polished metal sheet he'd taken along with him. He eyed the sun's position relative to *Minerva* and *Syren* and began flashing simple Morse code as best he could. He did this for another five minutes until he could see the first and then the second ship turn to port and in his direction.

C H A P T E R   9

BALABAC NAVAL BASE

Years before Connor Stark had gone through the ROTC program at Boston University, Commandant of the Marine Corps General Robert Barro said, "amateurs talk tactics, but professionals study logistics." Logistics were key to any military operation, whether it was water, food, clothing weapons, ammunition, or other materiel.

Stark had seen it fully in action when he was a lieutenant junior grade. His battle group was in the vicinity of a natural disaster off Africa. The ships immediately went into high gear, sending helicopters overhead to assess the damage and identify landing zones. Crews assembled pallets of food and water from one of the amphibious ships and began transporting them on LCACs—Land Craft Air Cushion—and helicopters. Medical personnel assembled to provide care for the local community. Few navies had such an extensive capability to provide humanitarian aid. It was because the materiel, the processes, and the platforms were the same, whether for a peaceful operation or a military assault. You had to get something from point A to point B. The same was true with what he was now witnessing with his own naval company.

One of the most welcomed sights he had was watching *Syren* and *Minerva* coming up from the south and taking station half a nautical mile off the base. Fisk had accomplished his mission. Both ships dropped anchor in the shallow waters four hundred meters apart, with *Syren* taking the north anchorage and Jaime's *Minerva* the south anchorage. Neither ship had helicopters aboard. Even in the commercial sector, they were too expensive to operate with the aviation support personnel needed to maintain them, especially in a maritime environment. Plus, despite the large flat deck that could accommodate two helicopters to land and take off, neither ship had a hangar. Instead, Stark invested in a suite of drones, all recommended by Jay Warren—the resident engineer, mad scientist, geologist, miner, and embodiment of probably a score of other talents that emerged from time to time.

Warren had taken Stark to Philadelphia to visit the drone company he wanted to work with. Warren could get sensors elsewhere, but he had needed a small company that could provide the platforms Highland Maritime could use in the field. Dragonfly Pictures had been around for a couple of decades, mostly in research and development for the government. But Warren, and then Stark, realized the opportunity in partnering with a small company. There was minimal bureaucracy to muck the works, and deals could practically be done on a handshake. Based on the money Stark's firm had made from the sale of the EMP rockets after the Sri Lanka mission, he could invest more in the company to expand Highland Maritime's capabilities.

Even without his binoculars, Stark could see the distinct profile of the DP-14 multi-mission unmanned aerial system (UAS) as its two rotors lifted it off *Minerva*'s deck. With a range of eighty miles and capability of carrying up to a two-hundred-pound payload, they could operate in up to forty-knot crosswinds, making them especially useful on the water. It was worth having two aboard each vessel. They were ideal for the ships' main decks. Each ship had twelve twenty-foot equivalent (TEU) containers, six to port and six to starboard, with a wide main passageway between them. Some of the containers were modified as extra crew quarters, a command center including a drone pilot station, Jay's personal research lab, and others as each mission set required.

The DP-14 drone, like the far larger, manned CH-47 Chinook helicopter used by the military for more than fifty years, had a rear rotor higher than the forward rotor. Capable of a speed up to a hundred knots, the first DP-14 arrived at the base only a few minutes after taking off from the ship. The rotors quickly stopped so Stark and Castillo could approach it and open the central cargo area. The first load was two hundred pounds of ammunition and a manila envelope addressed to Stark. He took it away just forward of the DP-14 and its nose-mounted camera as he signaled two of his people to unload and distribute the ammunition.

He sliced open the brown envelope with a pen knife and immediately recognized his cousin's handwriting on the plain white paper.

Connor,

   Bobby gave us all the details about the attack. We don't have any other details about that or other attacks in the region. We have maintained EMCON per your orders, but I know the situation has changed. We have been monitoring channel 16. The chatter from passing merchant ships started mentioning their concern about arrival times to Philippine ports because of nationwide power outages and communications blackouts. We have tracked at least seven Philippine ports on four different islands, including Mindanao, that have not responded to merchant traffic. You and I both know that doesn't make sense. A distributed network, especially among islands, shouldn't be affected to this scale. Our communications officer has his HAM radio on. He just made contact with someone from Leyte. We'll see what we can learn from that.

   By the time you receive this, Syren will have launched its TUAS to give us as much coverage as possible in case the attackers return.

   Olivia and I are standing by for your orders.

   —JJ

Stark thought for a moment about the TUAS—the Tethered Unmanned Aerial System—pulled out a pen from his vest, and placed the paper against the skin of the drone, scribbling out his response.

Jaime,

   Great job. Thanks for the resupply of ammo. Bring two more security teams ashore along with three days of food and water, four generators. Tell Jay to bring the portable TUAS and the satellite phones on the next RHIB. Have Olivia take tactical command of the ships. You, Fisk, and Warren should come ashore to meet. I don't

want to risk radio communications just yet until we have more
information.
—Connor

LE HAVRE, FRANCE

Golzari had taken a quick shower, napped for an hour, and grabbed his go-bag, including a couple of burner phones as well as Abdou Mansouri's identification. He changed into more casual clothes than he preferred and hopped on his motorcycle, a vehicle with decidedly more advantage given the insufficient parking spaces on Île Saint-Louis. Traffic was light on the E5 from Paris to Le Havre, except for a short backup due to a traffic accident near Rouen. Still, he managed to arrive in under two hours. He hadn't been to this port before since his previous job as a Diplomatic Security Service agent normally had him traveling through airports rather than ship ports since ambassadors and foreign ministers needed to get somewhere quicker than ocean transit could accommodate.

In the case of human trafficking, however, ports were much better for "business" than airports. It was nearly impossible in the post-9/11 era to traffic individuals, much less groups, by air. There were too many questions, too many requirements for the traffickers to worry about, too many eyes. Ocean transport, however, was ideal. Ships could carry many trafficked individuals and the security was usually far less stringent. In addition, unlike airlines, a ship could change flag, ownership, insurer, and identification many times during a criminal voyage. They also weren't bound to the same rules as airlines. A ship could arrange to change their destination en route or rendezvous mid-ocean with other ships.

Golzari passed the giant sculpture representing the port. It was an arch perpendicular within another arch of containers, each painted pink, green, red, blue, orange, or black. It made him want to vomit. He longed for something more classic and appropriate, like a giant Colossus of Rhodes. He parked his motorcycle near the first breakwater below the tall white tower with black lettering from top to bottom, "Le Havre Porte de L'Europe." Golzari didn't know how the harbor masters of Rotterdam, Antwerp, and Hamburg felt about that bold proclamation.

The Le Havre harbor master's tower was just inside the single quay for all traffic entering or departing the port.

As ships entered the port, the eastern concrete quay had a twenty-foot white tower with a red top and light, while the right quay had a similar structure except with a green top and light. Immediately inside the port to the east was a passage to a marina with hundreds of slips for sailboats next to twelve-story condominium buildings looking out over the English Channel. The ships then had to pass the harbor master's control tower before a fork at an island with a series of aluminum-roofed storage buildings. One set of terminals was to the left. Most ships proceeded on the right channel, passing gas storage tanks off their starboard and then terminals with a series of massive cranes to quickly unload the container ships.

Among the seven thousand ships that passed through this port annually were container ships, tankers, ferries from England, and cruise ships. If each of them trafficked only five people, that was thirty-five thousand individuals destined for servitude away from their homes and outside the law's eyes. Golzari couldn't search each ship; even the port authority's security couldn't do that. But thanks to his work in Paris, he had the name of a container ship—the *Strident Yingkou*. It was a Panamex ship, which meant it could transport between three and five thousand TEU containers. Some ultra-large container vessels could carry more than fifteen thousand containers. That is why, even in the twenty-first century, transporting cargo by sea remained the most inexpensive method for manufacturers and shippers.

Golzari had no method of searching five thousand containers that might hold trafficked persons. The ship hadn't yet entered port. It wasn't even on the horizon. If he notified the port authorities, he couldn't chance a leak since it was so lucrative to criminals who bribed their way through every step. It was possible that the ship's captain and crew didn't know they were transporting humans in modified containers that had food, water, toilets, and vents to breathe. Ship captains were normally European or American. The ships' crews were from developing countries, especially from Asia. Filipinos comprised the crew on a majority of merchant ships. Still, he couldn't chance meeting with the ship's captain and officers since he had no idea who was involved. For now, he'd assume the identity of Abdou Mansouri, the trafficker he had executed in Paris.

As Golzari paced along the seawall, one of his burner phones buzzed. He checked and it was a text from Emile. *Call me.* The former agent made certain he was out of hearing range of port workers and hit redial for the police officer's number.

"*Bonjour,*" said the voice.

"*C'est moi,*" Golzari replied. *It's me.*

"We've interviewed all seventeen that you found at the apartment building."

"Can you share anything?"

"I have to, *mon ami.* Without you, we wouldn't have known about this group and we wouldn't have had the opportunity to enter the building," Emile said. "I assume you're in Le Havre?"

"Yes, I arrived a few minutes ago. Are the children okay?" Golzari asked.

"Yes, yes. They've been overworked and underfed, but our doctors have said that otherwise they've been untouched. They're confused. And we couldn't communicate with them."

"What? What do you mean?"

"Damien, we first had to determine where they were from by asking them in their language. They don't speak any of the major Western languages—French, English, Spanish. They're all from Asia, and we had to track down what part by finding our own interpreters."

Golzari liked people to be succinct when reporting. Right now, all he needed to know was where the trafficked children were from.

"What did you learn?" Golzari asked, concerned, as he watched a catamaran pass through the quays.

"We have a native Filipino speaker who was confused because she kept trying to speak Tagalog to them, which is predominant there, but she can also at least recognize half a dozen other dialects spoken in the Philippines. She still didn't recognize what the children were saying to her. We ran it by other interpreters and they didn't recognize it either. We've called other regional linguists.

"What about maps? Could they point to where they're from?"

"Yes, we tried that. I don't think they've ever been exposed to a map—keep in mind most are very, very young. Since it didn't work, we're assuming they're from a remote region with a very limited school system if any."

"I understand. Keep me informed," Golzari said, frustrated by the mystery.

BALABAC NAVAL BASE

The boat repair facility on the south side of the basin had become the operations center. It provided more open space than the headquarters hut, and there was no blood on its corrugated metal walls or concrete floor. There were no windows on the first level; the few on the second level were accessible by a walkway around three sides of the structure. Stark leaned back against the frame of the two-story-high double doors wide enough to accommodate one of the Philippine Navy cutters or whalers if they needed repair work. One of the Highland Maritime four-meter RHIBs pulled up to the ramp as Captain Jaime Johnson planted her foot on the forward air tube and sprang from it as adroitly as she had diving from a three-meter springboard on the Naval Academy Swimming and Diving Team. Bobby Fisk followed behind her but waited for the RHIB to stop before he made his own cautious landing.

Stark went down to greet them as two more DP-14 drones landed a hundred feet away, delivering more supplies and equipment. He tried calling the naval base in Manila but only got an automated answer that the phones were not in service.

"Where's Jay?" he said gruffly as he approached the water.

Jaime slipped on her charcoal gray ballcap on, tucking her frizzy shoulder-length dirty-blond hair through the back adjustable Velcro strap.

"He was picking up something on the tethered UAS and said he'd be in as soon as . . . ," she started when another RHIB sped past the breakwater with the big, red-headed Jay Warren desperately hanging onto a crossbar with one hand and the other on a black plastic case with white letters on the side—"WARREN - Bola." The RHIB deposited him as he stumbled over the side, taking two loud, uncoordinated steps as Bobby caught him before he fell onto the concrete ramp. Warren breathed a sigh of relief, snapped his fingers as if remembering something, and turned to remove the black case from the boat.

"C'mon, c'mon," he said quickly to the others. "Let's get inside. Now!"

Warren was probably one of the few Highland Maritime employees who could be so informal and awkward with the senior leadership because, unlike most Highlands, he hadn't served in the military. He had, however, been a Navy engineer, which is how Stark met him while working on the FSF-1 *Sea Fighter* project.

When they entered the repair facility, Warren put down the case and told Fisk to help him close the double doors. One got stuck while sliding along the rail. With an extra push, the two managed to secure it. Commander Castillo and Lieutenant Santos watched the scene unfold, entirely confused. Stark and Johnson didn't exactly understand what was going on either.

"Okay, okay," Warren said loudly, looking up at the windows. Stark assumed Warren was assessing whether or not the mid-afternoon daylight was enough to do whatever he was about to do but then realized Jay was operating out of paranoia. Warren had breaking news that had delayed his arrival. He sped to the ramp, catching up to Jaime and Fisk, then closed the doors before speaking to Stark, but then he was concerned about the window.

"Shit," Stark said sharply.

"Yeah, yeah, I know, huh," Warren said in a loud staccato voice.

"Sir?" Santos queried.

"We're being watched," Stark said, removing his ballcap and bending the brim as he slipped it into his rear pocket. "How long, Jay?"

"I don't know, boss. I deployed the tethered drone when we started slowing around that last bend. It took a while for the sensor suite to detect it. It might have been sooner if we hadn't been in passive mode." Warren wasn't objecting to Stark's order. He knew the risks of being detected.

Stark crossed his arms and leaned against a worktable.

"What kind of drone?" Stark asked Warren.

"I can't tell. It kinda looks commercial. There's nothing special about it that I could tell," he responded.

"Captain Stark, what exactly does this mean?"

"It means, Commander Castillo, that the attackers are watching us. And it's probably what caught your attention above us earlier today. For all I knew, it could have been a cockatoo. I didn't think," Stark said, frustrated at himself for not considering every factor. And he realized he was blaming himself like Santos had blamed herself earlier.

"Lieutenant, have you heard anything about terrorist groups or insurgents using drones or using these tactics?" he asked.

She thought for a moment. "No, sir. This is completely different than any of the groups our military has encountered domestically. No history of drone use, but as you know, any individual or group can use them now. Combined with attacking the naval base, leaving, and then continuing to monitor . . ." she paused again.

"Something else?" Castillo asked his intelligence officer.

"If . . . if they were watching the whole day, then they know we took the base, but they haven't returned. That means they either could not or would not help the people they left behind," she reasoned.

"If they couldn't help and they haven't been back, it could mean their forces aren't nearby or that they don't have enough people to take us on," Johnson offered.

"They have two options—come in by sea or by air," Bobby suggested. "Once their vessel went over the horizon, it was too far to support them. And doesn't the fact that Team Four was only attacked by two people suggest that they don't have the force on the island to take us by land?"

"Maybe. And if they were close enough on land but chose not to act?" Santos slowly asked the senior team.

"Then it means," Stark said, "that they have been monitoring us. They've been watching us move, the number of people we have, how we patrol, the weapons we now have, and the fact that our two ships just arrived. Could they hear us talk, Jay?"

"I don't think so, boss. The drone was pretty high, and it looked like it only had a camera on it. No audio boom to pick up conversations."

"How high?" Stark said directly to Warren as he motioned with his chin toward the black plastic case.

"That's why I brought the twins with me," Warren said with an evil grin.

CHAPTER 10

LE HAVRE

Unlike an airport in which an announced arrival and unloading of passengers could be counted in tens of minutes, the arrival and unloading of a container ship was hours, if not days. Damien Golzari was, by his nature, an impatient man. Seeing a ship on the horizon en route to the port meant another hour or two before it reached the port. Once it reached the breakwater, its speed was probably less than six knots. By the time it reached its terminal, it could be another half hour by the time it tied up. Golzari wasn't entirely familiar with port operations, but knew the basics. He was cognizant enough of that shortcoming to recognize when he did need to reach out to experts. This was one of those times.

Golzari checked his watch and calculated the time on the east coast of the United States. He took one of the burner phones from his shirt pocket and sat back on his motorcycle. He dialed a number he had memorized.

"Operator," the voice answered in a neutral tone. In an era where there were only automated operators, the voice was a welcomed change. Technology had its role in the twenty-first century, as it did when he tapped into Abdou Mansouri's computer at the trafficking complex in Paris. But it also had its limitations. Artificial Intelligence was good, but it wasn't quite to the point of some futuristic science-fiction scenario where it was practically indistinguishable from speaking with a human. Golzari relied on human intelligence and human interaction. In his former job as a Diplomatic Security Services agent, he had to be able to read people and predict their potential to threaten someone under his charge, and he had to be quick enough to react. Few things frustrated Golzari more than an automated operator that kept providing him predetermined numerical choices but just as often didn't provide him the quick, efficient choice he needed.

"Code Echo Six Three," Golzari responded.

"Thank you, sir," the operator said. "How can we help?"

"Cynthia, please."

"Stand by."

The phone went silent momentarily before an alto voice answered.

"This is Cynthia—how may I help you?"

"Damien Golzari, Cynthia. I need some assistance," he said. That last sentence was not one Golzari often used or admitted to.

Connor Stark had ensured his private security firm's assets were always at Golzari's disposal based on the relationship they had developed in Yemen, Sri Lanka, and elsewhere. It had been a stormy association, at best, in the beginning but had grown into a respectful professional and personal friendship. One of the company's assets was Cynthia, its operational analyst, who had open-source information at her fingertips. She always had the night watch since much of the firm's operations took place on the far side of the world, up to a dozen time zones away. She was also the analyst most trusted to provide support alone.

"Certainly," she said.

"The container ship *Strident Yingkou* was due at noon at Le Havre. I am here now. It's almost two hours overdue. Do you have any information?"

"Stand by, Mr. Golzari." He heard the fast-paced tapping of keys. "It was delayed but is currently approaching Le Havre, scheduled for terminal Three-Seven. The ship should be within sight," she said as Golzari checked the waters off the port. Three ships were in the distance.

"It must be one of the ships I see now. Is there any indication of what caused the delay?"

"It briefly stopped off of Ponta Delgada."

"The Azores?"

"Yes, it reported some engine trouble," she said.

"Interesting. Can you tell me anything else?"

"Its last ports of call were in Madagascar, Thailand, Malaysia, and its point of origin for this voyage was Shanghai."

"Nothing in the Philippines?"

"No. Just Malaysian waters."

"Is that its normal route?" he asked.

"It . . . it appears that way. Huh, based on the track, the ship never intended to stop at Ponta Delgada," she remarked quizzically.

"What do you mean, Cynthia?"

"According to the track, it stopped in the Azores during each of its last five transits from Madagascar to Le Havre, and it remains there for just a few hours. Let me check something, Mr. Golzari."

"Certainly. I'll wait." The line went silent for a few minutes until she returned.

"The *Strident Yingkou* reported engine trouble each time it approached the Azores."

"Is that common?"

"No," she replied. "Newer merchant vessels don't experience many problems and certainly not at the same time and port during each voyage. That's not a coincidence. They're stopping there because they don't want anyone to know. Is there anything else I can do for you, Mr. Golzari?" she asked pleasantly. "We have a . . . logistics . . . company in Europe if you require anything. There's a standing note here from Mr. Stark to help you with any request."

Golzari thought back to the first days he knew Stark and how the barbarian punched him in the face in Ambassador Sumner's office in Yemen. Had Stark not been protected by the ambassador, Golzari would have arrested him for assaulting a federal officer. Now Stark's company had become a vital resource. Damien knew Stark wouldn't expect payment since it was small beans compared to what the firm received through its work, but Golzari didn't like debts and would have to pay somehow.

"Thank you for the kind offer. If I need anything, I'll text the details and a short list of necessities from the . . . logistics . . . company. Also, is Mr. Stark available?"

"I'm sorry. He's on assignment and is not due to return for some time," she said.

"Of course."

"Wait, there is one more anomaly, Mr. Golzari. That track for the ship off Malaysia? It's in the north, and it looks like the ship comes to a full stop in international waters for about an hour during each transit. I'm sorry I didn't catch that before."

"Not at all. That explains it and is very helpful. Please give my regards and my thanks to Mr. Stark when you speak with him."

"Safe travels."

Safe, he thought, was not a word he would use in this case.

BALABAC NAVAL BASE

Warren opened the black plastic box to reveal two drones resting securely in gray foam molded to the drone specifications. He called Fisk over and handed one to him as the younger man set it on the ground and unfolded its propeller blades. Warren did the same with the other, then reached for a third item in the box, what initially appeared to be a thick black cord. Within a minute he had fastened the ten-foot cord to hooks on the underside of the drones. Each end of the cord had a lead weight the size of a golf ball. Castillo and Santos stood back silently, observing the operation but intensely absorbed by it.

"Get the doors, Bobby," he told him. The sometimes socially awkward engineer often failed to see his requests came across as cold direction, but those who knew and had worked with him understood his idiosyncrasies.

Fisk pushed back each massive door on their rails as their weight caused them to clang into the frames. Warren removed the drone controller, synced up the two, and then flipped open its video screen. The first drone's blades started spinning and then the other as Warren tested the connection.

"You can control both simultaneously?" Castillo asked.

"Sort of. The first one is the primary that I control directly. I've already synced the second one to follow the lead on the first," Warren replied without looking at the PN officer.

The first drone lifted a foot off the concrete floor as the cord between the two drew taught, then the second drone lifted to the same height.

"'Fly, my pretties,'" Warren said with Wicked Witch of the West glee as the drones sped out the doors in nearly practical unison. The team walked out of the boat repair facility to watch Warren's Bola drones fly higher and higher toward their prey.

"How do they know how to find the drone, Mr. Warren?" Santos asked.

"Oh, they know because I told them. That drone that's been watching you? It's been flying a pattern. I programmed the first drone to follow that track and . . ." he paused, watching the controller's screen, "it's going faster than its target. Assuming whoever is operating it doesn't change the pattern too soon, our drones will catch up to it."

It took less than a minute for the twin drones to approach the target as the team kept their eyes locked on Warren's screen. The target changed course, but Warren followed it now and moved the controllers as nimbly as a teenager playing a videogame. He hit a button twice, and as he did so, the two lead weights dropped, taking with them the netting that had been coiled up in the cord. The Bola drones rapidly approached the target from either side. As they were about to pounce on it, Warren released the netting from his drones and ordered them to return to base. The target drone would never return home as it struggled like an eagle's wings caught in a noose. The enemy drone's blades stopped spinning as more netting enveloped the surveillance craft, and with that, it dropped from five hundred feet into the ocean.

"Not bad, Jay," Stark said to the proud red-headed engineer. "That solves one problem. I hope you have more of those in case they send another one after us."

"Don't worry, boss. I have us covered," he replied as the Bola drones returned to the basin.

"What now?" Fisk asked Castillo and Stark.

"We have a window, perhaps short, where we are not being surveilled," Castillo said. "We should take advantage of that."

All of them nodded in agreement.

"I think we need to remain at EMCON," Fisk offered. "They know we're here at the base and they've likely seen the ships, but if we can minimize what the other side knows, it would be to our advantage."

"I agree," Stark replied gravely. "I don't like it, but I agree. I'd still like to find out what's going on out there. Commander?"

"I agree, Captain Stark. Mr. Fisk said ships are still going through the channel south of here. Perhaps we can send out one of the whalers to rendezvous with a merchant ship," Castillo offered.

"Jaime, can you send someone?"

"Can do."

"We also need to know what's going on here. There are two pick-up trucks in the car pool. I'd like to take Lieutenant Santos with me and get a read on what's happening elsewhere on this island. We'll also need Mr. Warren. He has a different drone system that would fit in the back."

"That sounds reasonable, but I'd like to go with you as well. We can take both trucks," the Filipino commander said. "Captain Johnson has control of the boats, and perhaps Mr. Fisk can remain to take the tactical defense of the base."

Stark agreed. Both Jaime and Bobby had been under fire before. They thought clearly and tactically. He also worked well with Sivan Abraham whose experience with the Israeli Defense Force proved advantageous.

"All right, folks. Let's get kitted out quick and move out while whoever the hell is out there doesn't know what we're doing," Stark said.

CAMP DAVID

National Security Advisor CJ Sumner ran her fingers through her short, black hair, trying to read through the hard copies of memos on a variety of hot issues. But her mind kept returning to the Philippines. Nothing else in the world suggested that the Philippine situation was bigger than a cyberattack. No other country was experiencing widespread power outages. There was still no word from the Philippines on who was in charge now that their president was dead or even if anyone else in the country realized she was dead or, rather, had been assassinated.

While President Dunner rested, she had communicated with the secretaries of defense and state in Washington, less than a thirty-minute flight from the presidential retreat. Except for those short conversations, she was marking up the various memos by hand with a green pen while listening to "Piano Sonata in E minor" by the Norwegian composer Edvard Grieg. She had just finished editing another memo with some additional questions when her aide entered the sitting room of her cottage, going right for the television's remote control.

"What is it?" CJ asked.

The aide turned it to the BBC channel, showing the overhead video of some action on the ground.

". . . *Again, the breaking news at this hour is during a power outage in the Philippines. A mercenary company has apparently attacked a Philippine naval base, killing several Philippine military personnel. We'll have more details as they become available.*"

The short video was clearly from a drone, showing trucks exiting a compound and being ambushed and fired upon as personnel fell from the gunfire. Teams emerged from the north, south, and east. Some were in camouflage patterned uniforms, but half of them were in gray coveralls with darker ballcaps. The drone's video zoomed in as they gathered around the trucks and, although she couldn't see their faces, she recognized the gray uniforms as well as the one man who wore a beige fishing vest on top of his uniform.

"Oh hell," she said barely above a whisper, realizing everything had just become more complicated.

PART II

PART II

CHAPTER 11

BALABAC

Stark and Santos approached the first of the two available Ford F-150s from the car pool. Castillo went to the driver's side on the second while Jay finished unloading the portable tethered unmanned aerial system (TUAS) onto the cargo bed. Santos hopped into the cab's passenger side and laid out one of the maps she retrieved from the headquarters hut.

"Captain Stark," Santos said, turning to him as he entered the cab, "the tethered drone on your ship. I have a question."

"Shoot," he replied, looking for a key before realizing that it was a newer model that had a start button.

"Well, sir, you have drones. The island isn't that big—it's only ten miles long and five miles wide. Población I is only six miles from here. Why aren't we just using drones to see what's out there?"

"That's a great question, Lieutenant. The short answer is we are and will be. Warren has a tethered system in his truck that will give us a bird's eye view from a tactical perspective, and hopefully, we won't be surprised by anything. The tethered system on the ship can see out about thirty miles. But while those are important assets, you always need boots on the ground. There may be things the drones don't pick up. It's a risk, I know. Are you okay with that?" he asked with a simple smile.

She reflected on that for a moment, then nodded. "Yes, sir, I am. That's what we were training to do. Now it's the 'real deal,' I think, is how you Americans say it," she said with the first smile he'd seen from her since the training began.

"Plus, if we get into trouble, the trucks can drive a lot faster than geezers like Jay and I can run," he said lightly. But it also wasn't far from the truth. Jay was a large man, and Stark's best running days were years behind him. It was practically out of his memory how fast he had run in the Pentathlon. Since then, one of his knees had been injured during a terrorist attack in Italy that nearly derailed his early Navy career only a year after his commissioning.

In some ways, Santos reminded Stark of when he first met Ensign Bobby Fisk aboard USS *Bennington* in the Gulf of Aden. Stark had been recalled to active duty and had spent time with the young officer on the bridge at first and then in combat. She had the same level of professional competence but also a sense of human decency.

The engine roared to life. Stark turned to the back of the cab to check his go-bag. It had the standards of extra ammunition, knife, compass, binoculars, and a few tools of the trade Warren had as well for the training mission. He took the radio out and placed it in the storage compartment between the two seats. He turned it on to the predetermined frequency.

"Doc Brown, Doc Brown, Highland One for comms check," he said.

"Highland One, Doc Brown, read you loud and clear, out," came Warren's scratchy voice.

"Doc . . . Brown?" Santos asked.

"Warren's call sign is from a movie from the 1980s. *Back to the Future*," Stark replied as he pulled out of the car pool, waving Warren to follow.

"Ah. Classics," Santos said as she returned to study the map on the dashboard. Stark shook his head, remembering as a kid when he had seen it in the theater. His movies and music had now become "classics" to the next generation.

They drove out the gate onto the dirt road that circled the island. In another minute, they reached the perimeter where one of the teams had emerged the previous day during the firefight. After another hundred yards the heavy jungle vegetation made way for sporadic palm trees, a mile-long beach to the left, and low vegetation to the right. Once they were in the clear, Stark saw in his rearview mirror when Warren launched the tethered drone from his truck.

The tether had two benefits. First, it could remain aloft indefinitely, or at least as indefinitely as the ground-based power source allowed it. In this case, the portable TUAS had a series of batteries as part of its system. Second, its emissions couldn't be detected since all the data was transferred by one of the fiber-optic wires in the one-eighth-of-an-inch tether.

Warren radioed that the road ahead for the next three miles appeared to be clear.

"Doc Brown, Highland One, can you be more specific, over?"

"No people, nothing under the surface, over."

"Copy."

"What did he mean by that?" Santos asked.

"Mines, Lieutenant. The drone has lidar on it so it has some capability of detecting if there are any mines in the road or Improvised Explosive Devices. That was a lesson we learned from our experience in Sri Lanka. We still don't know who the attackers are or their full range of abilities. We know they had at least one drone, they have ships, and they had people ashore.

"If there are no IEDs or mines on the main road out of the base, that means that if they still have people ashore, they're thinking defensively."

"They're not thinking offensively?" Santos asked.

"It might mean they have no force or capability to plant mines and IEDs, or it could mean they have such an overwhelming force that they don't have to worry about defensive measures," Stark said, reaching for his sunglasses.

"Sun Tzu said if you attack the enemy, you should have three soldiers for every one of your enemy's," Santos commented as she traced the road on the map with her index finger. "We have nearly fifty people at the base now that you reinforced it with personnel from the ships. If they were watching us, should we assume they have at least one hundred fifty ashore—if they are ashore?"

"Good point, Lieutenant. Even on a small island it would be tough to maintain that size of a force. Like Napoleon said, an army marches on its stomach. A force that large would have to be fed somewhere, housed somewhere. It's just too large a group to remain covert."

The mysteries kept piling up, but many were based on unknowns and presumptions.

SOUTH CHINA SEA

Sergei Makarov felt a tinge of guilt and disgust as he watched the televised news using the short video of Highland Maritime's engagement at the naval base. Modern warfare wasn't only about kinetic weapons such as guns and missiles. It was now a broad-spectrum effort that involved cyberattacks, currency devaluation, and information operations. In the last case, the media sucked up whatever was given to them. All of them competed to have "Breaking News," but few ever took the time to verify a story before they released it. The newspaper reporters still did, of course, since they had time before their next issue, but televised news stations needed ever-new material to keep up with the attention deficit disorder of the masses.

A short thirty-second video could be expanded to hours of discussions among experts always on tap in case a story broke. All Makarov's contact had given the media was a video with a sentence that said mercenaries had attacked a Philippine naval base. From that, the screen showed six different experts. One retired general was an expert on the Philippine military. A former administration official in the US government discussed energy requirements and reasons for power outages. A professor at a Canadian university provided an overview of the history of mercenary companies, while another professor in Singapore talked about the major private security companies operating globally.

The anchor would make presumptuous statements or ask questions like "do mercenary companies have the ability to cause power outages?" None of them had any idea what was really going on in Balabac, but that didn't matter. They hadn't seen the entire video where the men and women aboard these ships had attacked and executed every Philippine Navy officer and enlisted personnel at the base. They hadn't seen the New People's Army (NPA) steal the warships. Because the video didn't show the basin, still new enough not to appear in internet searches, the "experts" didn't even know what base had been attacked. They named half a dozen scattered through the nation of islands that it "could be." But this base, still under construction, was so new that most outside the Philippine Navy did not know of its existence.

The onus for the operation had been firmly planted on some unnamed mercenaries. Makarov and his team had succeeded in the third phase of their mission. Still, he had some regret. This operation, this paid assignment, had no noble cause. He again flipped through the dossier on Highland Maritime, pausing on the biography of Connor Stark. *We are more alike than different*, Makarov thought. It was not a thought shared by his employer, but if it were, then the employer would not let on. His employer was like that. He never let you know what he was thinking. He didn't have to. He had the money and Makarov provided the services.

People like Makarov—and Stark—preferred to work their companies out of the public light and scrutiny. He didn't know how Stark had been so adept at keeping some of his previous activities out of the news, but Makarov respected that, even if once they had been on opposite sides. Now Makarov was employing a tactic he hoped no one would ever attempt on him and his colleagues.

The original video showed a clear shot of Stark's face as he looked up almost in the direction of the drone. It was only out of professional respect that Makarov didn't include that segment. And there hadn't been a need to name the company in the original story. That's not what mattered in this operation. The key had been to make it appear that a violent non-state actor had taken a Philippine military base amid a massive nationwide cyberattack, an attack directed from Makarov's ship in a compartment on the port side of the passageway. A team of specialists continued to insert themselves in various Philippine systems until the time was right to let the government and businesses return to their pre-attack condition. For now, the team started to release some of the systems, such as those used in hospitals, but Philippine media and major government communications continued to be the victim of the attack.

Makarov calculated that looting was starting to occur in the major cities and that the disruption in the supply chain would cause more harm than the good his employer needed in about three days as people began to run out of basic food and materials. His employer wasn't looking for permanent damage, just a brief disruption long enough for them to carry out their mission.

What he didn't expect was a disruption in his own surveillance. Stark's people had two drones that chased his down, netted it like an animal, and forced it to crash. He hadn't expected that and that was his fault. He read through Stark's previous tactics. Makarov should have known his firm was creative and innovative. Makarov had things to learn from Stark. Under different conditions, Makarov would have sought a job with Highland Maritime or offered Stark a position with his firm. The latter, however, would have been impossible based on who funded Makarov's ventures.

"Can we get another drone up?" Makarov asked the handler less as a question than an order.

"That was the only drone we had of that class. The backup has fewer capabilities," the man responded.

"Does it have a camera?"

"Of course, sir."

"Then we have something. How long?"

"It's packed away. It will take about twenty minutes to unpack and get it to the deck and another twenty minutes to set it up and connect it with our system."

Makarov wasn't pleased by this. That meant three-quarters of an hour at least, plus flying time to the island, where he'd be basing his decisions in the blind.

"Will that drone be as vulnerable as the first?" Makarov asked.

"To a degree, yes. I'm not sure how they found the first one. We didn't read any radar emissions from them. Until we know how they did it, our second one can be just as easily attacked and taken down."

Makarov still had the upper hand with the number of personnel he had. Stark had the advantage of better eyes in the sky. Makarov had three more days to accomplish his assignment. He would be paid, and then he would again have to ask himself if this one was the last.

LE HAVRE

Analyst Cynthia at Highland Maritime was correct. The *Strident Yingkou* was the next ship to arrive in the port. It wasn't as large as some of the others he'd seen as it passed through the breakwater. He counted the number of containers across and along the ship, then multiplied it by the number stacked atop each other. By his estimate there were fewer than fifteen hundred containers aboard, which was less than half of what a ship like that would normally carry. He wouldn't have time to inspect each one, and he still didn't want to tip them off. Then again, the ship was in port. It couldn't escape the authorities, could it? What would stop them? The closest French naval bases were in Cherbourg and Brest. By the time navy ships got underway and caught up to the ship, the traffickers would likely have dumped their cargo of humans.

Golzari checked the map of the port and memorized the route to terminal Three-Seven. It was in the most remote part of one of the channels, but with the slow-moving cargo ship trying to maneuver, Golzari arrived at the terminal before the ship did. There was more open space at this terminal, with only a two-story storage facility a hundred feet from the dock. Unlike the other terminals he passed, there were few dockworkers to help tie up the ship to the dock. As the ship's crew threw over massive fenders between the hull and the dock, those were followed by lines to dockworkers who tied them to the bollards closest to the bow and stern of the ship, and the engines gave one mighty roar to push it.

He kept the motorcycle and himself fifty yards away next to an old, wooden, single-room building that probably served as an office in years past but now appeared to be abandoned. In fact, few of the nearest structures appeared to have been modernized. There was also no identifiable port security here. If Golzari had to take a guess, key port authorities were on the take from whatever organization wanted illicit cargo entering the port, and all of it could be directed to this terminal.

The process to secure the ship and prepare it to deliver cargo might take another twenty minutes as he watched the dock's gangway tie up to the ship's quarterdeck. Golzari's phone buzzed as he removed it from his pocket and flipped it open.

"Yes?"

"How's Le Havre?" Emile asked.

"Loveliest port I've ever visited. I may buy a condo here," Golzari responded with his characteristic sarcasm. "The ship just tied up to the dock. It's at terminal thirty-seven in case anything happens."

"Don't take any chances," the police officer suggested. "We can call the port authority any time you're ready."

"I need more information, Emile. Give me some time."

"I have some news for you about the children you freed. It took a while to find someone who recognized the language they speak."

"And?" Golzari was growing impatient.

"It's a very localized language called Molbog, an Austronesian language that's spoken on only one island."

"Which one?"

"Balabac. It's the southwesternmost island in the Philippines."

Balabac, Golzari thought. *At least there is a lead.*

"Could the children tell you anything?" he asked.

"Every few weeks for the past year before they were taken, several families would disappear," Emile replied in a serious tone. "No one knew where they went. Then armed people came to their homes in the middle of the night and took them away to small boats, which took them to larger ships off the coast. The children were separated from the adults. They said they never saw the adults—their parents—after the first night."

"What do you think happened to them, Emile?"

"I don't know, but that's not up to the Sûreté. It's not a good answer but we have our limits. We can pass along the information to Interpol."

Golzari came up with a short list of what happened to the adults. If they were held captive like the children, there'd be no reason to free them and risk discovery of the criminal operation. Either they were sold into bondage themselves or they were killed. There was no third option.

"How many people are we talking about, Emile?"

"I have no idea. And neither do the children. A few of the older children said a lot of off-islanders with weapons arrived. They immediately shut down any communications—islanders couldn't access the internet, the only cell phone tower was removed, and they took the radio station. They started living in the homes of people as more arrived, and the native population was threatened. Suddenly large groups were forced onto fishing vessels. This group left Balabac a couple of months ago. They said they barely recognized anyone living there before they were taken. By the way, are you aware of what's happened in the Philippines?"

"What?"

"There's been a massive power outage. Something about a cyberattack but details are very sketchy."

"Thank you, Emile. I'll let you know if I find anything." Golzari flipped shut the burner phone and slipped it back into his pocket.

This human trafficking operation might be larger than he originally thought. If traffickers took an entire town, it meant an operation on a scale unheard of, possibly since the abolition of slavery in the nineteenth century. There had been large, forced migrations in communist countries, but those populations were displaced, not sent to other countries for servitude.

Golzari sat behind the old office structure, recalling all the details he had picked up from Abdou Mansouri's room, the contact names, and the payment transfers. He wondered if he had enough to bluff his way aboard the ship as he had when he entered the trafficking building in Paris. Mansouri was a localized trafficker. There was no indication in his room that he had ever gone to Le Havre himself. He did have a cover job at the restaurant and had to oversee the building where the trafficked children were held. He wouldn't have time to go to the port. He'd probably only deal with whoever transported them from the port to Paris.

He looked over his shoulder at the dock. There were no trucks here—yet. The gangway was now secured and one of the dockworkers ran up with some papers. The other workers left, probably to attend to another ship arriving or departing. A couple of the ship's crew loitered about on the deck, leaning against the railings. A cargo ship this size would have about two dozen crew members, mostly from developing countries. The ship's captain, first mate, and a few others—if the statistics held—were from Eastern Europe.

Golzari had a light jacket and secured his pistol in its holster as he did with his leg holster. He slid a sheathed knife into the inner side of his right boot. He had three more ammo clips in the pocket of his cargo pants. Now he'd play the odds.

CHAPTER 12

BALABAC ISLAND

The two trucks continued at a twenty-miles-per-hour pace on the dirt road that was more like two lightly trodden ruts. Most of the vehicles that had come down this road were used to construct the naval base. Trucks and construction vehicles arrived in Población I, the only town on the island. It had a population of less than ten thousand, as Stark recalled from weeks before when Highland Maritime planned the training modules for the Philippine Navy. There had never been any terrorist activity on this island compared to other Philippine islands. Maybe they were too far south and west to operate against the government. There was little on this island of value—at least until the construction of the naval base. *Is that what had really motivated a group to attack it*, Stark wondered. It wasn't even a large base, just an outpost.

Several short, fat animals with thin legs raced across the road twenty yards ahead of the truck.

"What the hell are those?

"Those are mouse-deer. They're indigenous to only this island," Santos replied after only briefly glancing up to see why he had slowed. Stark had seen strange creatures in the world indigenous to small islands. Once, early in his career, when his ship pulled into Guantanamo Bay Naval Base, he witnessed the odd animals colloquially called "banana rats" who descended on the outside movie theater after the film started and popcorn dropped on the concrete.

Stark pivoted his head to the left to make sure nothing or no one had spooked them from wherever they came from, but there was only beach, more palm trees, and tall grass. The window was down and he could hear the local birds, such as cockatoos. Those were the only ones he could identify from a trip to the National Zoo in Washington, DC, long ago. He had never been a fan of zoos since he didn't believe in caging up wild animals. CJ Sumner told him it was because he himself didn't like being caged up by anything or anyone. She was probably right.

Santos directed him to take a left at the fork in the road, heading due north since the right would take them to Población I. Most of the terrain around the island was flat except for the interior, which had a few hills. To their right were rows of coconut trees, one of the island's main agricultural products, but there were no workers that he could see, and Jay would have told him if the drone identified anyone.

Once he made the turn, Santos said they were only two miles from the cable crossing. Warren's voice crackled over the radio, telling him to stop here as there was something ahead. Stark stopped the vehicle, grabbed his weapon, and went back to the second truck, eyeing the drone tethered a hundred feet above. Because the power was coming from the batteries next to the winch, the drone itself didn't make a sound, which was another advantage of this system. Stark approached the right side of the cab where Warren was working the controls. Santos followed behind, slinging her weapon over her should so she could hold the map.

"What do you have, Jay?" he asked as Castillo turned off the engine to take a look at the screen as well.

"About a mile and a half ahead. I almost missed it since there's a lot of green cover," Warren replied in a tone that clearly indicated he was disappointed in not finding it earlier. "It's a building, probably aluminum. Big HVAC unit on its north face. The footprint looks about fifty feet by a hundred feet. No windows. I can't tell how many entrances. Hold on. There's a sign on the front. Let me change the azimuth a bit and . . . got it. I can't read the top line, but just below it says in English, 'Balabac Coconut Company.'"

"Okay, so it's a refrigerated warehouse?" Stark asked.

"How many food warehouses have armed guards?" Warren replied.

"What?"

"Two soldiers with rifles. Could be more people but there's too much vegetation."

"Commander Castillo, can you confirm those aren't Philippine military?" Stark asked.

Castillo looked as Warren zoomed in on one of the patrolling soldiers.

"No. No one in our military wears that camouflage uniform. They're wearing the same as the people who attacked the base," he replied.

"Thanks. Jay, when we were in Sri Lanka, you found me using one of the sensors. Can you tell if there are more people in the building?" Stark asked, recalling when he was held and tortured by the Tamil Sea Tigers.

"No, boss, not this time. In your case, it was an aluminum roof but wooden walls. This is aluminum walls and roof. My radar can't get through that," Warren said. His brow furrowed as he tried to find another way to get an answer.

"Lieutenant Santos, how far is that building from the cable crossing?" he asked.

"Less than fifty yards. That building shouldn't be there. And there's no road on the map leading to it. This map was updated six weeks ago to accommodate the new base," she said confidently.

"Any thoughts on what this is? Wait, Jay, shift the camera over to the left. Is that an antenna?"

"Yeah, yeah, it sure is. They've got comms. It might be the bad guys' headquarters. Maybe," Warren speculated. "But would it have been built that close to the naval base?"

"There's nothing there," Santos interjected. "It has no cleared road. It's just coconut plantations near there. The military would not have had any reason to go to that part of the island if they were busy building the base."

Stark pondered that thought. This was the first sign of the attackers. That building might help them find out who they were, and if it was their communications hub on the island, Stark might be able to learn what was happening off the island. There were four of them. He knew Jay could handle a weapon, but Stark was the only sharpshooter and most experienced with guns. Castillo and Santos were strict navy personnel who had some training. Nevertheless, they weren't ground-pounders. Then again, neither was Stark at one time.

"I know what you're thinking, boss," Warren said. He always seemed to be in tune with Stark's thought process. They had known and worked together long enough. "Crow's Nest has a signal jammer. It's not real powerful, but if anything goes down, they won't get a message out either by radio or Wi-Fi, if they have it."

"We should get a couple of the teams here. I want you three to head back to the base." Stark realized he was now issuing orders, but Castillo was deferring to his experience. "Bring back three teams with you. I'll see if I can get some more info about it. We meet back here in an hour."

Stark was turning away from the cab when Warren instinctively reached out and grabbed his forearm.

"No, you don't. You need someone to back you up," the big redheaded engineer said grimly. Warren remembered the effect of the Tamil torture when Stark had been left alone before.

"I'll do it," Castillo chimed in. "You may need someone who speaks Spanish or Tagalog."

"I should go as well," Santos added. "I went through communications school as part of my training." She hadn't missed a beat. There was no fear in her eyes. Concern for the unknown, maybe, but not fear.

"If something happens, no one back at the base might know what happened to us," Stark said in a low voice.

"Then we won't let anything happen," Castillo responded with a sly grin.

LANTAU ISLAND, CHINA

Hu Tao had to stop to catch his breath four times while his children raced up the 268 steps. A one-hundred-ten-foot bronze statue of a sitting Buddha rested atop the mountain, which drew tourists from China and countries that were either modern tributary states or would be in the future if China's—and Hu's—plans bore more fruit. His wife complained about his constant smoking. Now his lungs were demanding a break from the habit.

"Come, Papa," his daughter said, extending her hand to his. His wife was a few steps behind him but not winded. He knew she was there to make sure he'd fulfill his promise to the children to take them here.

They wanted a day-long adventure with him outside of Hong Kong, and Lantau Island was reasonable since it was only a short ferry ride from Kowloon.

The statue itself was less than thirty years old. The century-old Po Lin Monastery was to the left, where visitors were throwing snap pops on the ground. The sounds made Hu's burly security guard antsy. Although fireworks were more commonplace around the Chinese New Year, visitors still used them at Buddhist monasteries. They even used them at old Catholic cathedrals, like the ruins of St. Paul's in Macau. Hu was once told that the Jesuit priests, in order to teach indigenous populations about their religion, would incorporate local religious or spiritual rites and practices, hence the snap pops and firecrackers at anything deemed a religious shrine.

"Are you happy now?" he asked his daughter.

"Yes!"

Hu smiled. It wasn't something he did very often, but when he did, it was usually when he was with his children, especially his daughter, who exuded a life energy that was shared by everyone around her.

"A call," the guard said as he handed Hu the phone. Hu grimaced, having been interrupted by a joyful moment. He let go of his daughter's hand and told her to join her brothers in exploring the floors beneath the Buddha.

"Yes?" he said curtly in English.

"You wanted an update," came the voice with a Russian accent.

"And?"

"We took the base and did as you asked. We only left a few there. The private security firm and Philippine sailors regained control—as we planned."

"Excellent. I have been away from my office. How was the video from the drone?"

"Perfect," Makarov replied. "We edited just enough of it that it would play well on the news stations. They started airing it an hour ago."

This is what happened when Hu left the office to enjoy himself. Had he stayed, he'd have known immediately about the breaking news. But he could not say no to his children. He had planned this entire campaign, and sometimes he had to learn to trust his experts to carry it out when he was unavailable. He simply had to have the right people, something he had failed to do twice before in Yemen and Sri Lanka.

"What is the response?" Hu asked as he peered out over the island at one of the most magnificent views in the region. He was tempted to light a cigarette, but his wife was nearby, and his lungs were still recovering from the climb.

"The commentators have said little since they have little to go with. It's just all speculation in their world at the moment until we take the next step with that video," Makarov said dispassionately.

"Are you ready?"

"Two days. Will you be ready in two days?"

"Yes. We have most of the forces we need. We have a sense of the numbers at the base and offshore on the two security vessels anchored by it."

"Very well," Hu said, putting his hand in his pocket to stroke the Benson & Hedges cigarette pack. It was a small comfort to him until he could spirit himself from his wife's view.

"Are you maintaining surveillance on them, Sergei?"

"We were but Highland Maritime took down our first drone. We'll have the other one up soon," Makarov replied.

"How?"

"They had two drones carrying a net between them. Simple, but effective."

"Don't let them be 'effective' again, is that understood?" Hu said as his patience wore thin. "Do not underestimate his company."

"I understand. Is there anything else?"

"Yes. There are two. First, have your team release Manila now. Return power there, especially to the media outlets. In six hours, return power to the remainder of the country. It's time the next phase is put into place. How long will it take for Manila to return?"

"Fifteen or twenty minutes," Makarov replied without hesitating.

"Good."

"And the second?"

"Do you need Qin for the remainder of the assignment?"

There was a pause at Makarov's end. Hu knew Qin's value as a marksman and assassin, and Makarov would have preferred to keep him nearby. But Hu knew that Makarov wasn't asking his opinion.

"If you require his services elsewhere. . . ." Makarov began.

"I do. I need him to clean something up. A seaplane will arrive at your location shortly. I want Qin and his equipment on it. He will have instructions when he boards. You have your instructions, Sergei." With that, Hu ended the call without waiting for the courtesy of a reply. He wasn't in the courtesy business.

Hu took his wife's hand and led her below the Buddha to join the children as they toured the facility. Twenty minutes later, he excused himself to make a short call, receiving admonishment from his wife. But she had been with him long enough to know that these interruptions were commonplace. He was, after all, head of a major firm that afforded the family more benefits than all but a few in China.

The guard joined him outside as Hu dialed the phone number that was only now available on the networks.

"Hello," answered the meek voice.

"It's time, Felipe. Are you ready?"

"There has been so much confusion here, Hu. So much has been disrupted. Bandits have been running wild, destroying stores."

"Of course. This was to be expected. And now you must do what we agreed to."

"Yes, Hu. May I go?" he asked like a schoolchild asks a teacher to leave the classroom for the restroom.

"Yes, Felipe. Now."

CAMP DAVID

The Navy commander briefing the president and his national security team in the presidential lodge or the video teleconference from Washington set aside his notes and turned on the brief televised speech the new Philippine president recorded just a short time ago. Felipe Reyes had served as President Quinta's quiet vice president. A slightly-built man in his sixties sat at a desk in front of the camera. He clearly was uncomfortable in the limelight despite his decades in politics. Reyes had always been a back-bencher, according to the intelligence reports, not particularly popular or known outside his district, but a reliable vote for the party in power. They propped him up for his vote year after year.

The blue velvet curtains behind him had the flag of the Philippines on each side. The speech was live from Malacañang Palace, the Philippines' equivalent of the White House. It was both residence and office in Manila on the Pasig River. During President Dunner's state visit early in the administration, Dunner, Quinta, CJ, and CJ's national security counterpart met in the music room after dinner. Quinta was knowledgeable enough about Sumner's background to ask her to play a piece or two on the piano. Sumner noted that Quinta had not invited her own vice president to the state dinner.

CJ had seen a few clips of President Quinta from that same desk. Now Felipe Reyes, a politician who could barely handle getting reelected in his own district and was a shadow of a vice president, oversaw one of the most strategically placed countries in the western Pacific. And it meant that Quinta was indeed gone.

Reyes kept his remarks short. The first thing he confirmed to the nation for the first time was that Quinta's plane had been lost, likely due to engine trouble and that it was a tragedy that it occurred at the same time as the cyberattacks. He promised a full investigation to determine if the nefarious elements that had launched the cyberattacks had also taken down her plane. He promised to bring to justice those actors who had caused such widespread disruption throughout the country and ordered the military to take any action necessary against them.

Reyes' written words were meant to reassure the Filipino people, but his voice lacked authority, empathy, or conviction. That meant he'd serve as someone's puppet, but whose? The senior national security team had gone down in Quinta's plane except for the heads of their army and air force. There was the party in leadership and they knew how to manipulate him. Sumner speculated that Felipe Reyes would not be long for the presidency. Now that Quinta was gone, some other strongman—or strongwoman—would take advantage of Reyes' inability to act like a president.

Finally, Reyes called for all people to come together as Filipinos to re-store stability and security to their proud nation. After a "thank you," the recording concluded. Sumner looked to her right at President Dunner, who was focused on every word. His pen and notepad, always provided to him, went untouched. Dunner, despite his declining physical condition, was still mentally sharper than most in the room. His career as a skilled diplomat relied as much on his civil, decent demeanor as on his near-photographic memory when it came to the names of the people he met. It also helped him understand trends and geostrategic conditions. She was proud that he was her mentor during her own career through the ranks.

Dunner noted the briefer's earlier comment that power had been restored only to Manila. The intelligence community had no informa-tion on power and other systems on the other islands. Dunner was blunt.

"Can anyone in the intelligence community confirm if this was a coup?"

There was no answer at the table or on the video screen. Dunner was too nice to call out the CIA director, but the man on the screen knew he had to answer.

"Mr. President, at this time we don't have enough information to provide an assessment," the director finally said, breaking through the silence.

Sumner wanted to throw her head back in frustration, but Dunner had always taught her to remain cool, always smile, and never let them see you sweat or allow non-verbal signals to betray your thoughts. She could have predicted the exact words the CIA director would use.

"Thank you, Douglas," Dunner said as his thumb stroked his chin. "I appreciate that perspective, and I know your team will figure this out. I believe, however, that this was a clear coup, but not by Felipe Reyes. The man you saw in that speech doesn't have the capacity of dreaming this up or carrying it out. He was too scared of Quinta. He's never indicated in his entire career that he had the intellect, vision, or strength to do so. No, I believe he's a frontman for someone, and there has to be a reason that person—or people—wanted Quinta out. Douglas, I'd like you to provide me with an assessment later today on some options. Who had Quinta made an enemy? Of those, who had the ability to assassinate her in this way? Who of those had strong connections to Reyes? The heads of their army and air force weren't on the plane with President Quinta. Start there."

"Yes, Mr. President." Even through the video, Sumner could tell Douglas was miffed.

Dunner turned to the secretary of state. "I'd like you to contact the Reyes government if you can and extend my personal condolences on the Philippines' loss of their president and that we stand ready to support them in any way. With that, make an offer to provide humanitarian and technical assistance as I asked for earlier."

"Yes, Mr. President," the secretary said dutifully.

"Mr. President," CJ interjected, "may I suggest that the Department of Defense contact whomever they can as well to determine the Reyes government's intent to continue their participation in our naval exercise? The ships are only a couple of days from transiting the area."

"Of course, CJ, of course. All right, let's all get to it, ladies and gentlemen. Thank you very much for your time," Dunner concluded.

Sumner followed Dunner. "May I see you in your office, Mr. President?"

Dunner walked with her around the corner to the small office at the end of the hallway. He sat back in the black leather chair, eyeing the models of USS *Winston Churchill* and a *Seawolf*-class submarine on the shelf to his left.

"I know that tone, CJ," he said with a sigh.

"The Philippines, sir. There was a brief report in the news. They showed video of what they called mercenaries attacking a small Philippine naval base."

Dunner's eyes widened. "It's out? Why didn't the commander brief this?"

"Uh . . . I spoke to him before the brief and asked him to hold off on that until we had more information," she said apologetically.

Dunner paused and looked away from her. "I don't like that information was withheld from me like that."

"I'm sorry. But I believe the personnel in the video were from Highland Maritime Defense," Sumner conveyed in the softest of tones.

"Stark's company?" the president said, turning back to her.

"Yes. It's a sensitive issue, particularly since he sold us the electromagnetic pulse rocket materiel after the Sri Lanka crisis. I'd like to make some calls and get more information for you and the national security team."

"I'll give you some leeway on this one, CJ, but only some."

CHAPTER 13

BALABAC

The team had driven another half mile, then backed the two trucks just off the road in the first heavily forested place they came across. They grabbed their weapons and backpacks, then covered the vehicles with as much vegetation as they could before starting the trek down the road.

"Is the plan simply to kill them?" Santos asked Stark.

Stark thought that would have been an interesting question had it been posed in his college ethics course. When is it acceptable to kill outright? It was also a question that would have been answered differently at each stage in his life.

As an officer, he had killed terrorists out of revenge which led to his court-martial. In Yemen, he had killed out of self-defense. In Sri Lanka, he had killed insurgents to save innocents. There were other times as well, but each time deserved more explanation than "simply to kill them." Stark raised his closed fist. They stopped.

"Lieutenant, we're going to try to get into that building because it likely has some of the answers we're looking for. We—our teammates back there—are currently alone. It's been less than a day since that base was attacked. There is a wider problem—otherwise, the government would have sent ships or planes to find out why the base wasn't reporting back on a regular basis. We know that the people who executed everyone at that base are out there. Until we're no longer alone, I will do anything to make sure we all survive."

"Boss, we have the ships," Warren offered as he adjusted his hat with the strapped camera. "We could just extract everyone from the base and hightail it out of here."

"My sailors and I would stay, Dr. Warren," Commander Castillo countered. "That is our base, and this is our land and our waters we have been assigned to defend. Those sailors and those officers gave their lives trying to defend it. It's our responsibility now. It's our duty."

Stark motioned for them to move out, their weapons drawn and their eyes scoping for anything out of place or moving. Stark checked his compass with one hand, then led them off the road, where it began to clear. He estimated they were only a hundred yards or so from the building they had seen from the drone's video. He took out his binoculars and could just make out the building of corrugated aluminum. He hadn't caught it at first since it was painted green to blend in with the environment. Warren crouched beside him.

"Any thoughts, Jay?"

"Two guards and an unknown number inside. That pop gun you have doesn't have a silencer. If you take out the guards, then anyone inside knows we're here and might get a signal off to whomever they're working with elsewhere."

"Then we need to get whoever is inside out of the building. Do you have any of those smoke signals?"

"Is two enough?"

Stark hoped it would be as Warren handed them over.

"Take Santos and station yourselves on the west side of that building. Castillo and I will start it from the south side."

"Got it, boss. Be careful," Warren said as he motioned to Santos to follow him.

Stark and Castillo made it another forty yards when they began to crawl to minimize detection. The guards were chatting, though they were still too far away to hear any sound other than the calls of the wild birds. Stark waited until he thought Warren and Santos were in position, then pulled the tabs on the two can-sized smoke makers as he tossed them ten yards to his right. Twenty seconds later, two plumes of smoke began to rise. It took another twenty seconds for one of the guards to finally notice. He hit the other guard in the arm and pointed to what appeared to them a fire starting in the jungle. The other guard went to the door, opened it, and called inside. Two men and a woman ran out of the building.

The first guard started to approach the smoke to determine the cause. Stark waited until he was fifteen yards away, then stood with his gun pointing at the guard, telling him to freeze, hopefully a word spoken with conviction that was comprehensible in any language or anyone in the world who had seen a US cop show from the 1970s.

The guard began to unholster his rifle when Stark told him to freeze again. Stark pulled the trigger, shooting the guard in the shoulder and causing him to fall back. He swung the barrel around to the left toward the second guard, who now had his own gun out and pointed toward Stark. Three shots in quick succession dropped the guard forward. Warren, Stark thought, had just saved his life again.

Stark approached the first guard, now screaming in pain, and took his weapon. Meanwhile Castillo charged toward the building, his guns pointed forward in case anyone else emerged, as Santos called out to the man and woman in army fatigues who had come out when fire had seemingly threatened them. The burly Stark dragged the first guard by his other shoulder toward the building as the lighter man cried louder. When Stark reached the clearing by the door, he ordered Santos to cover the man, woman, and first guard as he motioned for Warren and Castillo to follow him into the building.

LE HAVRE

The dark clouds made way for a steady drizzle as Golzari casually approached the gangway of the *Strident Yingkou*. He didn't see any armed guards nearby, nor would he expect any to be visible. The merchant ship had to appear to conduct legitimate trade and not illicit cargo, like enslaved humans. If the ship were subject to inspection, and there was a small chance it would be, it couldn't carry weapons into a port like Le Havre. Given the amount of shipping that came through here and the limited number of port authority officials, it was unlikely that this ship would be subject to a search. Still, if the traffickers wanted to continue using this ship and port as they had, they had to reduce the risk. Firearms would be at the top of the list of high-priority contraband for inspectors.

A dark, pockmark-skinned crewman in light blue coveralls with a trash bag slung over his shoulder ambled down the gangway. The nametag read "Koffi," which Golzari recognized as a common name in Francophonic sub-Saharan Africa, most likely Côte d'Ivoire. Golzari addressed him in French.

"Hello, I'd like to speak with your captain," Golzari said with a smile.

"The second mate is up there," Koffi pointed with his thumb over his shoulder. "You'll need to ask him." Golzari thanked him and proceeded up the metal gangway that produced a small bounce with each of his steps and an accompanying clang at each end where it had been tied off. Golzari hated ships and never understood their attraction. It was probably why he never understood Stark's fascination with them or the sea.

A rotund Caucasian man in his thirties holding a clipboard greeted him coldly. Golzari wasn't wearing the uniform of Port Authority officers, and his unexpected arrival likely meant he wasn't a husbanding agent—the person or company responsible for ship services, repairs, and supplies.

"Yes?" he asked in French.

"I'd like to see the captain," Golzari responded calmly. "I have some business to conduct."

"What kind of business?"

"The kind of business I can only discuss with the captain."

The second mate considered the response for a few seconds, then motioned Golzari to follow. As they climbed the outside ladder, Golzari looked to the forward four-fifths of the ship's length, where the different colored containers—blue, yellow, orange, and half a dozen others—were stacked and would be unloaded and moved around like a giant Tetris game. What caught his eye were the top containers on the second row. Four across were the same shade of kelly green. No other ship containers were of the same color next to each other or, from appearances on the outer containers, those stacked atop one another. Perhaps it was a coincidence, but before Golzari entered through the hatch, his keen eye picked up screens about two feet wide on top of each of the four kelly-green containers. None of the other containers had them.

Once he and the second mate entered through the second deck hatch, they climbed the ladder three more levels until they reached the bridge, which nearly spanned the width of the ship. The blue linoleum tiled floor was sparkling from a deckhand on the far side with a mop and pail on wheels. A hefty older man in his fifties with a thick shock of white hair combed back sat in the captain's chair on the starboard side. His legs were fully extended as his socked feet rested on an extension of the bulkhead. His unlaced boots were placed on a nearby shelf. The captain had his laptop open to a website showing weather patterns off Europe.

"Excuse me, Captain," the second mate reverted to broken English, "someone to see you."

The captain slowly turned his double-chinned head toward the visitor.

"What is it?" he said. The deep voice was accented in what Golzari guessed was Russian, Byelorussian, or Ukrainian in origin.

"Excuse me for interrupting, Captain, but I have business to discuss with you—in private," Golzari said as he motioned to the mate and deckhand.

"Talk to my first mate," the captain said, turning back to his laptop.

"Captain, it's important. I just drove here from Paris to discuss . . . the recent shipments we received from you," Golzari answered.

"As you can see, we have thousands of containers, each with many items distributed throughout Europe. I don't track those, Mr. . . ."

"Mansouri. Abdou Mansouri."

The captain eyed him more carefully and gave no response. Golzari had made it this far and rolled the dice again. Since there was no evidence from the records at the Paris house that Mansouri had come to Le Havre, the captain likely had never met him. Then again, just because Golzari hadn't seen any indication of travel didn't mean Mansouri had never come here. Still, combined with the fact that Mansouri had a day job in a labor-intensive restaurant industry, made the chance of his traveling to Le Havre even more unlikely. How long could Golzari throw the dice until the house finally won?

"I know we've never formally met, Captain, but there is an urgency to this meeting. There was a problem with the last shipment of seventeen packages," Golzari said, cryptically referring to the children.

The captain picked up his phone and said something which was most likely Russian, then hung it up. He put his laptop to the side and reached for his boots, clumsily slipping his feet into them as he pushed himself off the chair. He leaned back against the chair as he tied each boot. *This is taking too long*, Golzari thought. *Is the captain getting ready to talk with me or stalling?*

His question was answered when three deckhands burst onto the bridge, two with batons and one with a large cooking knife. The deckhand who had been mopping pushed away the pail so quickly it fell over and spilled water on half the deck as he helped the others surround Golzari. The second mate pulled out a switchblade and held it to Golzari's neck.

For the first time in his professional life, Damien Golzari had allowed himself to be outmaneuvered, and for the first time in two days of rolling the dice, his luck had run out.

BALABAC ISLAND

Stark took three cautious steps into the rudimentary structure, clearly assembled rapidly by whatever organization he was dealing with. The dirt floor had footprints—those of the man and woman who had escaped with the thought of a nearby fire. It wasn't constructed for durability; it had been assembled as a temporary facility for whatever operation was occurring.

The entrance was in the middle of the building's hundred-foot length. Ahead was a ten-foot-wide corridor extending fifty feet to the rear of the building with double sliding doors. The interior walls were simple plywood. Stark felt the cool air and heard the low hum of an industrial-sized HVAC unit. There were no doors along the corridor, only frames with curtains. Stark noticed the dirt floor ahead had far more footprints than the men and woman could have produced.

He motioned to Castillo and Warren to remain outside and reached into one of his vest's left pockets for earplugs, then into another pocket for one of the three flash-bang grenades he carried with him. He lobbed one beneath the left curtain and then shifted to the left to pull out another, rolling it under the right curtain. Each would give him a few seconds advantage over anyone in those areas as they'd be temporarily blinded and unable to distinguish the sound of his moving.

First the left and then the right exploded, the curtains shielding Stark from the blinding light. There was no sound from the left area, but he heard cries from the right. He motioned to Castillo and Warren to follow him in as he pushed back the curtain with the barrel of his FNC rifle. As the smoke rose, he could make out the figures of at least five people and the light from computers and machines that lined the walls. All the uniforms were the same forest camouflage as the others, but only one had a weapon that she tried to orient herself with, desperately trying to face the curtain. She raised her weapon and got off two shots into the plywood and a third toward the curtain. Stark pivoted his rifle and shot her in the head when he heard someone behind him yell. Stark nearly slipped when he moved from the corridor's dirt floor to the rolled linoleum floor.

Warren emerged out of the corner of Stark's left eye and charged ahead, pointing his own rifle at the still-disoriented people on the floor to ensure they had no weapons or the opportunity to use them. Two were rocking back and forth with their hands to their ears, suggesting they had been closest when the grenade went off.

Stark called out for Castillo but got no response. He proceeded through the forty-by-fifty-foot area, checking behind and beneath the few desks. There were no windows for anyone to escape from.

"We're clear in here, Jay. I'm checking the other area," Stark said, looking for Castillo. The PN commander was in the corridor, sitting with his back against the far wall. Grimacing, he looked up at Stark, then down at his leg. Blood covered his thigh. One of the three bullets had hit him.

"Hold tight," Stark said as he entered the other area. There had been no cries on this side since it was devoid of people. On the left were banks of batteries. On the right were racks of water bottles and food.

Stark returned to the corridor, set his weapon down, and pulled out his Leatherman from his pocket. He unfolded the knife and cut off Castillo's left pant, exposing the bullet wound. From another pocket, he slipped out two green packages of QuickClot combat gauze, ripped them open, and stuffed them into the wound as he apologized to Castillo, who grabbed Stark's shoulder tightly and threw his head back in pain. Stark applied consistent pressure and now had to worry about the time needed to do so. It was recommended that pressure be applied for three minutes.

"Santos!" he yelled. "Bring those three in here! Jay, Castillo's been shot. I had gauze but no dressing. You got anything?"

"Goddamn fucking Bat Belt of a vest doesn't have dressing? Hold on," Warren shouted from behind the curtain. He tore the curtain from its rod, then marched the four prisoners to the corridor as Santos entered the facility with her three.

"Get them in that room," Stark said, motioning to the one with the batteries and supplies. Santos lined the seven against a wall as Warren rifled through the supplies until he found a towel and cord.

"That's all I got for now, boss," he said, handing it over to Stark, who maintained pressure on the wound. "And give him these for the pain. I always keep a few spare around when I go on assignments with you."

"Thanks," Stark acknowledged. "Take a look outside to make sure there aren't more bad guys en route. And check the guard I downed."

"Righto."

"Have you done this before, Captain Stark?" Castillo asked, gritting his teeth.

"Fucking up? Plenty of times. I'm sorry, Commander. We'll get you out of here."

"Stark, we came for something. At least let's find out what's here before you carry me away," Castillo said, managing a faint smile through the pain.

Two shots rang out beyond the walls and then silence. Warren's large frame filled the door frame.

"Next time you shoot a guy in the shoulder, make sure he still can't raise a weapon," he said. Stark knew it wasn't the first time Warren had

had to shoot someone, but it was far rarer for the mad scientist than it had been for Stark.

"Get those people sitting down against those industrial batteries," he ordered Warren.

In the minutes that Stark treated and dressed the wound, Warren expertly shepherded the seven prisoners, at the point of a rifle, to where Stark wanted them. After ensuring Castillo was okay for now, the Philippine Navy commander took his own weapon and pointed it at the door in case there were more out there while Stark joined Castillo and Warren.

Stark approached the seven prisoners. Five were men, two were women. None of them showed any indication of being scared. Most looked at him in stoic silence. Two had evident rage. One of them said something to the others.

"Quiet!" Stark commanded, hoping that was as evident as "freeze" in whatever language they spoke.

Santos moved toward Stark.

"I need to speak with you," she whispered. Stark and Santos backed out of the room and across the corridor.

"What is it, Santos?"

"When they spoke, sir, it was Tagalog."

"I thought you said the island's population only spoke Molbog," he said.

"That's correct. These people are not from this island."

CHAPTER 14

"Where are they from?"

"I can't tell," Santos admitted.

"Well let's find out," Stark said, about to head back into the room when he checked on Castillo. "Commander, how's the pain?"

"Mr. Warren's pills are starting to take effect," he said as he winced.

"We're only four people, Commander. I need your help." Castillo understood as Stark helped to lift him and told Santos to get his weapon. He brought Castillo into the room with the prisoners and sat him in a chair. Castillo was still in pain but accepted his gun from Santos.

Stark turned to the prisoner who had spoken to the others.

"You understand what I'm saying?"

He said nothing. He didn't sneer, smile, or cower.

"Let me rephrase that. You understand what I'm saying. That's a declarative sentence, not a question, fucker. It's a good time for you to speak up."

Still, there was nothing except now a smirk from the prisoner.

"Okay. Commander? I trust you'll do what you need to if any of them speak without being spoken to?"

"Of course." Castillo then said something else, probably in Tagalog.

Stark took Santos and Warren with him to the room with the computer terminals.

"All right, Lieutenant. Remember the training exercises we planned, specifically the FME module?"

"Yes, sir, I remember," the five-foot, four-inch officer said confidently of the foreign material exploitation training they'd had.

"Good. Because this is that module. We need to figure out what this place is and fast."

The smoke from the flash-bang lingered and was settling as the three of them walked around the room, leaving any written material to Santos since neither Stark nor Warren could read Tagalog or Spanish.

"Jay, is your camera on?"

Warren put his hand to the strap around his ballcap and pressed a button.

"It is now."

"Good. Get one scan around the room and then clear video of every monitor you can."

The forty-by-fifty-foot room had thirty terminals and monitors, with another thirty monitors above those. Most were cycling through codes. Some had maps of various Philippine islands. Each terminal had masking tape with one or two words written in black marker. One corner of the room had a radio transmitter and receiver that looked decades old.

"Jay?"

"Fuck if I know what this place is. If the island is as agrarian as we've seen and the Molbogs don't have that much contact with the rest of the islands, why this high-tech stuff? Except for that radio. Hell, that looks like the HAM radio on *Minerva*."

"Jaime said their communications officer was trying to speak with someone on Leyte Island through their HAM radio. If they're listening to traffic . . ."

"Sorry, boss, I can do a lot, but I don't have a license like that. It'll take a while for me to figure out."

"I can help," Santos said. "We used something similar in one of my communications courses. But about these terminals, Captain Stark, most of them are labeled by major islands in my country. I'm not familiar with the codes scrolling through, but if I remember my class correctly, these servers seem to be conducting a denial of service or distributed attack."

"Sorry, Lieutenant, I don't speak computer," Stark admitted.

"If I didn't know better, I'd say this is the hub for a massive ongoing cyberattack throughout the Philippines. See that one? That one says

'Cebu Island.' The next few are Mindanao, with terminals devoted to Davao and Cagayan de Oro. That bank on the far side are Manila and the major communities near it, but it's not scrolling anything like the other terminals. Some are launching multiple queries to utility companies, internet companies, and a dozen other types of targets. Military bases as well."

"That explains why the Philippine military hasn't checked on the base here," Warren observed.

"What about satellite phones? Why haven't I been able to reach our contacts with your navy?" Stark asked.

"Wait one moment, Captain," Santos said as she began typing on one of the keyboards. "Nothing is locked out. When you shot the guards, the computer operators ran outside. They did not take the time to secure their accounts. See here?" she pointed at one of the codes. "Captain, the cyberattack didn't attack the phone. It attacked the billing account."

"They went after the weakest link?" Warren asked.

"Yes. The navy has to pay a private vendor for satellite phone services. This particular attack essentially told the company that the navy was in payment arrears and shut off their services at nearly the same time as everything else went down."

"This is how empires fall," Stark said.

"That station in the corner," she continued, "is an uplink to a satellite, but I haven't had much exposure to them."

Warren took a closer look at the station.

"Ho . . . ly. . . ." Warren started.

"What?" Stark asked.

"Holy crap, this looks a lot like Bullhorn."

"Help me out here, Jay."

"Bullhorn has been in development by this mega-billionaire for a few years. It's a series of LEO—low earth orbiting—satellites. He had this idea of this constellation of about a thousand satellites, and the antennas would be the size of a friggin' toaster. Kind of like this one next to the station, but it's not what they proposed."

"Could someone else have launched and distributed a similar system without anyone knowing?" Santos asked.

"If they could, Lieutenant, we'd be in a whole lotta shit. I mean, a launch can't be hidden, but the payload could be for a while. Eventually it's all detectable by our ground tracking stations."

"Captain Stark," Santos offered, "this isn't a simulation. They really are attacking every island. That must be why this building was constructed so close to the cable crossing."

"It's not just a cyberattack," he replied. "Those people who attacked your naval base shot and killed everyone there. This is a coordinated effort. The question is still, who are these people? We've at least narrowed them down to Filipinos, correct?"

"Sir, there is no doubt the prisoners are from the Philippines. I just don't know which group they're with. As you know, we have several terrorist groups operating here. But none have ever taken a military base or had the ability to conduct such a widespread cyberattack. It just hasn't been their . . . modus operandi."

"There's a first time for everything, Lieutenant," Stark offered. "Can we stop it from here?"

"Maybe if we cut the power on the computers, but if there was a malware component to the attacks, I wouldn't know how to stop that. But there's one more problem—there are not enough people to operate these terminals. They are maintaining them, but I think everything's being uplinked to the satellites and run from somewhere else."

Santos maintained her composure. *This is one tough, savvy officer, keeping her head about her,* Stark thought. All she had been through in the past couple of days, and she was still performing like someone with years more experience. She turned to the HAM radio, put on the headset, and manipulated the dials to recall *Minerva's* direction, distance, and range.

Stark and Warren continued to walk around the room, trying to find anything. Stark thumbed through a green notebook with numbers to the left and writing in a foreign language on the right. The numbers went from 0000 to 2400, then started again. Stark took it to Santos, who quickly translated it.

"Logbook?" he asked, based on the numbers corresponding to military times he had seen all too often.

"Yes, sir. It notes the times of duties. They are very organized."

Stark looked closer at the times. "They received a communication thirty minutes before we arrived. Everything else is blank."

"Yes, sir. The communication confirmed this station would stop some of the cyberattacks in Manila." She scanned the earlier entries. "If this trend on the previous pages is correct, the next turnover for the guards and operators is in forty-five minutes."

LE HAVRE

"Who are you?" the *Strident Yingkou*'s captain asked.

Golzari, encircled by five crewmen, all of them holding a weapon of some sort, faced the rotund captain with the gruff Russian voice.

"I thought we established that, Captain. I am Abdou Mansouri, and we are both working for the same people."

"Why don't I believe you," he said, bending over to tie his shoelaces as his rounded belly caused him to momentarily lose his balance as his center of gravity shifted.

"Because you haven't met me before and because it was as a matter of concern that I had to risk coming here."

Golzari hoped to talk himself out of this because the more he considered the odds, the more he realized it was his only option.

"How do I know you aren't with the French government or another authority?" the captain asked as he rolled back into his swiveling chair. He planted an elbow firmly on the armrest and rested his rotund head in a cupped hand.

"Because, Captain, I would not have come alone. If the authorities knew about this ship and its cargo, they would have immediately boarded it with teams to detain you, your crew, and inspect every container like those four green TEUs," as his chin indicated their direction.

"Maybe the authorities are out there, and you are wearing a recording device."

Golzari put out his arms.

"Have your men search me. They will find two weapons. A gun on my left side and a gun on the inside of my leg." Golzari had just thrown the dice one last time. He knew they'd eventually search him and find his guns. He had no chance to use the guns. He was fast but not that fast. And these were not professional thugs. They were crewmen skilled to operate ships, not shake down people. That meant they were prone to mistakes out of ignorance, which was a big difference from being plain stupid. He hoped that lack of experience meant they'd overlook his knife. It was like a magician's trick. Focus the audience on what they expect to see and not what you don't want them to see.

One of the men patted him down in the exact two spots Golzari said they'd find the guns and took them away. They didn't take the time to look for anything else, just as he had hoped. That was the first break he got, but he knew he'd need a lot more to get out of here unscathed instead of gaining the information.

"What will it be, Captain? I came here to discuss a problem with the last cargo. We can do that. Option two is tossing me overboard and explaining to our employers why you killed their retailer from their very profitable Paris store. How much money will they lose before they replace me? What will they exact from you in that case? Are you going to compensate them for that loss? Or will they simply have you join me in this port's filthy water?"

The captain's eyes narrowed, considering the argument like a judge weighing those of the prosecution and defense. He rose from his seat and turned his back to them, looking out the windows in the distance from port to starboard. He returned to face Golzari and reached out his hand to the crewman who had taken the guns. The crewman carefully handed one to him, butt first.

"If our employers don't hold you to account, I have three teams of security at the store who know exactly where I am, what ship I am on, and who the captain is. And, Captain, I only hire Chechens."

That caused the reaction Golzari wanted. Every Russian knew what their country had done in Chechnya, the brutal massacres and the leveling of part of Grozni. Russians knew that Chechens hated nothing more than Russians and would gladly kill any one of them, or many at a time, in very creative ways. The captain looked Golzari in the eyes.

"Here is your weapon," the captain said, giving the gun to Golzari as he motioned to his crewman to give their visitor the other one then dismissed them all. Once they were left alone, the captain returned to his chair and gestured to Golzari to find someplace comfortable. Golzari was too experienced in tense situations to breathe a sigh of relief, but he promised himself a good cognac when this day was over.

"I may be Muslim by birth, Captain, but you wouldn't have any of the good vodka I hear about, would you?"

"Come," he said as they exited the bridge, went down the ladder one deck to his stateroom, and opened the door to small refrigerator.

"So, what is so important that you come here?" the captain asked as he poured two glasses. "You know I don't have any say over where the cargo comes from?"

"True, but maybe we can talk to our employers together since they may not listen to us individually. The last shipment from Balabac was horrible. Seventeen arrived in my charge, but three died the next day from malnutrition and some other ailment we couldn't identify. And we couldn't exactly call a doctor."

"Ha, true. I can tell you I only see them when I pick them up."

"How exactly do you transfer them if the containers are on top?" Golzari asked, knocking back the first drink.

"We cut a hole in the top of each one, then weld it back when they're in the TEU. Since we make the transfer at sea, we have no cranes on the ships. That's it? That's the only issue? A few of the thousands we've transported have died in your care? Isn't your profit margin enough?"

Golzari casually leaned back on a console like he was talking with an old friend. "Is it ever enough money? Men like you and me do all the work, but most of the money goes to the top men."

"Very true. But they'll have to find a new source soon," the captain admitted.

"New source?"

"Yes, this was the last cargo from Balabac Island. More than two hundred kids in those four containers."

"Why the last one? Not that I'm complaining since we can surely find better products elsewhere."

"I was told by the Chinese vessel that there were no more on the island," the captain said, tilting his head back with the second shot. Before he put his glass down, Golzari had taken out the gun from his shoulder holster and pointed it at him.

"Now, Captain, let's have an honest conversation, shall we?" Golzari locked the door.

BALABAC ISLAND

Forty-five minutes until the changing of the guard. That confirmed there were a lot more of the bad guys on the island. If there were two guards and five people in the building, that meant three or four shifts per day. Stark lined up the pieces in his mind. If they were coming from the village, they'd take a couple of vehicles.

"Okay, get on the radio. You have fifteen minutes. After that, we're getting out of here in case they get here early. Jay, we have to get Castillo out of here. How long until you can get to one of the trucks and be back here?"

"Once I get to the truck, it's only a few minutes, but it's getting there that . . ." Jay didn't say it. He was older than Stark and enjoyed a lot of good meals.

"Don't worry."

"You're the one who raced in the Olympics, boss," Warren said with an air of levity. Santos's head lifted since she could hear the conversation even through her headset.

Stark had four problems. The first was that the relief was coming on watch in under an hour. The second was that Castillo was in no condition to walk or run. Third was that they had prisoners in the other room who would tell their reliefs everything. And fourth, this facility—this place hidden in plain sight as a refrigerated warehouse for goddamn coconuts—was a key part of a massive cyberattack on the whole of the Philippines. Warren wouldn't make it to the trucks and back in time. Santos was needed on the radio.

"Sir? I think I have *Minerva*."

"Jay, how heavy would you say Castillo is with his uniform?"

"One sixty, one seventy, maybe?"

"That's what I thought. There's a clearing about sixty yards back. Can you get him there?"

"Oh, yeah.

"Lieutenant, give *Minerva* our coordinates. Tell them we need an immediate medevac and to send one of the DP-14s to a clearing sixty yards south of this building." He added a quick summary of their situation, which Santos relayed to the ship. "And tell them we may need backup. We'll need a couple of teams to hoof it since there weren't any more trucks at the base."

"Connor," Warren said in an unusually formal voice, "that could take an hour and it'll get dark soon."

"I know . . ." Stark knew what that meant. He was the only one available to reach the trucks. They were a mile away. On a good day with sneakers, he could run a seven-minute mile on a track—significantly slower than in his athletic years and when he still had two good knees. On a mostly dirt road running with boots in coveralls would be fifteen minutes at best. Another five minutes to get back. That left only about twenty minutes before the relief force arrived. Running as part of the Pentathlon in the Olympics was less pressure.

"What about the prisoners?" Warren asked.

"I know, Jay. I know," Stark said, uncharacteristically frustrated, especially since he had gotten them all into this situation.

Castillo had to be treated, and Jay had to get him to the landing zone for the DP-14, where its empty cargo bay designed for supplies or a two-hundred-pound person could be transported. Stark needed Santos at the radio for a few more minutes, and the prisoners needed to be monitored, plus everything else, like what to do with this station. Stark should have taken more people with him, but there wasn't any more time for second-guessing.

"Jay, get Castillo to the LZ now and give me all his ammo. After the DP-14 takes him away, I want you to hightail it to the trucks and go back to meet up with the teams and get them back here."

"You're not pulling an Alamo here, are you?" Warren retorted.

"Just get back here with the teams. Go!"

Stark shifted to the other room as Warren carried Castillo out. He was alone with seven prisoners, all looking at him, most of whom seemed to want to pounce on him. Insurgents always had a certain level of hate that obscured their rationality and ability to work civilly with others. So which were these? One of the terrorist groups of the Philippines or someone else? Did they think he would shoot them? Hell, did *he* think he would shoot them?

He remembered hearing about an episode in Afghanistan where a Navy SEAL team had granted clemency to a shepherd boy instead of killing him during a mission. The boy reported the team to local Taliban fighters. And, for that moment of mercy, the team had been repaid with death. If Stark and Santos left these people behind, they could tell their relief force about them. But what could they tell them? That four private security and PN officers killed two of their own? They would have the names of the two officers, and they undoubtedly overheard Warren and Stark use names.

Warren's Bola system had taken out the drone that monitored them at the base. What information could the prisoners share that wasn't already known to whoever was in charge? What would it really matter? And so it came down to a simple decision—the chance that they'd spill something he hadn't considered or to execute them in cold blood. Stark had killed repeatedly regardless of his early career when killing someone in close range was anathema to him. Despite the past decade, where he had killed more people than he now remembered, it had always been in self-defense, in response to an attack, or, in some cases, when there was no other choice but justice at the end of a gun. But killing unarmed prisoners wasn't something he was ready to do, if he ever would be. Or is this what he had become?

For ten minutes his mind raced through discussions about ethics and the tactical situation in which they found themselves, starting to find some answers to the questions of the past thirty-six hours.

He looked into each of their eyes as they looked up at him from their seated positions. Some were full of anger, some of fear.

Connor Stark, the former navy officer who had raised his hand to support and defend the Constitution and what it meant, now raised his weapon and began shooting.

CHAPTER 15

The prisoners instinctively raised their hands to their heads and dropped to the floor as the bullets sprayed above them, piercing the industrial-sized batteries that supported the building's HVAC and computer systems. Metal shards bounced off them as they remained frozen, fully expecting the next rounds were going into them. Stark remembered the basics of what Warren had once taught him during their earlier FME training days. Industrial batteries had lithium-ion batteries and hydrogen. When the bullets' kinetic energy went through the panels and into the batteries themselves, the hydrogen ignited and released gas. The energy released wasn't a spark like a flint lighter but a friction spark. Any burst of fire was momentary.

While that destroyed the effectiveness of the batteries, it also had the consequence of causing concussions for anyone near those batteries, like getting slammed against a wall at high speed. The shooting stopped momentarily while Stark reloaded his weapon and emptied another clip into the remaining batteries.

Out of the corner of his eye, he saw Santos run in with her own weapon raised until she saw what he was doing. Stark finished off another clip and popped in a new one. Smoke rose from the battery compartments as they hissed. With the second round complete, he didn't know if they were dead or simply unconscious. In either case, at least they had a chance of surviving.

"Santos, how are you doing in there?"

"It would be faster if I used your method, Captain."

She wasn't smiling, but Stark was damn sure of two things. First, she hadn't hesitated to run toward the gunfire when she didn't know what it was, and second, she had a dry sense of humor despite everything happening. If she hadn't been a PN officer, he'd have offered her a job with Highland Maritime Defense.

"Go for it," he said as he turned back to check the pulse of each of the prisoners. The male guard was starting to come around, turning over, his eyes still closed. Stark drew back and struck him once in the head with his meaty hand to knock him out. They were all alive, at least for now. If they had anything to do with the attack on the naval base, as they surely did the cyberattack on the country and wanted to complain, they could take it to their union leader to complain about the dangerous work.

He walked back to the server area where Santos was methodically putting a few bullets in each of the terminals and towers. An operation like this took significant planning—months, maybe a year or two. Stark doubted that the attackers would have a spare bank of computers and terminals on a distant island like this. They had built this place as a one-shot, one-kill facility. It was a facility of the attack, not the originating source. Neither he nor the Highland Maritime team had the ability to find a satellite where they were receiving transmissions from another site. It was all beyond his Luddite mind to understand. At least he knew to turn to the experts when needed.

"Are you done?" he asked as she depleted her third clip like a pro.

Santos scanned the room at the shattered screens and twisted equipment. She fired three more rounds into the radio equipment.

"Yes. I am done."

"Let's get out of here.

He stopped at the door, holding her back with his free arm, as he checked to the left and then the right. It was clear, for now. Nearly a hundred yards ahead, he saw the distinctive frame and twin rotors of the DP-14 drone carrying Castillo in its compartment on his way to be treated on the ships. Warren was out of sight. Stark and Santos began a quick-paced jog once they reached the dirt road. After eight minutes, they heard vehicles in the distance behind them get louder and then fade away as they apparently turned. In a few seconds, the relief force would arrive and realize what happened. He hoped the relief didn't have more than three or four guards based on what they had seen earlier.

Stark knew he was slower than the officer, who was two decades younger.

"Go, Santos. Go as fast as you can and don't stop until you reach the trucks," he ordered. She paused, her wide brown eyes speaking volumes about her composure and courage. He knew that she'd keep his pace if he asked.

"Go. I'll be right behind you."

Santos's twenty-five-year-old, thin frame bolted ahead of him, and she soon disappeared around a bend.

Stark picked up his pace, but between his age, his boots, his nine-pound weapon, and the level of activity the past couple of days, he recognized that even adrenaline wouldn't help him get to the finish line. When he competed in the Pentathlon at the Olympics, the cross-country running portion was four thousand meters. It had been reduced to three thousand at a later Olympics. Now he was struggling with about fifteen hundred meters to the truck; he estimated he had already reached the two-thirds mark. Age caught up to you at the most unexpected and inconvenient moments.

He heard vehicles coming up behind him fast. Based on how loud they were getting, he wouldn't make it the last five hundred. He could easily dart into the vegetation to the left, which was thick at this point, while beachfront could be seen off to the right beyond the groves of palm and coconut trees. He might be able to lose them that way. But if the vehicles reached him, they'd still have a chance of catching up to Santos and maybe Warren. It was imperative that his teammates get back to report to the base. It was vital that they be saved from this.

Stark veered off to the beach side of the dirt road and assumed a prone position behind a medium-sized rock as he pulled out the remaining clips. He had two left. In the Pentathlon, he had used a 4.5mm air pistol from ten meters at a target. Now he was using the 5.56mm rimless bottlenecked intermediate cartridges of his FNC. It had a range of up to four hundred meters. He adjusted the rear sight to a distance of two hundred meters since that was as far down the road he could see before one of the bends. He could hear the vehicles speeding up. He wouldn't have to worry about the second clip. He wouldn't have time to reload. He might be able to take out one or two if he was lucky.

The first of two gray pickup trucks, whose make he didn't recognize, came around the bend. He took a deep breath, sighted one of the soldiers hanging over the cab from the back, exhaled, and took the shot. With a muzzle velocity of more than three thousand feet per second, the bullet impacted his chest before they heard the shot. The soldier fell backward and off the truck. The pickup slowed and then stopped as two soldiers and the driver started firing back. The second pickup deposited another three. They hit the ground, making it more difficult for Stark to sight them. All he could do was aim for the movement of any vegetation he hoped they were crawling behind.

That was when his final round fired. He fumbled for the new clip as he saw them advancing to take advantage of the pause. They were standing now, running and shooting in his direction as he wished the rock would have been larger. As he tried to insert the clip, the jungle to his right exploded in more gunfire.

LE HAVRE

The captain, if anything, kept a neat cabin, or at least the steward did. Despite his nicotine-stained fingers, dried skin, and hoarse voice from decades of smoking, the cabin seemed clean of yellowed walls, suggesting that smoking was only allowed on deck. The bed was made, its sheets and blanket taut. The desk beside it had a simple lamp with a beige lampshade and probably was part of the ship's supplies. He had a loud, ticking analog clock rather than a digital clock. This was a captain who didn't trust the power to go out and relied on an old wind-up clock instead to keep the time and wake him. The desk on the aft wall had a computer and two photos, one with him and a woman about his age and size and another with them and three children in their twenties or thirties. The walls were bare except for a poster of Vladimir Putin smiling and waving to a crowd and a certificate in Russian—probably some maritime license—where Golzari could make out a name in the center, Vasili Antonov. The trash was empty. That and the made bed indicated that the steward had already been in the stateroom that day and would not immediately return.

Golzari remained standing. He pointed the gun toward Captain Antonov, seated in the Barcalounger nine feet away. If they were going to have a discussion, Golzari didn't want either of them talking so loudly that they would be heard outside. He made it clear to the captain that if he called for help, he would die. The captain understood and didn't care to risk his life. He was a mariner who simply transported cargo, regardless of that cargo. He also wasn't one to risk his life for the cargo in a few TEUs compared to the thousands of other legitimate units that drove the lifeblood of much of the world's economy.

"You are not with any law enforcement agency, or else you would have arrested me on the bridge, and the ship would have been swarmed with your colleagues," Antonov observed. "So, will you answer me now as you should have on the bridge? Who are you and what is your business here?"

Antonov wasn't stupid. Just as Golzari had kept talking to stall for time, the captain would do the same, knowing that a ship in port was just as busy as one at sea, with crew requiring checklists or approvals to be signed by the captain. They would eventually come looking for him, and Golzari didn't have a way out since the porthole was too small for anyone's frame.

"How long have you been transporting Molbogs here?"

Antonov refused to answer, shifting his weight in the chair. Golzari reached into his pocket and pulled out a silencer, attaching it to the barrel and pointing it at him again. "First the legs, then the arms, then I start selecting more . . . uncomfortable . . . targets, Captain. Answer the questions." The captain squirmed for the first time.

"What do I care? This is the last shipment. Eleven months."

"Why the Molbogs from Balabac?"

"I don't know. Picking them up was easy for me, but I supposed someone didn't think so many people would be noticed."

"You transported thousands. You didn't think people would notice?" Golzari asked in a hushed tone, trying to lower Antonov's volume unconsciously as well.

"It's a small island. It's in the distant reaches of the Philippines."

This bothered Golzari. How could the population of an island simply disappear and no one in government notice?

"What were the names of the ships you picked them up from?"

"The fishing vessels had no names."

"They were all fishing vessels?"

"Yes. Not the big industrial fishing vessels you see in the Indian Ocean and not small coastal boats. Each brought a few hundred aboard." The captain started tapping his finger on the chair. He was getting nervous.

"How did you communicate with them?"

"We didn't until we were tied up alongside each other."

"Were they armed?"

"Yes. There were guards in uniforms."

"Uniforms?"

"Yes."

"What kind?"

"Nothing like a sailor's uniform. They were army uniforms. Green and black patterns."

"Anything on them like ranks?"

"No. They had nothing on them."

"How did you know where and when to rendezvous?"

"I would be notified in port."

"Which one?"

"Shanghai."

"Who hired you?"

"I don't know."

"One more time, Captain." Golzari chose not to point the gun in the direction of his leg but further up to get right to the point. The captain straightened and reflexively covered his crotch with his hand, though it would do nothing to stop a bullet. It was the sign of a man whose self-control and logic had given way to fear and desperation.

"I don't know. Each time we pulled into Shanghai, the port would load those containers, and someone would come aboard with a note for the time or coordinates of the next."

"Tell me about the person," Golzari said impatiently as he knew each minute that passed might draw the crew to the cabin.

"It wasn't the same person. It was a delivery service, so it was someone different each time."

"What about the first time? How did they initially contact you?"

Antonov was pensive, trying to remember the details. He pointed to the two drawers on the right side of his desk.

"The paperwork is in there. It was when the containers were first placed on the ship. I was told never to move them and how to use them."

Golzari knew enough about shipping that each TEU had its own identification number painted on the outside which would trace their history from the manufacturing site and where it passed through each node in the supply chain worldwide.

"Get them—carefully, Captain," Golzari said, moving back to allow him space without allowing Antonov to turn his back to him. Antonov bent down, opened the bottom drawer, and immediately went to a folder labeled by month and year. He laid out the folder on his desk and sifted through half the stack before removing two sheets, setting them aside.

"Here! Take what you want!" Antonov said loudly. Golzari motioned him back to his chair as he briefly looked at the paper and shoved it in his pocket. There was a knock at the door as Antonov waited for Golzari to instruct him.

"Captain?" came the voice from the other side.

Antonov said something in Russian as Golzari heard the metallic friction of a key inserted into the lock.

SOUTH CHINA SEA

Hu was nothing if not prompt. No sooner had he hung up the phone than the fishing vessel's captain reported that a seaplane was landing and had radioed to transport the passenger immediately. Qin never asked Makarov why he was leaving for another assignment, but that wasn't his role. Qin silently packed his few belongings and climbed down the ship's rope ladder to the awaiting boat, which took him for the abbreviated ride to the seaplane just fifty yards off the fishing vessel's port side. A hatch opened and a crewman helped Qin aboard. The hatch closed as the propellers' revolutions increased their speed. The seaplane moved slowly at first, and then as the engines reached their desired levels, it lifted off the surface of the water, gradually gaining elevation and distance, eventually banking left toward an unknown destination. Makarov continued to lean against the railing to rest and think for a few moments amid the ruckus of the soldiers talking and playing dice games on the deck.

"Sergei!" Toni called as she bolted from the aft hatch. Makarov turned back to the once beautiful woman whose external looks to him faded as he got to know her. He had been on enough assignments with her to understand her. She was an expert in computers, but she was devoid of principles, this American. She liked the money, but like a lifelong drug or alcohol addict, the only thing she truly loved was the immediate satisfaction from whatever thrill life offered, not caring about the consequences to herself or the people around her. Makarov had seen it all too often—the addict's only true love was the addiction itself.

She ran to him and took his arm.

"We have a problem," she said emphatically, pulling him to the interior as the soldiers made way for them. They raced through the passageway and down to the largest area on the ship devoted to the mission. The doors were already open to the space, cooled for the three dozen computer servers and an equal number of operators. Makarov closed the door behind him.

Toni brought him to the largest monitor.

"Look! We're down!"

"Manila?" he asked.

"No. We released that earlier, but you told us not to stop the attacks elsewhere for another six hours. Our links to the island are gone. It wasn't all at once. It happened within the space of about three minutes. Their link to the satellites just faded out," she said as she tried reestablishing the link herself.

"We need to find out what's happening at Site B. Is the drone up yet?" Makarov asked. Toni picked up a headset and dialed the drone control room one deck up.

"It's en route," she said. "ETA is now ten more minutes because the wind has picked up from the east, and its running into a headwind."

"The sun is setting, Toni. Does that drone have infrared?"

"Yeah, we had it on both drones. But since we lost the other one, we'll have to time the pattern for this drone a lot better. We'll only have coverage for an hour, then recall it to recharge each time we want to use it," she said, calling up a different application on the computer.

"How long will it take to recharge the batteries?" the Russian asked the former US Army and CIA case officer. She had skills, but she had no character. Both served his company well.

"Ninety minutes to two hours," she responded unapologetically.

Makarov calculated time and distance problems. The four ships were maintaining station at what they referred to on any communications as Site A, now forty miles west by northwest of Balabac Island. These $50,000 drones could fly at sixty miles per hour absent headwinds. Most commercial drones could remain aloft for thirty minutes. His drones— or, rather, now drone—was modified to fly for nearly two hours. Toni was right. Between launch and recovery, they'd only be able to remain in a pattern for an hour. This had been his mission. He should have planned on additional drones, but he didn't expect Highland Maritime to have the capability of taking down either of his. That meant he might lose this one as well. If that happened, he was completely blind from the air.

"Can we uplink directly to the satellite from here instead of relying on Site B?" he asked her.

"No. Site B tapped directly into the cable to the other islands. It was a direct connection. We might be able to relaunch some of the attacks, but it will take time. The malware seems to be effective, especially with the utility companies."

During the initial planning for this operation the previous year, Toni had explained that sometimes the simplest efforts were the most effective. In the case of most of the utility companies, the team of Chinese cyber specialists in this room had inserted code to indicate that no one in key areas had paid their bills and so the utility companies' automated system shut down all accounts on a key date which had occurred nearly two days ago. Several of the attacks exploited weaknesses in automated, bureaucratic systems. Others were more sophisticated, but none that were known to the US or its allies as those the Chinese government or its companies had used in the past. Until Makarov knew what happened at Site B, he'd hold off updating Hu.

"No. Most of the goals have been achieved. The next phase begins tomorrow morning anyway. Find out what you can about Site B and fill me in. Then let's get some rest. I want everyone ready.

"Sergei, are you sure?"

"I'm sure. We have only one thing left to do and then we're done."

CHAPTER 16

BALABAC ISLAND

One by one the attackers fell along with the sun over the western waters. Two tried to get up and shoot but both were knocked back by another hail of bullets from the familiar sound of Highland Maritime's FNC rifles until there was silence. Four figures wearing gray coveralls rose from the vegetation and walked onto the dirt road, their rifles pointing toward potential danger. Warren moved toward Stark as Bobby Fisk and two other Highlanders crept toward the downed attackers, prepared to defend Stark in case more were on their way.

"You okay, boss?" Warren asked.

Stark's prone body slumped closer to the ground out of relief until he felt a sharp pain in his ribs. He deliberately rolled over to his back.

"I . . . I think I'm hit, Jay," he said, trying to recall the last time he'd been shot and what that had felt like.

Warren hovered over him and unzipped the vest and the coveralls, exposing a dime-sized fresh blood stain, and pulled out a translucent plastic shard. He shook his head and tossed it aside.

"I need to check your bat vest before you go out next time. The compass must have split when you dove behind the rock. You're fine."

Stark felt like an idiot, but with so many pockets on this vest, he needed to rethink what he took with him next time. His hand latched onto Warren's thick forearm, letting it lift him off the ground like a human crane.

"Thanks. How did the others get here so fast?"

"Mr. Fisk watched the first DP-14 lift off to medevac Commander Castillo, then he ordered the other three DP-14s to the naval base. He figured that if it can be used to extract someone, it could be used to insert someone. He and two other guys under 190 pounds—they ditched their body armor—crawled into them as delivery vehicles and met me at the trucks."

Stark's initial experiences with Fisk on the USS *Bennington* weren't wrong. That young officer was innovative, bold, and capable. After the Yemen episode, Stark had pulled strings at the highest level, getting Jaime back into the Navy and with her own command. Another string had Fisk assigned to her ship, the USS *Charles Stewart*, where they all worked together in Sri Lanka. After that, the wheels fell off the cart. Rossberg, who had been the inept commander of *Bennington* and then involved in transporting doomed ships to Sri Lanka, was apparently promoted to rear admiral and assigned to the Bureau of Naval Personnel, where he had taken vengeance on them, derailed their service, and drummed them out. Jaime had worked for Highland Maritime before, and since she was from Port St. George, the decision was easy. Fisk had to be recruited since he had offers from a shipping company. Highland Maritime won and was better because of the continually evolving officer who was the perfect team member as Jaime's executive officer on *Minerva*. And if Stark ever had the opportunity, he'd make the same offer to Christina Santos.

"Bobby!" Stark yelled. "Search them and then drive their trucks back to the base." Fisk waved his arm to acknowledge the order.

"C'mon, Jay. Let's get to our trucks and Santos."

"What do you mean? She was with you," Warren said, confused.

"I told her to run ahead since I couldn't keep up. You seriously didn't see her?"

"Sorry, no."

Stark knew when Warren was kidding. This wasn't a time for that and he wasn't kidding.

Now it was Stark's turn to be confused. There was only the road and the beach to the right. It was a straight, easy shot back to the trucks. If the enemy in the vegetation had taken her, why didn't they take him as he passed as well or simply shot him? He hadn't heard a shot, so it was possible they used a knife and dragged her into the heavier brush.

"Dammit, Jay, we need to go find her now." Stark picked up the clip he had trouble with earlier, slapped it into the magazine well, and began to march off toward where he thought she might have been taken. Warren grabbed him by the shoulder and stopped him.

"The sun's down. It'll be too dark."

"We have flashlights. Let's go," Stark said, emphatically pulling away from the larger man.

"Connor, we go in there without knowing where she is and not knowing where more of the bad guys are, and we'll be caught too," Warren reasoned. Fisk and the others had finished sweeping the bodies and were heading toward the trucks as one of the men hopped into the cargo bay.

"We can't leave her out there," Stark said, nearly resigned to the facts Warren had just pointed out.

"We didn't bring our night-vision goggles. We can't go blind at night with our numbers, and we're low on ammo again. We'll send a drone with infrared." Warren said in his most reassuring tone.

Fisk and the others had just risked a drone ride to come to their aid. How many times in his career had someone helped him?

"Jay, remember in Sri Lanka when the Sea Tigers had me tied up in that building?" Warren nodded at the thought of the torture.

"You guys found me and came back for me."

"Boss, we had the ships back then. Hell, we had Navy helicopters. We don't have what we need." Fisk and the trucks closed in and stopped at the arguing duo.

"We need to get the hell out of here and back to the base," Fisk shouted out the window. Stark explained the situation.

"Captain, I'm with Dr. Warren on this one. That search area is just too wide."

"Turn off the engines. We're going to find her," he said, rejecting their advice. They did as he directed and got out of the vehicles. Warren mouthed the word "fuck," then he said it aloud as he looked back in the direction of the computer facility but above the tree line.

"That's not a bird, boss," he said, pointing up. The others followed the path of his arm.

They could barely make out a drone in the distance speeding from the ocean toward the disaster the building had become, thanks to Stark's team. It was only a matter of time before they were seen. If they could be seen, they could be tracked. If they could be tracked, more people could be vectored on their position. Warren and Fisk were right. Stark reluctantly accepted that they couldn't immediately help Lieutenant Christina Santos.

"Let's get the hell out of here," he said.

WESTERN PACIFIC

The bridge of USS *George HW Bush* was dark except for the lights emanating from the oscillating scopes for the operations specialist and digital readouts for course and speed. Normally a lieutenant surface warfare officer would serve as officer of the deck (OOD) for major combatant and normal operations, but this was no ordinary exercise. *George HW Bush* was leading and coordinating one of the largest multinational fleets during peacetime. This large-scale exercise (LSE), now steaming a hundred nautical miles southwest of Palau, was nothing new to the US or its partners. LSEs took place almost annually so that the US and various partnered navies could simply practice integrated navigation and simple maneuvers and test communications, the latter of which were especially problematic since each navy had its own standards and not every ship could communicate in the same way with every other ship.

Commander Lynn Henry, the ship's navigator, scanned the seas with her night vision binoculars, comparing the location and distance of each ship around her with the radar in front of her. *Fifty ships*, she thought, *can be a nightmare given the differences in training standards, experience, language barriers, and the unexpected—the factors that every SWO worries about.* Henry had been selected as the next executive officer of USS *Charles Stewart*, a Flight III *Arleigh Burke*-class destroyer, arguably one of the most successful shipbuilding programs in the US Navy's history.

She was grateful she had artfully avoided the inherently-flawed Littoral Combat Ship program, despite being pointed in that direction by several of her previous senior officers. There was a reason there were no LCSs among the US Navy's complement during this LSE—they were already being decommissioned because they lacked the duration needed for Western Pacific exercises. Henry would have added they also simply sucked, but since the flag officers and their Public Affairs Officers were incapable of handling or telling the truth about the program, she kept her opinion to herself. That's probably why she had made commander and was on track for her own eventual command.

A shift on one of the tracks caught her eye. One of the LSE ships seven nautical miles off her port bow was picking up speed. The command directions for the evening had all fifty ships maintaining course of two-five-five degrees and speed of seventeen knots until 0700 when the admiral—or rather one of his senior captains—would provide more information for the day. The ship was now at twenty-two knots and on course of three-zero-zero. She checked the hard copy of the ships' positions. That was a Philippine Navy ship. She grabbed the mike and set the ship-to-ship radio for channel one-four.

"Philippine Navy ship *Jose Rizal*, you are off course. Please respond." She unclicked and told her junior officer of the deck to call the admiral and the captain up to the bridge immediately. She could handle the ship's navigation and working with other ships, but given the Navy's recent history of OODs not informing their captains when something was amiss in the middle of the night and colliding with other ships, she erred on the side of caution.

There was no response from the PN ship. Another ship was now off course and speed, this one just behind the *Rizal*. It was *Antonio Luna*, *Rizal*'s sister ship. Soon, four more ships around the fleet followed suit. All were PN ships, and all had taken a general course and speed in accordance with the *Rizal*. She checked radar. The fleet had been spaced apart enough at night that she did a quick calculation and told the quartermaster and his UI sailor—under instruction—to check the maneuvering boards, or mobords. The PN ships weren't in immediate danger of colliding with other ships just yet.

"*Jose Rizal*, please respond," Commander Henry said calmly and firmly. "You are off course." Still nothing.

"Captain on the bridge!" said one of the watchstanders as Captain Will Porter, clad only in gym shorts and a blue T-shirt, burst through the aft hatch.

"SITREP, OOD," he said.

"Sir, all four Philippine Navy ships shifted course three minutes ago to three-zero-zero and increased their speed to . . ." She checked the radar. "Now they're at two-four knots. Quartermaster?"

"Moboards complete, ma'am. None of the four ships are on track for colliding with any other ship in the formation so long as the remaining ships remain on PIM," the quartermaster said loud enough for everyone on the bridge to hear.

"Sir, *Rizal* has not responded on channel one-four," Commander Henry said, again looking through her night vision binoculars.

"Great. Did you inform the admiral?" the captain asked.

"As soon as we called you, sir," Henry responded.

Porter got on the radio. "Any Philippine Navy ship, this is *George HW Bush* actual. You are off track of our agreed-to plan. Please respond."

"Admiral on the bridge," the watchstanders said loudly but in a different manner than when the captain arrived. Captain Porter and Commander Henry knew the team well enough to detect a hint of fear and exasperation.

The five-and-a-half-foot admiral casually entered the bridge, stopped, surveyed his domain, and clasped his hands behind his back. He had a graying mustache, trimmed neatly so it drew attention to the center of his face rather than his shallow cheeks. Instead of the standard blue coveralls, he arrived wearing his service dress blue uniform. He wore the three gold stripes of a vice admiral on his sleeve, a rank he had been promoted to just months before.

"Why have you called me up here in the middle of the night?" his high, nasal, mousy voice bellowed as best it could. Henry gave him the abbreviated situation report.

"What?" he asked incredulously. "That's not right. That should have maintained formation with us. What did you do wrong, Commander?"

Henry ignored the accusation. She had served under him once before and hated every minute of it, along with the rest of the wardroom and crew. He had been a lot thinner then. She had hoped never to see him again, and then somehow, someone in the Pentagon replaced the original exercise commander.

"Give me that mike," he ordered the captain. The admiral swayed as he spoke, thinking he was still on some age of sail ship of the line.

"This is Admiral Rossberg aboard US Navy aircraft carrier USS *George Herbert Walker Bush* to the Philippine Navy ships. What are you doing? Why are you leaving?"

"This is *Jose Rizal*. Our ships have been ordered to terminate our participation in this exercise and return immediately to Manila Bay. Our new president has also asked me to convey to you that the large-scale exercise is no longer welcomed in Philippine territorial waters and may not transit through any of our straits. *Jose Rizal*, out."

"Your orders, sir?" the captain asked.

"They don't tell us what to do. Only the Pentagon does. We continue with our remaining ships on course." With that, the admiral turned and left for his stateroom. Commander Henry was grateful that she would not see or hear Vice Admiral Daniel Rossberg for the remainder of her shift.

BALABAC ISLAND

Lieutenant Christina Santos had never been in better shape in her life. She had less than twelve percent body fat, she could outrun any other female officer and many male officers taller than her during their semi-annual tests, and she could carry half her own bodyweight if need be. If her training there and elsewhere weren't enough, she had been tested more in the past two days than in her career and elsewhere.

After she passed the bend, Stark behind her, she sped another fifty yards. When she heard the distant sound of speeding vehicles, she darted left into the jungle and kept going another twenty yards, then dove to the ground so she couldn't be seen but could keep an eye on the dirt road.

She heard the heavy pounding of booted feet and heavy breathing as the figure of Captain Connor Stark raced passed her position. A minute after that, two pickup trucks slowed and stopped when one soldier riding outside the cab was blown back by a gunshot. The soldiers got out of their vehicles as a few shots and then more were fired. She backed out of her position, and when she was well away from the trucks, she turned and ran for the next twenty minutes.

Santos only slowed because sunset had given way to dusk and then to darkness beneath the canopy of the jungle. She had no compass, no water, no light, and no food. She had a couple of extra ammo clips with her but little else. She knew the island had crocodiles, but those would be close to the shore and she was heading increasingly inland. There were treacherous or poisonous animals to speak of. The most dangerous she knew of all held weapons.

The wildlife calls grew louder the darker it became. She was now directionless but kept inching her way through the vegetation where minutes seemed like hours until there were fewer leaves, bushes, and trees. Though the sky was clear, it was a moonless night, and there was no ambient light anywhere. The only reason she knew she had reached a large clearing was when she raised her head to the sky and took a moment in this chaos to appreciate the unencumbered view of thousands of stars.

She laid down her rifle, pointing it away from her, then squinted as she turned 360 degrees, trying to distinguish any features around her. At least the gun pointed her in a direction. She retrieved it and kept walking, firmly planting each boot on the earth to ensure she didn't step in a hole or rut to avoid twisting an ankle. She made it to the end of the clearing, where the overgrowth darkened the way ahead.

By slowing her tempo, she had more than caught her breath, and her heartbeat was slower than it had been during her initial run and the adrenaline rush. As she took her next step, a light appeared to her left just a dozen yards away, then another to her right as two more flashlights lit her up. She couldn't see who held them, but the lights from each side allowed her to make out the distinctive shape and size of rifle barrels as she gradually lowered her own.

CHAPTER 17

Golzari saw Antonov's eyes shift from fear to satisfaction as the stateroom's door cracked open as someone asked for the captain again. Golzari had positioned himself behind it. When it was halfway open so that the person could see Antonov sitting in the chair, Golzari threw his weight against the door, throwing the man against the wall, and then whipped the door fully open, providing him with an unobstructed view. It was a steward, a few inches shorter and slighter than Golzari, who was stunned by the swiftness of the action.

Golzari pulled him in and threw him to the ground, glancing toward the passageway to check for others, then closed the door. His attention was diverted just long enough that Antonov pushed himself off the chair and propelled his massive body across the room toward his captor. Fortunately, his weight and age slowed him long enough that the former Diplomatic Security Service agent, with cat-like reflexes, swung his pistol toward the captain and instinctively put three bullets in his chest. The captain died immediately, but his weight was so overwhelming that it kept on until it pressed Golzari against the wall and fell on him. Golzari struggled to extract himself from the body as he noticed the steward rise and move toward the door.

Golzari's left hand was wedged beneath the wall and Antonov's body, momentarily losing his grip on the gun. Instead of chancing a shot go wild, he dropped the gun and grabbed the steward's ankle, trying to pull him down as well. The steward's arms desperately reached out for the door but fell a few inches short. The steward struggled to get his ankle free from Golzari's grip but only managed to lose his balance and fall backward, knocking over a standing lamp. Golzari retrieved his gun and shifted himself from beneath Antonov's body.

The steward rose again, but instead of moving toward the door, he moved further into the stateroom and cowered on the bed. He put out his hands and said something Golzari didn't understand, but it was the universal language begging him not to shoot him. The man was a steward, unlikely to have been a part of the trafficking network, and only by accident on a ship that held these people.

Golzari regained his composure and stance.

"Get on your stomach," he told the steward as he made circles with his free forefinger, indicating that he should turn over. The steward did so, acknowledging verbally in broken English. Golzari perused the room for anything he could use to bind the steward's hands. Finding nothing apparent, he opened the closet and took a belt. He slipped his gun into his holster, noticing some dampness on his chest for the first time. It was Antonov's blood when he'd fallen on him. He tied up the steward's hands as best he could but knew it wouldn't last. Hopefully, the steward was too inexperienced or scared to try. Golzari put a facecloth in his mouth to prevent him from shouting.

He checked and still had the documents in his pocket. Now it was a matter of getting off the ship before anything else happened. His shirt was dark enough that someone might not notice the blood. Golzari opened the door as he heard the steward cry through the facecloth. Golzari entered the passageway, closed the door behind him, and retraced the steps he'd taken from the bridge and then back to the exterior. He passed only one crewman in the passageway a deck below, but the man who had been on the bridge paid little attention to him as they exchanged simple nods.

Golzari made it outside and casually walked down the starboard ladder to the quarterdeck, where two more crew, including Koffi, were talking. He gave a simple wave to them and thanked them for their help and walked down the gangway, its metal again clanging, calling attention to two other men talking next to a lorry at its base. Golzari was ten feet away from the dock when the men looked up at him. The second mate said something to the driver. He couldn't make out all words, but he heard "Abdou." The other man closer to the lorry shook his head, then called to a third man in the truck's passenger seat. Golzari realized that his cover was blown. The truck driver knew the ship's captain and the real Abdou Mansouri since he was transporting the people in those containers. The second mate called up to Koffi and the other crewman, who made their way toward Golzari.

Scanning up and down the dock revealed it was just Damien and five men. He took out his gun, planted his feet on the gangplank, and took the first shot into the second mate's head. The lorry driver dove back in the cab as the passenger came around with his own pistol. He shot twice at Golzari but both missed. Golzari returned one shot that punched his opponent dead center in the chest, dropping him.

Golzari hopped onto the dock and kept his gun raised as he followed the driver, who reached for something on the far side of the cab. He took the first shot. The driver cried out in pain and reached back to where the bullet had entered. Pulling the driver out of the cab and throwing him on the ground, he surveyed the landscape again. Two more trucks slowly emerged from behind the warehouse and turned toward the ship. Koffi and the other crewman, unarmed, ran back to the ship.

The former Diplomatic Security agent quickly jumped into the cab when he saw a clipboard with invoices and handwritten notes. He ripped them from the clipboard, then bolted back toward where he had left his motorcycle. He took the burner phone and called Emile, telling him to get as many police to this terminal, that people were in the cargo bays. Golzari knew they wouldn't get there in time if the other two trucks were determined to get rid of the "evidence," so he reloaded his weapon and ran back toward the dock. The trucks stopped in front of the gangway.

From thirty yards away, he began unloading his weapon toward the cabs. He wasn't firing to hit anyone, he was firing for effect, and the desired effect he wanted was for the trucks to assume he was law enforcement and try to escape. Both lorries began moving again and sped off. He went back to his motorcycle, keeping an eye on the ship where the crew scurried about. He waited until ten minutes later when he heard sirens approaching the dock. Satisfied that he had disrupted this ship's activities, he turned on the ignition and made his way out of the port.

BALABAC NAVAL BASE

By the time Stark and the others returned to the naval base, twilight had given way to dusk and the darkness of a distant island. The security teams at the base maintained minimal lights so as not to present targets to anyone in the jungle. An electrified wire had been mounted two feet off the ground fifty yards from the southern and eastern fence lines. Tripod-mounted infrared cameras had been set up on the hill Stark and Santos had been on when they witnessed the base in the aftermath of the attack. One drone with an IR sensor was flying a pattern beyond the base.

The wind had picked up and with it the waves. With *Minerva* and *Syren* stationed where they were, the whalers couldn't make it out of the base without the danger of swamping. However, the Philippine sailors had completed the repairs on the Australian *Armidale*-class vessel *Townsville* and had finished refueling it. Years of running small boats off the Maine coast had taught Stark never to chance taking on the sea because the sea would always be more powerful than you. Stark left Sivan Abraham in charge of the joint security teams to defend the base. They had enough sensors to warn them if the base was attacked and to be reinforced by the ships' crews. Stark, Warren, Fisk, and a few others got underway with *Townsville*, though he wasn't sure of the legality of a private security company taking command of an Australian vessel, even if it had been on loan to a government that had questionable authority at this point. Stark operated the vessel without running lights or radar, using only NVGs to ease it out of the basin and into open waters.

Using only the ship's compass, he steered for the position of the security ships and maintained a steady speed of six knots, calculating how soon it would take him to rendezvous. He asked Fisk to take one of the flashlights and communicate to *Syren* that *Townsville* would approach and tie up to them starboard-side to. The light flashed in Morse code to acknowledge the maneuver. Olivia, the ship's executive officer, had thought to take five glowsticks and mount them on *Syren*'s starboard side. It was just enough on this clear night to give Stark some perspective as he maneuvered his vessel alongside. Olivia's own experience as the commander of a ship in the Royal Navy had proven as invaluable as Jaime's ship handling days on US Navy ships, *Minerva*, and, back before the Yemen incident, one of Highland Maritime's security ships, *Kirkwall*.

Thoughts of *Kirkwall* continued to plague Stark, especially on nights like this, so similar to when Jaime, Stark, and their colleagues were attacked and sunk by pirates in the Gulf of Aden. *Kirkwall* was one of Highland Maritime's first security vessels assigned to protect supply boats from pirates in the Gulf of Aden. Had it not been for the courageous actions of a few officers aboard USS *Bennington* defying Captain Daniel Rossberg, the survivors of the attack would have died. Stark remembered the name of every Highland Maritime Defense employee lost that night. He had made the calls to their families. He never forgot what their voices sounded like or what they told him.

Fisk and Warren handled the bumpers and lines with *Syren*'s crew. When they were tied up, Stark shut down the engines, relying on *Syren* to maintain station for both vessels. They cross-decked with the crew welcoming their captain back. It was a fifty-fifty chance which ship Castillo had been flown to for treatment; as chance had it, he had been delivered to *Syren* since it was closer. Stark told Warren and Fisk to get a shower and hit their racks for some rest while they could as he made his way to medical.

The corpsman sat next to the resting Castillo, who was beneath a clean white sheet that covered most of his body except for the wounded leg. The wound had been cleaned and Stark assumed the bullet was removed since he saw ten stitches on Castillo's thigh. Translucent gauze and jelly protected it from infection. Stark had seen this before with his own people.

"Can I wake him?" he mouthed silently to the corpsman, who nodded and left the bay.

"Commander?" Stark said softly as sat on the stool. Castillo opened his eyes.

"Renaldo. It's Renaldo Castillo," he responded.

"Thank you. It's Connor. I have some bad news, Renaldo."

Stark recounted the events after Castillo had been medevac'd and how sorry he was that Santos had gone missing.

"Thank you, Connor. I've worked with her for nearly two years. She is most impressive. Don't underestimate her. Maybe she hasn't been captured. Maybe she's in hiding until the morning," he said hopefully.

"I hope so, Daniel. We have a drone up now over the base. I'll see if we can get another one near where she was lost. We won't give up on her."

"I know. She is my responsibility. She is one of my people," he said, closing his eyes again. Connor knew the look of losing someone in your care, and he empathized with him.

"Get some rest. We need to get ready for whatever is out there. I'd like to pull everyone back to the ships. We can run *Townsville* as a shuttle."

"No," Castillo said emphatically. "I told you before—it's a Philippine Navy base. I will not allow it to be surrendered. You and your people are under no obligation to defend it, Connor, but I am and so are my sailors."

"No. We're in this together, Renaldo. We'll stand with you."

Castillo gave Stark his hand and clasped it firmly. "Together. We'll keep it working together," he said, drifting off to sleep.

CAMP DAVID

Secret Service agents followed the president and National Security Advisor Sumner as they strolled after breakfast in the winding paths emanating from the Aspen Lodge. Agents ahead of them kept the paths clear of any other military personnel or the small force of civilians who maintained some of the buildings. President Dunner was religious about his morning regimen. After a light breakfast and a morning brief, he exercised for thirty minutes. His preferred exercise was walking since, as CJ knew, he could contemplate and, if he was with someone, have a discussion instead of a bullet-laden Powerpoint presentation on whatever the topic of the day was. CJ suspected the gently-paced sound of his cane tapping the path had the same effect as the metronome when she played the piano.

He had some domestic issues he needed to discuss with the treasury and labor secretaries later this morning, but he wanted more time for the Philippines—again. Dunner and Sumner ate toast and poached eggs while the chief of naval operations briefed them via the VTC on the latest developments.

Four Philippine Navy warships had left the large-sale exercise as President Reyes and the new government recalled them. Reyes had earlier announced that no warships would be permitted to transit Philippine waters. This posed a problem since the fifty ships—now forty-six with the departure of the Philippine ships—were scheduled to transit the Balabac Strait separating the Philippines from Malaysia. Nearly two dozen countries in the world were recognized as archipelagic states—a nation that consisted largely of islands. Indonesia and the Philippines were the best and largest examples.

Any nation's warships, through international law, were permitted a right of transit through what was formally known as an Archipelagic Sea Lane Passage, which meant that, at some point, warships could be in territorial waters within twelve nautical miles of a land mass. But there were limitations. Warships had to proceed without delay, not use or threaten force or engage or conduct other operations. It was a simple transit only. In reality, if the conditions were violated, few nations had the ability to stop whatever warship wanted to engage in other activities.

If anything positive was occurring, the cyberattack began to abate. Malware was still creating problems, but the severity of the continuous attacks had been cut as if someone had turned off a switch.

Dunner stopped momentarily buttoning his cardigan sweater, the last his wife had given him for Christmas before she passed. Some of his media opponents had joked about the consistency with which he wore it. It generated social media memes. Accounts devoted to pictures of the sweater proliferated. Late-night hosts started a *Where's Waldo?* parody with the president's sweater. Dunner's polite disregard and downplaying of the sweater was of the many reasons CJ respected his character. The president never told the media why he wore it, and he never shared the reason with his press secretary lest they go through back doors to counter the joke. Sumner knew because she had been present at the gift exchange and how much younger he looked or was back then. CJ knew that when he wore that sweater, he was comforted by his wife's memory, if only for a short while.

"CJ, I said we were continuing with the exercise, but that was before Reyes basically told us to go to heck. What do you think?" He resumed his walk in the woods.

"Mr. President, these exercises are months, sometimes years, in the planning. All the participating navies are those we would have to—or rather hope to—coordinate with should there ever be a war with China. Exercises like these are necessary not only to build goodwill and send a message to mainland China, but every navy has different platforms, systems, and capabilities."

She briefly recalled how little she knew about navies until she and an equally young Lieutenant Commander Connor Stark shared an office when she worked for Senator Padraic O'Rourke and Stark was their military fellow. He had educated her then and again in Yemen.

"That means," she continued, as she put her hands in her pockets as the mid-autumn chill was in the air, "this is an opportunity to deconflict differences in those capabilities, learn how to conduct basic maneuvers, and identify possible opportunities to purchase systems or software that are more compatible with each other. I think your initial direction was correct. We press on."

They walked a few more minutes as the path wound around toward the landing pad for Marine One and the Marine Barracks. Dunner breathed deeper to enjoy the cool, crisp air after another miserably humid summer in DC.

"You know that would have been easier with President Quinta in charge, but now with Reyes and his stated position, we risk alienating him. Is this exercise worth that? Couldn't we just change the direction of this armada? If I recall from the brief a few days ago, they were going to steam through the Sulawesi Sea closer to Indonesia, head up to the Sulu Sea in Philippine waters, then transit that strait between Malaysia and the Philippines, continue through the South China Sea, and then conclude with many of them having a port call in Singapore."

CJ herself didn't remember all those details and she'd been at the same brief.

"What if," he proposed, "we modified their path? After the Sulawesi Sea, they could head . . ." Dunner stopped for a moment as the lifelong diplomat recalled his geography. "Southwest to the Java Sea, then north-west to Singapore? I know what you're going to say, CJ. It avoids the intended show of force against China and their militarized islands in the South China Sea."

She smiled broadly, showing her perfect white teeth. "Yes, Mr. President. If we exercise that option, we are signaling to the Chinese that the Philippines has the power to change conditions that are favorable to China."

"Don't they?" he asked rhetorically.

"Yes, they do. How will this look to our partners in this exercise? Will they view it as our respecting a change in government and a diplo-matic request, or will they see it as a chink in our collective armor? Our embassy and consulates have reported that there have been some riots and looting but nothing to suggest widespread support or opposition to Reyes. People are just struggling to survive there."

"The CNO mentioned the ships were thirty hours from Philippine waters," the president responded, "and then another six hours until they approached the strait between them and Malaysia. We have some time on this one. I'd like to chat today for a few minutes with the heads of gov-ernment for each of the participating nations. Just a friendly call to thank them," he said with a wink as he grabbed her arm. "C'mon, Madam Ambassador, I'll race you back to the Lodge."

CHAPTER 18

SECURITY VESSEL *SYREN*

Although the wind and waves had picked up, *Syren*'s size and beam minimized the effects of the motions that might cause seasickness in some of the less experienced crew. Even Stark was prone to it under the right—or wrong—conditions. He quickly showered, changed into a fresh T-shirt and shorts, and lay in his rack without turning the light off.

After checking in on Castillo, Stark toured the ship to check on all stations to see if there was anything new he should be aware of. Olivia had things under control, as she always did as the XO and often acting CO. He left standing orders in the command center to wake him with any change, but that was difficult to do since they were still mostly operating in the blind. The drones were now their only saving grace, and they'd be blind without them. The technicians refitted the tethered unmanned aerial system—Crow's Nest—aboard *Syren* with additional cameras and sensors. The larger unit could remain aloft in the light sustained winds they had been experiencing, and the tethered units didn't have to return to recharge. They constantly received power from the ground station or, in this case, the ship.

The drone operator would collect information throughout the night and report to Stark and the senior team half an hour before sunrise. Stark decided to release the ships from their EMCON. The bad guys knew they were there. It didn't mean they'd use active radar just yet, but it was time to start receiving more information from the outside. It would have been a greater risk to remain in the dark.

Santos was out there somewhere. Stark hadn't been fast enough to keep up with her, and he made the decision not to slow her down, leaving her alone for those minutes between him and the trucks. Those minutes had been crucial. She was dead or a prisoner or lost. Or maybe, as Castillo suggested, she was just hiding out until she could make her way back to the base or someone found her. Without her skills, Stark wouldn't have known the attackers weren't local Molbogs. He wouldn't have had any idea that the building near the cable had been conducting cyberattacks nationwide. And then, like a seasoned professional, she remained calm as shots were fired around her. The Philippine Navy needed people like her. Hell, the US Navy or Highland Maritime Defense needed people like her.

He turned to his side, his eyes wide open although he was exhausted. His desk was on the other side of his stateroom. One of the photos on it was a headshot of Maggie and had replaced an earlier one he had of her. This one was black and white, which was too bad since it failed to capture the color of her hair and eyes. It had been taken by a vacationing photographer in Port St. George. She never sat for photos. The photographer caught her as she was taking a break from the pub and on the deck overlooking the harbor. She was brushing back her long red hair as the sun was setting. It caught every feature of her face—her slightly turned-up nose, her wide mouth, the inch-long scar from a childhood accident. It was lunchtime on the East Coast, and she'd be busy serving locals and people visiting "from away," as the locals called anyone who hadn't been in Maine or Port St. George for at least four generations. Like Maggie. And she was from really far away for the locals.

Maggie never asked about his missions. She had a bartender's way of letting people offer up information. That's how it had been with her and one of the reasons he confided in her. But she never hid her feelings about his missions. She had lost family members in all the twentieth-century wars the United Kingdom had fought, from World War I to the Falklands. When she and her brother moved to Port St. George from Scotland, she hadn't anticipated being involved with someone who was as much at risk as any of those family members. Maybe that's why she never agreed to get married or even live with him in the same house. Until he was no longer involved on the operational side of Highland Maritime Defense, they'd maintain a comfortable status quo in their relationship. It was the only way she could protect herself from losing someone closer than they had become.

She was probably right. He had never recovered from all the losses going back to the terrorist attack in Naples when he was a junior officer and his fiancée was killed. It happened again when he was a mid-grade officer and lost two mentors to Canadian terrorists in Quebec. Later there was the Highland crew in Yemen and Gunny Willis in Sri Lanka. Would Christina Santos join the ghosts who haunted him every day?

For now, all he could do was push on and get out of this as he had before. All he had to do was return to Port St. George, walk into the pub, and see Maggie. *One step at a time, one crisis at a time, and one day at a time,* he thought as his mind focused less on the past two days and wandered among memories, possible futures, and disjointed images and illusions as his body finally gave in to the reality of biology and drifted to sleep.

FISHING VESSEL *SISON*

Makarov could tell the paramilitary troops topside and wandering around the four ships were getting restless until the sea state changed. They were no longer singing as they were too occupied puking their guts out from seasickness. Most of them just wanted to lie down somewhere—anywhere—and curl up in a fetal position. It was no laughing matter. He'd need these troops soon and it was not uncommon. He had watched an old documentary about the Allies' Normandy invasion and the seasickness as the soldiers crossed the English Channel. He was in command of four ships—two large fishing vessels and two now-former Philippine Navy cutters—and was coordinating with the New People's Army ashore, all of whom he had been responsible for transporting for the past year.

It was no easy logistics task. The first step had been to identify a suitable island from which they could operate. The New People's Army was more than fifty years old, but its members were scattered throughout the

Philippines, making their goals more difficult. They had the distinction of being the world's oldest, continuous communist guerilla group. It was Hu Tao who developed the plan to unite all of them to increase their effectiveness. The Chinese government wanted the US to be so embarrassed by the event that China could exert more control and influence in the region than before. It was Sergei Makarov whom Hu had assigned to carry out each phase.

Makarov's sources in the intelligence community mentioned that the US would conduct a large naval exercise with more participating partners and more ships than in years past. It was scheduled to begin in Hawaii and end in Singapore, with several transits through straits, including Balabac Strait. Makarov spent a week on the island with Toni, where they posed as a journalist and photographer for a travel magazine, although there were no tourist hotels or facilities. They hired a local Molbog who could speak some English. They casually shared the new government's interest in the small forgotten island with a proposed new base on the western side for patrol vessels. There were only nine thousand Molbogs on the island.

Makarov and Toni set up a shell company with help from colleagues in Hu's organization so they could construct an unobtrusive building near some coconut groves. They kept the building empty for months, except for the computers, servers, and batteries. Then came the transportation network. Fishing vessels would arrive at night from other Philippine islands both large and small. A few fellow Filipinos took up residence. Then a few Molbog families would leave "voluntarily," and soon people were disappearing by the scores. The New People's Army infiltrated Población I within days, using the same tactics every communist insurgency used—taking over radio stations, the police station (all of three people and two bicycles), and the local government building that employed four people. They controlled all communication to the mainland. To the rest of the Philippine government, there was nothing wrong with the people on Balabac Island. Even when the naval base started construction and the government shipped in materials to the town's port, only NPA guerillas posing as Molbogs had contact with them.

They had to do something with the Molbogs. When the fishing vessels took them to sea, the NPA soldiers killed the adults, collected the bodies in fishing nets, and sank them with lead weights. The children were transferred to a passing cargo ship that rendezvoused with them and took them to Europe to work. Makarov wondered more than once if he would have changed his mind about the trafficking if he had children of his own, then he would just shake his head and dismiss it lest he had second thoughts. But he wasn't as bad as the man he knew only as Jean-Pascal, a French ex-pat with a secluded compound in the Azores. He had some association with Hu Tao in the past, so Makarov and Toni paid him a visit—the only visit—to make this experienced trafficker an offer for more people than he had handled before. What was better, Hu's company would pay him to do so. Jean-Pascal would make money just for using his transportation network and then more profit actually selling them throughout Europe.

By the time the US-led armada got underway from Hawaii, Makarov had cleansed Balabac Island of all native Molbogs and replaced them with nearly six thousand NPA members led by Colonel Jose dela Cruz. He wasn't particularly charismatic, but he served as a useful tool given everything Makarov and Hu were doing for them.

The real icing on the cake was when Hu and Makarov learned that the private security company Highland Maritime Defense would conduct some training with an element of the Philippine Navy in the weeks leading up to the multinational exercise. President Quinta herself had added the component for reasons unknown to them. It was Makarov, however, who came up with the idea to make this work to their advantage and help Hu get revenge on the firm that had thwarted him twice before. Makarov worked with a New People's Army soldier planted in the Philippine military who convinced their leadership to hold the exercise on Balabac Island because of the new naval base.

Everything had fallen into place. The NPA had executed the Philippine Navy personnel at the base, and when they left just enough of their sacrificial members to be killed by Highland Maritime, Makarov and Toni edited video of the action to make it look like mercenaries had taken the base. Now all he had to do was take out Stark's force. To do so, he first needed to speak with Jose dela Cruz immediately. The destruction of the building that facilitated the cyberattacks meant that the Philippine government and economy were reconstituting themselves sooner than the schedule demanded.

"Come on, Toni," he said to the blond-haired American sipping a cup of coffee nearby. "It's time for dela Cruz to put on his show."

OFF BALABAC NAVAL BASE

"You look like shit, boss," Warren said, handing a steaming cup of coffee to Stark, who, despite falling asleep, had been restless for the few hours he was in his rack. Stark was dressed in a clean set of gray coveralls but wore the same boots as yesterday. He left the all-purpose vest in his stateroom as he recalled Warren's suggestion. Still, he felt a bit naked not having immediate access to all the tools he liked to have on him and that the vest afforded. They were topside, waiting for Jaime Johnson and Fisk to arrive on one of *Minerva*'s RHIBs now that the sea had calmed again in the blue hour as they awaited sunrise over Balabac Island.

Johnson and Fisk's small boat pulled into *Syren*'s aft bay as Stark and Warren headed down to the command center. Olivia Harrison was waiting with the primary drone pilot and the communications officer who doubled as the intelligence officer briefing them. The auburn-haired ex-Royal Navy officer mostly kept to herself, preferring ship operations rather than any activity ashore wherever Highland Maritime Defense was working. It was a convenient relationship, but Stark was already thinking of handing over command of *Syren* to Harrison after this mission. He'd miss ship command; nevertheless, he was now too involved in all other aspects of his company to properly devote to the ship and its personnel.

He heard Fisk and Johnson coming up the passageway aft when the corpsman poked his head in.

"Sir, I have a patient who would like to be part of this brief."

Stark smiled and welcomed Commander Castillo as he hopped in on two crutches toward a chair Warren pulled out for him. He plopped onto the seat, simultaneously exhaling loudly.

"I hope I didn't oversleep!" he said cheerfully.

"Clearly we need a new corpsman who respects the rest of their patients," Stark retorted. "Great work, doc."

"Anytime, skipper. It keeps me employed," he joked as he left to make way for *Minerva's* leadership team.

"Looks like everyone made it through the night," Jaime said to her older cousin. They all took their seats facing the comms officer and the screen behind him. Oliver Riddle was normally pale, but his white face was even more so and sullen. Perhaps it was just that he had worked the night shift.

"Good morning, Captain Stark. As you directed last night, we opened up comms less than an hour ago. The cyberattack you interrupted yesterday had been ongoing for more than a day. As near as I can tell, around the same time that happened, the president of the Philippines, President Quinta, died when her plane went down en route to Davao City, which would have made it roughly when you all went ashore on the eastern side of the island.

"Her vice president, Felipe Reyes, was immediately sworn in and vowed to restore security and get whoever carried out the cyberattacks. Reyes claims that it was the cyberattack that caused the crash. There's already speculation that it was an assassination, not just a consequence of the computer attacks."

"President Quinta supported our involvement training with the PN component," Stark commented. "I don't think it matters what Reyes thinks right now. Sounds like he had too much on his plate to worry about what we're doing."

"Um, not really, Captain. It's bad," Riddle said as he clicked an arrow on the screen as a BBC report appeared. A chyron with black letters in a white ribbon on the lower portion read, "Mercenaries Attack Philippine Naval Base." The anchor spoke over a video showing an overhead perspective of gunfire and battle as troops in gray coveralls and others with military uniforms advanced and shot several others in uniform. The anchor claimed that several dozen Philippine sailors were killed defending their base from an attack by a mercenary company that had taken it for unknown reasons.

The leadership from both ships were stunned. Not only did they prefer to work out of the media's attention, but the media were completely wrong about what had happened. Stark's teams were saving the base, not killing Filipino sailors. Warren pushed his chair back, raising his hands to his head, saying, "Ho-leee fuck . . ."

"Continue the brief, Oliver," Stark said, trying to maintain his composure.

"The New People's Army, a communist insurgent group that's operated in the Philippines for decades, announced a half hour ago that because of the mercenary attack and the nationwide inability to defend itself against the cyberattack, they no longer have confidence in the Philippine government. Captain, they declared secession from the rest of the islands and said they were forming a new government whose first mission will be to rid the island of the mercenaries. I supposed that's us, sir."

"I suppose," Stark said, still focused on the frozen image of the screen of the battle just two days ago. "Anything else?"

"Our drone flying a pattern over the base didn't detect any activity. Our tethered drone was looking for any movement in the direction of where Lieutenant Santos went missing. It didn't detect anything within a one-kilometer radius except for small animals. I'm sorry, sir," Oliver Riddle directed at Castillo, who was motionless.

There it is, Stark thought. The attack was inevitable and imminent. Somehow the New People's Army had enough people to think they could declare secession. But that would require consensus among the population. What did the local Molbogs think of that?

"Just another administrative item, Captain. We got a note from Cynthia at headquarters. She wanted to let you know that a Mr. Golzari called and accepted the firm's offer to support some work he's doing in Europe."

Stark perked up. "Golzari? What kind of work? And what kind of support?"

"He had some questions about a ship called the *Strident Yangkou* in Le Havre. He later texted her, asking for a flight to the Azores and some supplies, including weapons. He didn't go into many details other than to provide her with a link to a local French news clip about the ship being detained in port for human trafficking. That's all we have for now."

For now. For Stark, it was enough to absorb—*for now.*

CHAPTER 19

EASTERN ATLANTIC OCEAN

The Dassault Falcon hummed easily at its cruising altitude over the eastern Atlantic. Aside from the two pilots and one flight attendant, the privately chartered jet had only one passenger who spent the first part of the flight sleeping. Damien Golzari was awoken by the flight attendant an hour before arrival. After he left the port and ensured he wasn't being followed by law enforcement, he stopped his motorcycle to review the papers he had taken from Captain Antonov and the lorry driver. The driver's papers listed the destinations in Paris, Brussels, Amsterdam, and Munich for the trafficked children. He'd call Emile about those so he could help his colleagues in those cities. It also had an address on São Miguel, the main island of the Azores.

The captain's two sheets of paper were different. On the back were scribbled the latitude and longitude coordinates for each time the *Strident Yangkou* came to a full stop in the South China Sea forty miles from Palawan Island. It had no ship names with which it rendezvoused. Antonov told the truth on that count.

What the sheets did have, however, were the serial numbers for the cargo containers that were used for every voyage. He texted Cynthia at Highland Maritime and asked for a flight from Le Havre Octeville Airport to João Paulo II Airport, a few miles from Ponta Delgada on São Miguel. He'd also need the ammunition and other supplies they had discussed earlier. Although it was a long shot, he also provided her with the serial number of containers. She had access to a database through one of the shipping companies that worked with Highland Maritime. The containers belonged to a shipping company in Shanghai called Zhaoxiang Shipping, Ltd.

His next text was to Robert Witherfield. He hadn't spoken to him in more than a week, which was sure to set off a "where have you been and why haven't you called" series of texts or calls, but he'd have to settle that later. They had known each other since their days at the Cheltenham School, and they had worked missions together since Robert worked counterterrorism and counterintelligence issues for MI5 in London. Golzari asked him for any information on Zhaoxiang Shipping, Ltd. and provided the four container numbers to him as well as Antonov's name and that of the *Strident Yangkou*. Then he apologized for not being in contact, but he was on assignment.

He made a brief stop at a convenience store to buy a water bottle and a few protein bars, then waited until Cynthia told him where to meet the privately chartered jet. It was out of the way and didn't require to be checked in, which was good since he still had both his guns on him, and as an Iranian-American, he had experienced the brutality if law enforcement mistook you for a Muslim terrorist any time after 9/11.

An hour later, the Dassault Falcon arrived, its flight attendant escorted him to the plane, familiarized him with the craft, then showed him the luggage that had arrived for him. Golzari had to admit it. He'd hated Stark and his mercenary company when he'd first encountered them in Yemen, but it was far more efficient and helpful than the government he had served for twenty years until someone found a way to force him from the Diplomatic Security Service.

"We'll be landing in thirty minutes, Mr. Golzari. Please let us know if we can ever be of service again," the attendant smiled pleasantly. He was sure a private charter jet like this was accustomed to more demanding customers. All he wanted to do was get some sleep and rehydrate.

The plane landed smoothly at the airport named for Pope John Paul II, taxied, then dropped him off. Golzari hailed a taxi, entered, and said "hello" and "thank you" in Portuguese. He could say those two words or phrases in nearly thirty languages. It served him well on his travels. He found natives were more responsive to requests if you at least greeted them in their language in their country. The Azores were an autonomous region of Portugal, so the words were as helpful here as in other places where Portuguese was spoken, such as Brazil, Mozambique, and Angola.

The driver said something, then spoke in English, clearly recognizing Golzari's own language.

"Hotel Álvaro Póvoas," Golzari said.

The cab driver snapped his head back in surprise. "Hotel Álvaro Póvoas?"

"Yes, please."

The driver shrugged his shoulders, looked in the side mirror, then drove off. A text came through.

Can you talk? It was from Robert.

Not now. Fifteen minutes?

Certainly.

In his twenty years with the Diplomatic Security Service, Golzari had traveled to or through nearly every country in the world, protecting his charges. He had been to the Azores only once for an overnight. The views were excellent since São Miguel was so mountainous. In fact, there weren't any beaches on this archipelago formed by volcanoes, which is probably why tourism wasn't as abundant from Europe as it could have been.

The cab slowed in a rundown section of Ponta Delgada that, judging from its colonial architecture, might have been more affluent decades ago.

"Hotel Álvaro Póvoas," the cab driver said as he double-parked in front of the older building. The meter spat the fee as Golzari paid him the appropriate amount in euros. He grabbed his medium-sized luggage and checked in. No one else was waiting. There wasn't much activity here, nor could it have been. The lobby was the size of a bedroom, built for nineteenth-century functionality on a provincial island rather than to impress new guests. It was cheaper than most of the hotels he queried. It was a place whose staff would not ask questions.

He took the stairs to his room on the second floor overlooking the narrow street but didn't check for surveillance devices as he might have elsewhere. He called Robert.

"Where have you been and why haven't you called?"

Golzari rolled his eyes, and then the thinnest smile appeared on his lips because he knew Robert so well, and he knew Golzari.

"I'm sorry?" was all he could muster.

"I forgive you. You needed something and I believe I found it. You always run in interesting circles," the British agent said in his smooth tenor voice.

"How bad is it?" Golzari said.

"Zhaoxiang Shipping, Ltd. Has a spotty history. It owns ships, containers, and a few of its own terminals, not only two in China but others in Namibia, the Dominican Republic, and Turkey."

"That didn't take you long to learn," Golzari recognized.

"It didn't have to. We have a file on it. It is involved with illicit commerce. We've seen drug running, some arms to developing nations, but nothing so major that we needed to intercede. At least not here in the UK or our territories."

"They've been involved in human trafficking for the past year from a small island in the Philippines," Golzari said, thinking that was pretty major.

"Interesting. Well, the *Strident Yangkou* is owned by another shipping company, but it was originally owned by Zhaoxiang Shipping."

"When did they sell it?"

"Eighteen months ago. Your friend Antonov came aboard a few months later. He didn't have ties to the old company, that we can tell. However, we did find that a few years ago Zhaoxiang Shipping was collocated with another company in Hong Kong, and at least three members on its board of directors went to the other firm."

"And what was the name of that firm?"

"Zheng R&D," Witherfield said slowly, punctuating each syllable.

"Zheng R& . . . oh."

"That's right."

Golzari remembered where he first heard of that company. It was in Singapore when he was investigating the death of another agent. Zheng R&D had stolen technology to help the Tamil Sea Tigers. They employed a sniper named Qin.

"I owe you, Robert."

"Anytime. See you in London sometime soon?"

"Soon."

PRIVATE SECURITY VESSEL SYREN

The command center was deathly silent after the brief, some stunned by their being exploited by the media in a false story, others by the announcement by the New People's Army that it intended to take the base. While the surveillance drones still showed no movement in proximity to the base, the island was too small to think an attack was days away. It was hours.

"Commander?" Stark turned to the Philippine Navy officer. Castillo was deep in thought and paused a few seconds before selecting his words.

"Thank you," he said. He looked at the floor to collect his thoughts. "We can only assume what has happened to the Molbog population here to be so dominated by the New People's Army. We have two choices. We can abandon the base to the NPA in which we hand them a major victory, or we try to stop them. As the senior officer of my government on Balabac, I can't allow them that first option. My people would not permit that, and the military will come here eventually. The NPA are likely at Población I. It is not days but hours when they will be able to attack. The Philippine military can't get here that soon, even if they hadn't been disrupted by the cyberattack.

"Captain Stark, Highland Maritime Defense has already exceeded its mission. You all came here to help us train. You fulfilled that contractual requirement. It has been a trial by fire. My sailors and I are grateful for you standing by us, for retaking the base two days ago, and for disrupting the cyberattack. But this is our fight. You are Americans, and British, and French, and Nigerian, and many other nationalities. You are a company. I cannot expect you to stay. The NPA doesn't have dozens or hundreds of people—it has thousands. And if it has, in some way, transported them here, then we are outnumbered. I told you before that I will defend this base, as will my sailors. I know the odds, but I also know my duty.

"You and your people need to leave on *Syren* and *Minerva* now. This will not end well and you are not required to be here. I thank you for your training, your courage to stand with us, and your friendship. But you need to save your people."

Maybe it was the lack of sleep or a quirk in the ship's HVAC system, but Stark's eyes began to water. A few weeks ago, he didn't know Commander Renaldo Castillo. In training with this surface warfare officer, he watched him listen, learn, and act. They had become more than business associates or partners. They were friends. And they were friends who were threatened by a dangerous non-state actor.

"Commander, we don't have a lot of time," Stark began. "You are not going to fight this alone." He grabbed the closed mic and told Riddle to patch him through ship-wide on both *Syren* and *Minerva*. He started when his communications officer hit two switches and gave him the thumbs-up.

"Highland Maritime, this is Connor Stark. We're expecting an attack on the base by the New People's Army, probably today. Our Philippine Navy partners are defending it from that attack. I am joining them. I hope to use all the assets we have at our disposal, but I want to be clear—I do not expect anyone to remain for this one, given the odds. But we've faced challenging odds before together. Anyone—and I mean anyone—who doesn't want to be part of this operation, this is what we'll do. Any and all personnel from *Syren* who opt out will go topside in five minutes and will be transferred to *Minerva*. Anyone from *Minerva* wishing to remain for this one, please go topside for transfer here to *Syren*. *Syren* will remain on station with any crew and security teams from the two ships. As soon as all personnel are transferred, *Minerva* will return to headquarters.

"If anyone is thinking about staying, understand that we may be looking at hundreds of insurgents coming our way. We've seen what they can do. If you want to stay with me and our Philippine partners, then the New People's Army will see what *we* can do. *Syren* actual, out." He released the transmit button, then glanced up at the digital clock on the bulkhead. *Five minutes*, he thought.

"Commander Castillo, we should probably start thinking about tactics. You have twenty-seven sailors between the ships and ashore. . . ." Stark caught himself as he thought about Santos. "I deeply apologize. Twenty-six."

"I want to stay," Fisk said, raising his hand.

"Thank you, Mr. Fisk," Stark replied with a nod.

"You got no chance without me, boss," Warren said with a crooked smile beneath his red mustache and beard.

"Captain, I'm sorry but . . ." Olivia Harrison started to say.

"It's okay, XO. I need you to transfer to *Minerva*. Since Bobby's staying here, Captain Johnson needs someone on board with her."

"But I'm not going, Connor," Jaime Johnson interjected, unusually using his first name in the company of others rather than his organizational title.

"Yes, you are," he countered but he didn't share the real reason. She was a single mother with three children—his nephews and niece. She was needed back in Port St. George in a way Stark and others without children weren't. He always hoped Jaime would take over the company if anything happened to him. Maybe it was time.

"Not everyone is staying for this ride, Jaime. You and Liv need to get out of Dodge with our people. Let's remember that the NPA has a couple of Philippine Navy cutters they stole from the base. If they try to stop you, I need an experienced team on *Minerva* to take our people home safely. Agreed?"

Jaime thought about it for a moment, gently pulling her right earlobe as she bounced her leg. Normally, his younger cousin was far calmer than Stark could ever be. He saw that momentary tug of war in her mind.

"Aye, sir," she finally agreed, meeting his eyes, those same kindly and supportive eyes that had looked out for her cousin when they were kids growing up.

Stark began to run through the situation. He had four minutes to think and wait.

SOUTH CHINA SEA

"The plan was to wait!" the black-haired dela Cruz shouted at Makarov on the video monitor.

"The plan had to be modified," Makarov responded coldly. "No military operation ever follows the plan with precision. That's why we have to adapt."

"Bullshit cocks," dela Cruz snapped, now waving his arms. "You! You said we had six more hours after Reyes' address."

Bullshit cocks? Makarov thought, perplexed by the idiom.

"Colonel, I . . . ," Makarov continued before he was interrupted.

"No. No more 'Colonel,' Makarov. You will address me by my proper title now that the New People's Army has established our sovereignty as the People's Republic of Balabac and formed our provisional government. You will address me as 'Chairman dela Cruz.'"

Oh fuck, Makarov said to himself as he tried to maintain his composure. A little victory had gone right to this third-tier guerilla's head. Dela Cruz had never had much success other than kidnappings, murders, and petty theft. Once Makarov and the resources of Zheng R&D were brought into play, his people were consolidated, a plan was put in place, and they had just taken over a fucking island. This new overly-inflated ego could pose problems. The operation was nearly at its apex and, despite the loss of Site B and its ability to continue the cyberattacks, by every measure, the past year had been successful—with very little thanks to "Chairman" Asshole.

Jose dela Cruz had operated like a typical insurgent, always wanting the whole pie that was out of his reach instead of actually eating a piece of it. It had taken Makarov—with an additional meeting with Hu Tao more than a year before—to convince the guerilla that, in reality, he would never lead the Philippines but that he could take a manageable island. It was dela Cruz's female lieutenant during that meeting who commented that in John Milton's *Paradise Lost*, the serpent—or Satan—said it was better to rule in hell than serve in heaven. Dela Cruz agreed and the lieutenant was henceforth referred to as the Serpent, or *Bitin* in her native Cepuano tongue.

"Chairman, the change in plans was due to your not providing more security at the site. If you had, the attacks would have continued. As it is, we are adjusting our plan."

Makarov hit the mute button as dela Cruz began to yell, stick his middle finger at the camera, and produce other movements that might be described as non-verbal communication as the Russian simply watched him go on as the two uniformed personnel at his sides stood passively. They should now be at the town hall, the center of their new government. A flag was hung behind dela Cruz. Fortunately, it wasn't the NPA's flag—a white triangle and a gold star at each vertex with an AK-47 atop a spear in the center, all on a red background. Toni was better at optics from her CIA training and, with a great deal of persuasion by dela Cruz's two lieutenants, the little dictator agreed to the new, less warlike or intimidating flag behind him. It had a powder-blue background with a dark blue single star in the middle.

To the Chairman's right was his deputy, a lifelong member of the NPA who had orchestrated most of the attacks for dela Cruz. Unlike his boss, he was reasonable, listened to ideas, and knew how to carry them out.

On his left was "Bitin." Makarov hadn't seen her for months, but she was as coldly efficient and intelligent as dela Cruz was maniacally petulant and boisterous. At first, he wondered how two such individuals could take orders from someone like dela Cruz, then he realized the Soviet Union had had its own problematic leaders. Perhaps people just wanted to be led by narcissistic, megalomaniacal crazies.

A minute later as dela Cruz appeared to simmer down, Makarov took him off mute.

"Chairman dela Cruz, I apologize for pointing out reality, but let's discuss the next step. We have momentum and we should not cede that. And we don't have to be concerned at this point about the Philippine military arriving from other islands."

"How is this possible?" dela Cruz skeptically asked as his beady eyes narrowed.

"That's left to others to contend with. But you'll know soon. For now, we need to take the base back."

"I agree. Ernesto?" dela Cruz said, turning to his right, "how many do we have?"

"Chairman, as of three days ago we had an island population of six thousand, three hundred twenty-two. That includes our soldiers and their families. We have eight hundred fifteen soldiers divided into four battalions. In addition, we have one hundred eighty on your four ships."

Makarov thought to point out that the numbering scheme was different than how many soldiers one would find in the Russian Army.

There, eight hundred soldiers might be four or five companies. But this was a guerilla army. There were no rules. Except when most of the guerillas on your ships were still recovering from their seasickness.

"Thank you, Ernesto. Bitin, what about the enemy force?" dela Cruz asked, spinning his chair toward his other side.

"The enemy is composed of two forces," she said matter-of-factly, her hands clasped behind her back. "Their ships, *Minerva* and *Syren*, each have a crew of twenty-six sailors. Each ship has an additional ten specialists plus fifteen security professionals. The ships have equivalent capabilities. Each has a tethered drone, two untethered drones with surveillance packages, and two drones that have no sensors but can carry supplies. The Philippine Navy complement is twenty-six. They are all at the base, along with ten security professionals from the private security ships. Combined, they have a total of one hundred twenty-six, so our force outnumbers them nearly four to one, sufficient to mount an offensive."

"Excellent. Excellent. When do we attack the base, Makarov?" dela Cruz asked.

"Send one battalion now. Have twenty of them take the road toward the north side of the base. The rest should approach from the east. Both should attack at 1100, so send them now. They will press the attack until they take the base or run out of ammunition."

"Why don't we send everyone?" Ernesto asked.

"Because you don't need everyone. Bitin just said there are a couple of dozen only at the base. The rest of your battalions will remain in reserve. The fishing vessel *Tiamzon* with us is serving as the ammunition ship. It's better if we resupply the troops from the sea rather than Población I in case any country has the idea of countering us there. All our troops have boarded one of the fishing vessels and are underway. And here is what you will do with the reserves. . . ."

CHAPTER 20

OFF BALABAC NAVAL BASE

Seventeen. Seventeen of the crew aboard his ships had chosen to stay. That was nearly half the combined ships' complements. He wasn't disappointed. That was more than he expected. Given what they were about to face, he would have preferred if all of them had left. He didn't want to lose any of his people—or Castillo's. Seventeen. It wasn't like the crews could be combined. He was losing capabilities with that loss. All three drone pilots, for example, were leaving. That meant Warren was the only one who could fly them and Stark couldn't use him in other areas. As soon as the numbers came in, Warren said he was picking up a six-pack of soda and a pound of beef jerky to get him through the flight operations alone. Most of those heading out of the area were newbies, mostly on their first assignment with the company.

The RHIBs from both ships started the personnel shuffle. Stark, Castillo, Fisk, and the senior security officer, Sivan Abraham, debated their battle plan in the command center. Stark once observed that every time Abraham was internally figuring out movements, she'd run her left hand through her short, spiked hair. Everyone had a tell. As for the short hair, she had once told Stark that she eschewed long hair because the less your enemy had to grab in a fight, the better.

Oliver Riddle, the communications officer in his third year with the company, was trying to do too many things at once since his assistant had been one of the seventeen to leave and *Minerva*'s backup comms officer hadn't yet arrived.

"Shit," Riddle said.

"What's up," Stark said, putting a firm hand on his shoulder to reassure him.

"Captain, I'm really sorry. I just caught this since I'm trying . . ."

"Oliver, it's okay. Help is on the way."

"No, it isn't, sir. The Philippine Army, Navy, and Air Force will not be helping us to defend the naval base or retake the island."

"What do you mean?" Castillo asked as he swung his wounded leg around.

"The new president of the Philippines, Felipe Reyes, just issued a statement that his government will '*respect the decision of the citizens of the People's Republic of Balabac to secede due to the centuries of colonial and imperial interference. The Philippines have endured enough bloodshed from the tools of imperialistic nations, and the PRB has a right to protect itself from the tools of imperialist nations, such as the mercenaries now at the former Philippine naval base on Balabac. My government hopes to work with the PRB in the future.*'"

"That is insane," Castillo said. "No one in my government would condone that. The Philippine people wouldn't allow us to recognize a state run by guerillas who have fought us."

"There's something else going on here, Renaldo. Do you know anything about Reyes?" Stark asked.

"He's the vice president and used to be a senator. I don't follow politics so that's really all I know."

"For now—whatever the political reason—any help from the Philippines military is off the table. And with Reyes' statement, there's now no reason for you to be here. According to the Philippine government, this base doesn't belong to the navy."

Castillo's face sank at the realization that his government had just caved to a terrorist organization—one of many that had vexed the Philippines. And now they were surrendering sovereign territory to them. He rubbed his lips back and forth with his forefinger in thought.

"Connor, you were an officer in your navy, correct?"

"Yeah, for a while," Stark said, pensively recalling the only job—the only vocation—he ever wanted.

"You swore an oath about enemies foreign and domestic?"

"Yes. When I commissioned and each time I was promoted."

"Is there not also something in your system where you should not obey illegal orders?"

"Yes."

"I see," Castillo said softly as he cast his eyes down momentarily.

"Renaldo, I once paid a great price for challenging the decisions of my superiors." Stark thought back to when he was about Castillo's age and had taken actions that led to his court-martial and discharge from the Navy.

"Aren't some things worth paying the price?" Castillo asked.

"Some things. We each determine what that is. Sometimes it's the right thing to do, sometimes it's the wrong thing. What are you willing to risk for your decisions? But I can tell you this right now—we can abandon the base to the NPA and get everyone home."

Castillo planted one of his crutches on the deck and used it to push himself up to a standing position a few feet from Stark. He grimaced with pain as the meds were wearing off, but he seemed a little taller.

"If the NPA takes this island, then the Moros and Abu Sayyaf and a half dozen other terrorist organizations will have a precedent to do what they've done here. You came here to train us. What good is training or exercises if we don't take a stand when it matters? Felipe Reyes is either wrong or he's made his decision based on faulty information. We stand here."

Commander Renaldo Castillo of the Philippine Navy straightened his blouse and asked Riddle for a video recorder.

NEW YORK CITY

The anchor cut away from a ten-minute story about the Kardashian family and what they wore to a gala in New York City when the words "BREAKING NEWS" appeared across the screen. She shuffled some papers and read the monitor.

"We have breaking news this hour as we update an earlier story about the Philippines and the attack by mercenaries on a naval base. This video was just released to us and we'll play it for you now."

The video showed a trim man with short black hair in a gray and black camouflage uniform with two suns sewn on. It was clearly filmed on a ship as the background showed water and land beyond that.

"*My name is Renaldo Castillo. I am a commander in the Philippine Navy, and I am recording this at the naval base on Balabac Island. I wish to correct the misinformation that has been presented. We were on a training exercise two days ago when we discovered our base had been attacked, its personnel executed, and its ships taken. We fought the attackers who are part of the New People's Army. They claimed mercenaries attacked the base. That is a lie. It was the NPA that did so. Because the information my government based its decision on was false, I implore President Reyes to reverse his decision recognizing the so-called People's Republic of Balabac and send forces to . . .*"

"We're breaking away from that unverified video. Again, we can't confirm the validity of the person who alleges to be in the Philippine Navy or to actually be at the island, but if we have any confirmation, we'll certainly report on that. In the meantime." She turned to a reporter, "let's talk about the breaking news on public backlash to Chloe and Kim's bold decision to wear . . ."

PONTA DELGADA, AZORES

The temperature in the Azores rarely ever fell below sixty degrees, which limited Golzari's options when hiding his side holster and Glock. He had a history of purchasing finer clothes, but his wardrobe was back in his Paris apartment. His suits and coats had been specifically tailored at a discreet store in London to make his guns less obtrusive. A good tailor could do that. Instead, Golzari had to find the closest clothing store and buy a light blazer off the rack. He rented a car and made sure to familiarize himself with the laws to decrease the chance of the local police pulling him over. He could not exceed 100 kilometers per hour on the expressways (few as there were) or 50 kilometers per hour in localities. He crossed his fingers that nothing happened to result in chasing someone or being chased.

The sun shone brightly on the square in Ponta Delgada, full of locals skateboarding, smoking, or playing chess. Tourists walked haphazardly and pointed at buildings, trees, and statues as they photographed them. Some took selfies with whatever structure they found of interest. Golzari was always paranoid about being in the midst of so many phones and opportunities for surveillance—what normal people called taking photos of items and people of interest to them. He had a newspaper, and whenever a phone swung anywhere in his direction, he casually raised it to hide his face. He had a problem with that in Paris when he first started to play piano on Pont Saint-Louis. Old habits die hard.

At the center of the square was a gazebo with a white base, painted iron railings, and a single set of stairs. Its roof, like most of the roofs he'd seen on the local buildings, was comprised of half-round terracotta tiles. A classical guitarist played a piece—Sonata 42, if he wasn't mistaken—by the eighteenth-century Portuguese composer Carlos Seixas. The black and white tiled square was fraught with dizzying wave patterns on one side and more symmetrical shapes on the other. From his elevated vantage point, Golzari could see the port and the Atlantic Ocean just above the two-story white, blue, pastel green, and golden mustard painted homes in the square.

He finished a protein bar and an iced tea, careful not to spill any on his new blue blazer, pretending to himself that it was worth more than he had paid. Golzari broke out the papers again. He had practically memorized everything on the sheets, including an address at Ponta Delgada. That address was diagonally across the square from him, a modest home with a man he had seen enter earlier.

Golzari sent a simple text to a number he hadn't called in a while and hoped it wasn't disconnected.

It's me, he wrote.

Three dots appeared a few seconds later, then the reply:

Me who.

Me, your favorite ex-husband, he replied.

No dots appeared for a long minute as he kept his eye on the house.

What the hell do you want? Melanie Arden answered.

I'm texting you some dox. He sent images of more than a dozen papers he'd taken from Paris and Le Havre.

A few more minutes passed when the phone buzzed.

"Where are you?"

Melanie was always straightforward—more so since their divorce. The last time he'd run into her was in Sri Lanka where she had been on assignment as a freelance reporter.

"Ponta Delgada," he said softly. There was no one within thirty feet of him, but he lowered his head while he watched the house.

"The Azores? Are these documents what I think they are?"

"I don't know how much time I have, Mel. I'm not here in any official capacity." He told her everything—the name of the restaurant where the little girl worked, the address of the trafficking house in Paris, information about Abdou Mansouri, the ship, Antonov, the trafficking of Molbogs from Balabac Island, and why he was here.

"Is that enough for a story?"

"Are you kidding me? Do you know what's happening in Balabac right now?" She shared as much as she knew based on the breaking news stories and what she'd been able to gather from her sources.

"Mercenaries wearing gray coveralls and dark ballcaps? Stark's company?"

"That's what I'm told," she said crisply.

"They displaced an entire island population with New People's Army. This will end poorly," he answered. "Mel, take this number down . . ." She did as he asked.

"Whose number is this?"

"Caroline J. Sumner."

"President Dunner's national security advisor?"

"Yes. I met her in Yemen and was later her personal security officer. Tell her who you are . . . if you don't mind."

"Were we married long enough for me to mind?" she said with a half-snort.

"Can you get the story out soon?"

"Really soon, given everything that's going on out there. Thank you, Damien."

"I owed you, Melanie. Must run," he said as he turned off the phone.

Golzari waited long enough for the man in the house to reemerge after lunch and now here he was. He was about five foot, eight inches tall and wore work boots, faded blue jeans, and a long sleeve blue shirt. The shape of a pack of cigarettes protruded from his shirt pocket. According to the sheets, a man named Silva lived there.

Golzari crumbled the napkin and sandwich wrapping, rose casually, and walked down the steps toward Silva. The man walked a few blocks to his car, a white Citroën with two wheels on the sidewalk, as were other cars. Golzari accelerated his pace as the man opened the driver's side door. After the man entered and put the key in the ignition of the pre-keyless vehicle, Golzari ensured there was no one nearby and gently tapped on the passenger side window with his knuckle. He smiled broadly. The man rolled down his window.

"Hi! I'm from the States and I think I'm lost," Golzari said in his best impression of an Ugly American accent. "I'm looking for the Church of Misericordia. Can you help?"

"Ah, you are very in wrong place," he responded. "You have to go . . ." The man instinctively twisted left and threw his arm to point backward—exactly what Golzari wanted him to do, which was why he chose the Church of Misericordia in planning this. With swift precision, Golzari reached for the door lock with his left hand, opened it with his right, and plopped himself in the passenger seat before Silva turned back to see what had happened.

In a crisis situation, people revert to one of three actions: fight, flight, or freeze. Golzari's nature and training had him in the "fight" category, responding to an action. Others would run away. Then, there were those like Silva, who were part of the "freeze" type. With Silva not knowing what to do, Golzari managed to slip out the Glock from beneath his blazer and point it at Silva's gut.

"Let's go for a drive, Mr. Silva," he said. "And please keep it under fifty kilometers per hour as we are in town."

Silva, further confused by the Middle Eastern man threatening him, just obeyed and drove up the street.

"Who are you?" Silva finally blurted out.

"Someone who has been made . . . unhappy . . . by your business."

Silva said nothing. He wasn't one to think quickly on his feet or show fearlessness, however misplaced, like Captain Antonov.

"Tell me about your work, Mr. Silva," Golzari said coldly as they drove around another square lined by trees.

"I'm a simple man. I work in a warehouse."

Golzari pressed the gun barrel into Silva's ribs, causing the car to swerve momentarily.

"What is the work in the warehouse, Mr. Silva?"

"We just move cargo to and from ships." Silva was beginning to break already as he whimpered. He was in his forties. Golzari had seen the type before. The man had a wedding ring. At one point he might have been a decent man just trying to make a living who found himself working in a place that was advantageous to nefarious characters. Golzari had no idea what the unemployment rate was in Ponta Delgada, a city of nearly seventy thousand people, but sometimes people looked the other way just to keep their job. Golzari saw a sign for an expressway.

"Let's talk about that cargo from the *Strident Yangkou*, and let's talk about Jean-Pascal."

Silva looked over at Golzari with abject fear in his eyes.

"Focus on the road, Mr. Silva. Let's begin . . ."

WASHINGTON, DC

President Dunner and National Security Advisor Sumner flew back to the White House on Marine One earlier than expected. The helicopter's pilot, a Marine major, landed the craft so lightly and expertly on the front lawn that Dunner and Sumner didn't even know when they touched ground. The president left the craft with one hand firmly planted on the handrail and the other holding his cane. The Washington, DC, version of the paparazzi began snapping photos as soon as Marine One landed and would do so until he entered the White House. They didn't have enough B-roll of Dunner even though he'd done the same thing dozens of times since taking office. It had been drizzling for more than an hour, but the paparazzi didn't care. They needed product for their news agencies.

As Dunner put his foot on the ground, he switched the cane from his right hand to his left and turned to raise his hand to return the salute of the Marine. In doing so, Dunner's left foot slipped on the wet grass. His leg flew up as his body twisted to the right, and he fell backward. The Marine, who was still ramrod straight saluting his president, reached out for him but he was too far away. The president continued his fall as his right temple slammed against the end of the metal handrail, bouncing off it and again hitting, catching the corner of a step before he rested on the ground. The first Marine moved toward the fallen president as the second yelled something to people in the cabin. Sumner, waiting for the president's salute just inside the door, saw this unfold and raced out. The paparazzi immediately started texting the images and videos to their agencies for more breaking news. Nothing like this had happened since President Ford's old football knee gave out from under him as he descended Air Force One. That incident paled in comparison.

A gaggle of aides bolted from the White House, some waving arms, yelling for an ambulance. The paparazzi kept snapping away to capture this moment for posterity. In the next few seconds, all the cable news networks would break from their story to show pictures of the frail, falling president. They'd then launch into discussions about his being one of the oldest people to become president, the comparison of his fall to his poll numbers on domestic issues, they'd find a presidential historian to reflect on the history of presidential accidents, a medical expert would speculate on the nature and effects of the injury without having even treated him or seen the extent of the injury.

What none of them would say was that a good and decent man who never hurt anyone in his life had tried to return a salute and, due to poor weather, had slipped and fallen.

Sumner wanted to get to Dunner but the Marines were there, and the last thing the president needed was more people except the on-duty physician who was racing across the lawn. She leaned against the frame of Marine One as the aide who accompanied them and hadn't witnessed the fall, immersed as she was on her phone, tapped Sumner on the shoulder and then pulled the national security advisor back inside.

Sumner said nothing, stunned as she was and concerned about the president. The aide showed her the phone's viewscreen. Sumner grabbed the phone and scrolled down the story as her jaw dropped, although all she really needed to know was the headline:

"China First Country to Formally Recognize New Island Nation."

PART III

CHAPTER 21

Stark, Castillo, Fisk, Abraham, and Warren stood around the tactical table that looked like a raised garden bed on legs. Warren had seen the technology from a firm in Virginia and modified it for training purposes. A digital image was input with an SD card next to a keyboard and the four-by-eight-foot table copied that. It then modified the image into three dimensions, providing a holographic topographical representation. Warren input an overhead image of the general area to include *Syren* and *Townsville* on one side and the base with its perimeter on the other. Warren zoomed out briefly to show the entire island. Stark marveled at the technology before realizing that *Minerva* and its crew weren't represented on it.

Based on the latest drone sweep, about two hundred NPA soldiers were making their way to the base. Some were on the dirt road Stark and Warren had been on, while others were coming through the interior. Warren used a stylus to draw a large circle around the holographic representation of those soldiers and then drew an arrow from the circle to the base. A display screen directly above the box at head level changed, and up popped an estimated number of soldiers with a minimum and maximum walking time based on their direction. Since they were all on foot, the estimated time was two hours from now.

The display also showed the number of blue forces, although there were two shades of those—the blue forces that were the Philippine complement and the light gray forces of Highland Maritime Defense.

"Sivan, what's your assessment of the naval base defense?" Stark asked.

"The NPA is lightly armed—nothing more than AK-47s that the drone could see. They had backpacks. Could simply be water but we need to know more. I don't know why they're sending only a portion of their force. I suspect the majority are staying in Población I for now to secure it in case. This force still outnumbers us enough, but we've managed to dig some trenches—four each on the southern, eastern, and northern sides of the base, each large enough for teams of three," Abraham said as she drew lines with her own stylus where the trenches were.

"With luck, I think we can hold off that force," Abraham continued. "Plus, our folks are more experienced in coordinated operations. Their bastards are from dozens of islands and haven't had a history of working together in groups larger than a terrorist cell. But if they come in with more, we need to look at other options. Even if they haven't trained as a regiment or battalion, the numbers have an advantage—like Soviet soldiers during the Second World War. As a fail-safe, we're going to have the whalers and the two RHIBs *Minerva* left behind for us tied up but running. That way, if the NPA gets through the fence line, we have a chance to get our people out."

"Thanks, Sivan. That drone we saw yesterday heading toward the computer building came from the water, not from Población I," observed Stark. "Did the cutters have drones aboard, Daniel?"

"None," Castillo said, swaying on his crutches. "They were *Jacinto*-class offshore patrol vessels given to us by Hong Kong when they were turned over to the Chinese in 1997. They could have brought drones aboard, but I don't know if they'd have had time to practice on them. They're lightly armed with a 25mm naval gun and a couple of 20mm Oerlikon cannons. It's enough to rip into your hull." He didn't need to say they'd rip through *Syren*'s sailors as well.

"We know that they have the *Jacinto*s as well as the big fishing trawler we saw a couple of days ago," Stark said, having Warren add those three vessels to the map. "We don't know what else they might have. Then again, they might not know we got *Townsville* operational. Oliver?"

"Sir?" responded the comms officer, removing his headset.

"Call up the map of commercial shipping between here and . . . and the first set of Chinese islands that they built. So . . . about a one-hundred-nautical-mile diameter."

Riddle connected to the commercial vendor Highland Maritime Defense had contracted with for additional services. A map of the larger region—the eastern South China Sea near Balabac and Palawan—appeared on the widescreen. The contours of the coastline and islands appeared in green, while the blue water was dotted by rectangles with pointed ends representing nearly every ship in the region. Different colors were used for freighters, tankers, sailing vessels, fishing vessels, ferries, and other types of craft. Each ship over seven hundred tons was required to have Automatic Identification System (AIS) transmitters, which helped in navigation and determining what vessels were nearby. This posed a problem during the height of the Somali piracy crisis since the pirates were savvy enough to more easily find their prey viewing an AIS display. The shipping companies started turning off their AIS so they couldn't be found.

Illegal fishing trawlers likewise turned off or didn't have AIS aboard so that state law enforcement officials couldn't track them, which is why more ships were needed to patrol, like the construction of the Balabac Naval Base. Warships also didn't always flash AIS.

The screen started a sped-up two-day loop of marine traffic in the South China Sea. Stark and Fisk moved closer to it, trying to find any anomalies. They found one nearly simultaneously.

"There," Fisk pointed. "Riddle, can you zoom in right here?" The comms officer obliged. The shifting patterns were nuanced but there was a small "black hole" that the commercial ships were avoiding through minor changes in course and speed. The black hole shifted during the two-day period as if any ships in that hole were moving slowly in a box pattern.

"Drone, Warren?"

"Sorry, boss. One-armed bandit here without other pilots."

Stark nodded, acknowledging his engineer's challenge.

"Sivan, does it make sense to divide our forces? We take *Syren* and *Townsville* to the *Jacinto*s and fishing vessel and keep as many ground forces here to defend the base?" Stark asked.

"Two skillsets, Captain. The ship operators have had basic firearms training, but you can't take them off the ship if you want to keep the engines running. And our ground-pounders aren't much good unless you're planning to board another vessel. Are you planning on boarding, Captain?" she said in her deep, throaty voice.

"I don't think so, but can you spare a team of five for a couple of hours? If we get underway now at top speed, we'll reach that black hole in three-quarters of an hour, and then another back here."

"You thinking of frying them, boss?" Warren asked.

"Would that be with the 50mm guns you have?" Castillo asked, perplexed. Stark silently chided Warren, who shrugged his shoulders. Castillo was with another government and the weapon Highland Maritime Defense had wasn't known beyond a few people. Still, the weapon was intended for times like this, and since they might be in their last battle, Stark decided to share the company's greater secret.

"Renaldo, what I'm going to tell you is not for public consumption," he began.

"I understand and will not share anything you tell me, Connor."

"Thank you. Do you remember when the Tamil Sea Tigers made their return a few years ago?"

"Of course."

"*Syren* was there, and Highland Maritime was on the ground as well. The Sea Tigers had found a mine with pure hafnium, an extremely rare early element, that could be used for an Electromagnetic Pulse weapon," Stark said.

"Yes, I remember. They took out the Sri Lankan Navy. One of their officers briefed us on it."

"What they didn't brief you on . . . Highland Maritime managed to get a supply of that hafnium. Warren made his own rockets with them. We've used them before. We might be able to employ them out there. We have two types—an anti-ship variant and something smaller."

Castillo could only bring himself to say, "Oh my . . ."

"Can I have a couple of the smaller rockets, Captain?" Abraham asked and didn't have to wait long for the nod of approval.

"Bobby, your thoughts?" Stark said.

"There's a reason they needed those *Jacinto*s otherwise they wouldn't have made the effort to take them. The ships and the ground force might be caught between a rock and a hard place with our backs to each other but no way to support each other. Do you know what I mean?"

"I do," Abraham said. "He's right. Take the ships out there. We've got all the ammo from *Minerva*'s supplies and half of *Syren*'s."

Stark considered that for a moment and then reversed himself.

"No, they might not know *Townsville* is operational. Commander, I leave *Townsville* to you and return to its pier. I have an idea."

USS GEORGE *HW BUSH*

Admiral Daniel Rossberg imperiously walked down the passageway to the bridge with the ship's captain, Will Porter, who towered above the flag officer but retained the thin, muscular frame of his basketball days at the Academy. Rossberg's short, overly stout body shape, by contrast, resulted in jokes among the crew whenever they saw C-3PO and R2-D2, although they respected their C-3PO and wanted nothing more than to toss R2-D2 overboard.

Rossberg's flag aide, a Navy lieutenant, who was just a couple of steps behind them, cursed the Bureau of Naval Personnel detailer who had condemned him to two years by Rossberg's side. He had four hundred seventy-two days and three hours left, and every one of those days felt like a month.

"Come on, come on," Rossberg barked impatiently, as much as he could with his nasal voice, even though Porter could have taken two stride lengths for every one of the admiral's.

They arrived for the latest coordination meeting with the commodores of the other participating squadrons, all on VTC, while the room had the ship's company senior officers and senior enlisted as well as the squadron leaders.

"Attention on deck!" the sailor closest to the hatch said as the admiral entered.

"Seats, seats," he said as if annoyed by the traditional recognition that the senior officer had arrived.

Rossberg settled in the blue chair with the gold ship's crest; he was the only one in the room in service dress blues with medals, not ribbons. Ahead of him, the wide screen displayed the captains and commodores of each partner nation. Commander Lynn Henry, the ship's navigator, who was also the point person for all the other ship's navigators, stood to one side of the screen with a camera facing her. She wore the ship's blue coveralls, beige belt, and gold ship's crest belt buckle. Normally the Operations Officer would have conducted the brief, but because of the complexities that had occurred, the captain asked the Navigator to do it.

"Permission to begin the brief, Admiral?"

"Permission is . . . not granted, Commander."

All heads in the room turned toward the admiral.

"Sir?" Commander Henry asked surprisingly.

"You're not properly dressed," he said. "Where are your service dress blues, Commander?"

"Sir, we're all in coveralls during ship operations and . . ."

"And you will go back to your room and change immediately. You will show me respect and you will show respect to our partners on the screen," Rossberg said. The partner naval leaders were all in shock since they had heard everything.

Commander Henry left and ran down the passageway to change as Rossberg and the other leaders waited, even the partnered leaders who sat in stunned silence, each in their own coveralls, digital camouflage, or khaki uniforms. They had no choice but to be quiet since Vice Admiral Rossberg just pushed a pen around instead of at least engaging them in small talk.

She returned six minutes later and took her station near the screen.

She had just opened her mouth when Rossberg waved his hand for her to start.

Commander Henry discussed the proposed passage of the Balabac Strait and the fact that the new Philippine government had refused permission for the fleet to transit Philippine territorial waters, hence the reason they had changed the PIM to shift further south in the Celebes Sea, closer to Indonesian waters. She mentioned that the New People's Army had declared independence and that not only had the new Philippine president accepted that, but the People's Republic of China had as well.

While that might not have stopped the multinational force, the People's Republic of Balabac had announced that they were an island, not part of an archipelagic state, which meant that they were not subject to the same international maritime laws. And as an island state, they refused passage for any multinational naval force through their waters. China had subsequently issued a public statement endorsing this interpretation of international law and that they intended to support and defend the People's Republic of Balabac, positioning their naval forces in the strait if necessary.

"Well, the United States doesn't recognize them. And neither does any other country here. We're going to do what we were told to do and proceed on the original course."

A green light appeared under the image of Captain Takahashi of the Japanese Maritime Self-Defense Force aboard JS *Kirishima*.

"Admiral, I'm sorry, but my government has informed me that we need to reconsider our participation in this exercise. Until we can assess the . . . legal . . . ramifications of this transit and China's intent, my government does not believe this exercise is in any participant's best interest, so we will be leaving the formation. I'm sorry, Admiral."

The video cut out. Several other green lights appeared as captains and commodores echoed the Japanese sentiments and, one by one, ships pulled away from the multinational force until only the US Navy remained and Vice Admiral Daniel Rossberg sat in front of a blank screen.

BALABAC NAVAL BASE

Sivan Abraham jogged to each trench, speaking with her Highland Maritime Defense security personnel, checking their defenses, inspecting their weapons, and ensuring they had sufficient ammunition at the ready. Since they were no longer at EMCON, each of the trenches had a radio so she could issue orders as the battle ensued. She was no stranger to combat and military operations, which was why Stark had hired her. Her first experience was boarding the *Karine A* in the Red Sea as it carried fifty tons of ammunition and weapons bound for Palestine. Abraham had participated in no fewer than twelve known operations during the Second Intifada and Lebanon War as well as missions few were aware of. Since the personnel from Highland Maritime Defense were the most experienced, they were in the trenches as the first line of defense.

Her last check was behind one of the Quonset huts, where she had set up a small launch platform. The irony was rich since she had remembered so many Palestinian rockets raining their hell on Israeli businesses, schools, homes, and families. In Sri Lanka, the Sea Tigers had designed their rockets based on the Palestinian Qassam rockets. She doubted these would be of use. According to the information from an earlier drone pass, the NPA didn't have tanks or any vehicles, at least for now.

Meanwhile, Castillo was reviewing the positions his sailors had taken closer to the basin behind jury-rigged shields made of sheet metal several layers thick. Their job was to provide covering fire for the Highlanders in case the NPA began to overrun the base. Several sailors were manning the boats in case a full extraction was necessary. Castillo hopped as best he could with his crutches, and his presence managed to bolster the confidence of his young sailors, who were more comforted with him at the base than on *Syren*.

One of the Highland Maritime security officers had the controls of one drone zipping back and forth. The NPA soldiers were just a few hundred yards away now, just beyond the outer perimeter of the vegetation. Some marched down the road from the north, while the majority were coming from the east. Abraham couldn't figure out why they were divided and, if they were, why they didn't cover the southern flank as well.

"All positions hold your fire," Abraham said into her radio. "We are not wasting ammunition firing into the jungle. We do not fire and waste ammunition. Make them come to us. And wait until I give the signal."

They waited until the first shot rang out from the jungle, then another, and then a hail of fire.

"Hold," she said again.

FISHING VESSEL *SISON*

The drone made one low pass over the naval base as Makarov and Toni saw every position the defenders held. The NPA from Población I had taken their positions north and east of the base. The base held its gunfire.

"Smart," the Russian said. "They don't have an unlimited supply of ammunition and they're waiting for better targets." He grabbed the handset. "North and east units, advance."

With that, the drone gained elevation to watch the battle unfold. The forty or so NPA soldiers from the road began crawling and firing, moving just a few feet at a time. The hundred and ten from the east did the same. The naval base still didn't return fire, but they couldn't restrain themselves forever. At what point would they start returning fire?

The minutes went by until both flanks reached fifty yards. That was when the defenders peeked out of their trenches, looking for the easy targets first. A few NPA soldiers went down. That was not surprising. The NPA were guerillas with less experience and formal training than those security professionals at the base. He noticed, however, that it was only the people in the trenches firing, the security dressed in gray coveralls and black Kevlar vests. It was the Highland Maritime Defense personnel in the first line of defense. That was smart. The best shots were those in that first line since the Filipino sailors would not have had the same training. For all Makarov knew, they were even worse shots than the NPA. He wouldn't have blamed them if that were the case. They were sailors. They were supposed to drive ships like he himself had done in the Russian Navy. They weren't Army soldiers or Marines.

But the NPA were just terrorists, insurgents, guerillas, whatever people wanted to call them. They were like the Chechens or Mujahideen for the Russians and the Soviets before them. To Makarov, they were fodder like the Russian prisoners given to a mercenary company in the Ukraine war. This battalion would be slaughtered for the greater good. They just didn't know it.

He pressed the button on the handset again, "North and east units, charge."

BALABAC NAVAL BASE

"What the hell are they doing?" Abraham said aloud. "They're standing up and charging. That's suicide." And that, she realized, was the intent of this wave. They were being sacrificed to force her people to expend their ammunition and hopefully take some of them out. They were fifty yards from the fence line, and the trenches were another thirty yards from the fence line to the base. That meant they had about ten to fifteen seconds before the NPA reached the fence line.

"North and east trenches, weapons free. I repeat, weapons free."

The trenches responded with a blithering volley taking down more NPA soldiers as some reached the ten-foot-tall chain-link fence only to die on it. A few NPA soldiers had cutters with them as they tried to help others gain entry.

Abraham relied on the north and east units as she looked back toward the ocean, which was clear, and then the southern flank. Were they trying to pull her folks from the southern trenches and create an opening? She decided to keep the southern trench units where they were. The NPA soldiers were falling rapidly. She heard a few yells but couldn't tell if they were from the fence line or the trenches.

The NPA to the north were nearly gone, but the eastern attack had breached the fence line in two places. She high-tailed it and joined the defense as she radioed for reinforcements from the northern trenches now that that threat had been temporarily eliminated.

One of her people had been shot, a bullet grazing his face. It would take some plastic surgery when they got out of here, but he'd survive. She had seen a lot worse. She raised her FNC and took aim at an NPA soldier, hitting him in the stomach. Two others were only ten yards away when one of her trench mates took them out. They were the last ones. Some hundred fifty NPA soldiers lay dead or seriously wounded between the jungle and the trenches. Her teams had probably expended a thousand rounds. And still there were more NPA soldiers somewhere out there.

FISHING VESSEL *SISON*

Makarov smiled as he watched the battle. He had identified at what point the defenders would open fire, some fifty yards from the fence. What was better is that a dozen NPA soldiers managed to get through the fence and almost to the trenches. That was with only one battalion. Highland Maritime would have no chance against the three battalions held in reserve, plus a surprise he planned.

CHAPTER 22

Silva spilled everything to Golzari as the road on the main expressway passed the Azorean tea plantations. Silva made fifty percent more money by taking a boat to the *Strident Yangkou* along with two of his coworkers whenever the ship was anchored off the town's waters. They always approached from the oceanside of the ship to avoid the transfer of people— *"people," in this case, meaning trafficked individuals,* Golzari thought. They were told to take photos of any women older than seventeen and text them to Jean-Pascal. Part of the deal of trafficking people was that he'd have his selection of two or three young women for his private estate to work or . . . work.

Golzari realized that Zheng R&D wouldn't have cared if he skimmed "profits" from the top. The actions in the Philippines weren't about making money in the trafficking business. It was about displacing a population and building contacts in illicit networks around the world. After a year, Jean-Pascal had more than twenty young women working at his estate on the side of a mountain overlooking the Atlantic Ocean.

According to Silva, Jean-Pascal Belanger only had about a dozen security officers working for him, with three or four on duty at any time. There was a fence around the property about ten feet high and was off one of the side roads so you couldn't see the house if you were passing in a car. Silva said there were no cameras, but motion sensors were along the walls. Besides the young women and the security, several people worked for him during the day—a chef, a butler, a maid, a landscaper.

Jean-Pascal Belanger was a French ex-pat who arrived on the island a decade before. Back then he was in legitimate commerce, as were they all. He served as an agent to several shipping companies passing through the Azores. It started with simple drug shipments, then more. Belanger made enough money from drugs to buy the estate. That's when other networks noticed him and when, last year, someone reached out to him about shipping people. The real money rolled in and he hired security to protect him, but he didn't think there was any real danger except for common thieves, and he didn't want to be disturbed.

That's the key, Golzari thought. Belanger had only been in the black market a short time in a backwater place compared to the bigger markets. The security were probably locals with as little experience as him. Any hired gun worth his weight was employed in the better-paying markets in Europe, Central and South America, Africa, and Asia. Hired guns didn't mind their job so long as the money was worth the risk. It sounded like the risk was low here, but so was the pay. Golzari had seen real money and the security it bought. Maybe this was the last break he needed. There was only one problem and he was sitting in the driver's seat, babbling about his family and how he needed to make sure they were taken care of.

Golzari had the address for Jean-Pascal Belanger's estate, a general lay of the land, and a man who was part of the trafficking network who could talk.

"What does your wife know of your work, Mr. Silva?" Golzari asked with an evil smile.

"Noth . . . nothing. She wouldn't approve. I have daughters the same age as some of those girls," he stammered.

"You have daughters, Mr. Silva? Forget your wife. What would your daughters think? Or do they socialize with these young women you pro-cured for Jean-Pascal?"

"No, no, of course not. They can't know. I just do it to help them and now I have to or I would be . . ."

"Shut up, Mr. Silva," Golzari said, pressing the gun into the man's gut as he looked at a map. He pointed to a position on the map. "Look at this. You know how to get here?"

"Yes, it's a remote place, but I know where it is."

"Drive there now."

Fifteen minutes later, Silva turned onto a side road and then another after that. Golzari hadn't seen a house for a couple of miles. They were on the eastern side of the island near the Reserva Natural Lagoa de Fogo. Other cars were just as absent. When they had driven another few minutes, Golzari told him to park near a clearing. The car stopped and Golzari told him to get out of the vehicle. Silva didn't move.

"Get . . . out . . . of . . . the . . . car."

Silva opened the door and walked away from the car as Golzari did the same.

"Stop right there and keep your back to me, Mr. Silva."

"Pl . . . please don't kill me. My family . . ."

"I'm sure there are a lot of families who didn't want to leave Balabac Island or have their children sold into slavery, Mr. Silva. You've been part of that."

"Please!" he implored as his body began to quiver.

"You have a wallet? Throw it to your left."

Silva reached into his right rear pocket and did as he was told.

"Take your clothes off and throw them to your left," Golzari ordered.

"What? Why?"

"Just do it!"

Silva did as he was told, first tossing his work shoes and then the rest of his clothes.

"Move forward until I tell you to stop." Silva went five more paces before Golzari ordered him to stop. He went over to the clothes. It was the smell that caught his attention first, and then he realized Silva had pissed all over himself after he got out of the car.

"Kneel," he said as the man obeyed.

"Please!" Silva said again.

"I want you to think about your wife and your daughters right now, Mr. Silva."

The man's ample mid-section shook with ripples as Silva could no longer contain his crying.

"I want you to think of them as you count to one hundred. Then you may do as you wish. But if you ever tell anyone about this or if you help

Jean-Pascal and people like him again, I will have my associates in Ponta Delgada pay you and your family a visit. Do you understand?"

"Yes, yes," Silva said through his heavy sobs.

Golzari tossed the clothes in the trunk and put the wallet next to him and drove a mile back from where they had come. He stopped again, tossed the clothes a few yards off the road under some low brush, and then continued on to meet Jean-Pascal Belanger.

PRIVATE SECURITY VESSEL *SYREN*

"You doing okay, Bobby?" Stark asked.

"All set, Captain," Fisk said at the helm.

"Don't eyeball the waves and break my ship," Stark said half-jokingly.

When *Syren* had been in the Navy's service, Stark had ensured a surface condition sensing radar with an appropriate angle of declination was mounted above the pilothouse. It provided information on the direction, speed, and length of waves to minimize the impact of a wave on a hull. On container ships, it helped account for wave and pitch.

Stark had taken an educated guess on the position of the NPA ships—at least the two former Philippine *Jacinto*-class cutters and the fishing vessel that was twice their size. He expected them to be about forty nautical miles—give or take ten nautical miles—from the island. *Syren* was making forty-five knots. He'd arrive in the area in about an hour, but *Syren* had its tethered Crow's Nest system up. *Syren* could make close to sixty knots for short sprints—hell, he'd even managed once to get her to sixty-five knots on her first trial before she started shaking apart, so they spec'd her out for sixty knots—but Crow's Nest could only keep up at forty-five. The advantage was that Crow's Nest allowed him to look over the horizon, and if he was correct, they'd see the NPA ships before they saw him.

Stark settled in the captain's chair, a chair that he first sat in aboard FSF-1 *Sea Fighter*—as *Syren* was originally called when it was designed and built by the Office of Naval Research—when he was a young lieutenant commander offered a chance to test out the ship. A thin brass plaque above the window in front of him read, "Save the crew if you lose the ship." It was the ship's unofficial motto when it was built. Few officers, especially junior officers, had a chance like that, and Stark jumped at it, despite the mark it put on him by some senior Naval Sea System Command officers who hated the project because it wasn't built by them. Moreover, it showed up the problems they had with the Littoral Combat Ships. FSF-1 was faster, more capable, and more innovative than LCS. It was also a hell of a lot less expensive.

He switched to his headset so that all the key crew were on the network simultaneously, then he reached for the monitor and keyboard, its arm extending so that it was close to him. He tapped in the URL for the commercial shipping site and typed the firm's password. Traffic would get heavier in the coming hour, and he needed to know how much room he had to maneuver.

"You awake, boss?" came Warren's voice over the network.

"Do I need to be?"

"You better. Crow's Nest is picking up three vessels. Two look a helluva lot alike *Jacinto*s. Bearing is zero-three-zero degrees off our starboard bow at two-five knots heading on course one-two-four degrees."

Stark's display didn't show those ships since their AIS was off, so he pictured the scenario. If both he and the NPA ships maintained course and speed, they'd see each other on the horizon in a few minutes. They'd pass within a nautical mile. He asked his navigator for a moboard to confirm.

That would be too close for Stark. The two *Jacinto*s had weapons that outranged anything *Syren* had.

There was something else on his screen. It was another anomaly well to the north of their position. The commercial shipping pattern had an unusual gap northeast of Hainan Island in China.

"Comms, Captain. Can you see what I'm looking at?"

"Copy, sir. I see your screen from down here."

"Do you see that break just northeast of Hainan? Can you loop the past two days like you did earlier but just focus on that area?"

"Yes, sir, and . . . there you go. You should see it now," Oliver said efficiently.

There it was, indeed. It wasn't just a gap. It looked like a goddamned parting of the Red Sea that started north of Hainan in . . . Zhanjiang. Commercial shipping was being rerouted, as some ships to the east slowed to single-digit knots, and those to the west were increasing their speed. Zhanjian? *Shit*, he thought.

"All hands, this is the captain. It looks like we've got an unknown number of Chinese Navy ships coming out of Zhanjiang, the home of their South Sea Fleet. If I'm tracking this correctly, they're on a course of approximately . . . one-seven-five straight for Balabac Island. That's a distance of a thousand nautical miles, but it seems they got under yesterday."

Stark did another calculation. Assuming an average of twenty-five-knot speed and the time and location that pattern started . . .

Shit, he thought again. PLA/N—the People's Liberation Army/Navy—as it was formally known.

"We could be looking at Chinese Navy ships between twenty and fifty nautical miles behind the NPA ships," he said into the headset. "China has already stated their support for the NPA, and I think they're sending ships to back up their support."

Was that the plan all along—for the NPA ships to meet the Chinese warships? This changed everything. He wasn't in a position, even with some EMP rockets, to take on warships. China now had three aircraft carriers. If one of those was in the mix, that added another layer of complexity since he had no air radar, and then there was the possibility of subs, and not even Jay Warren, with his box of tricks, could detect a sub. One might be below them right now and they'd have no way of knowing. And, since China publicly supported the NPA, which emerged from the "mercenary" attack on the naval base, *Syren* was as much of a target as his people at the base itself.

"Got'em, boss. That's definitely them dead ahead," Warren said, his voice higher than normal, like it was every time he got excited.

"'Them' who? The NPA or the Chinese warships?"

"Two *Jacinto*s and a fishing vessel.

"Helm, come right, steer course zero-nine-zero." Fisk repeated the order as was the requirement to ensure the conning officer or OOD was heard correctly. That new course wasn't enough, but now he was trying to buy some time.

POBLACIÓN I

"Every one of them? Every one of them! Dead! An entire battalion was not just defeated—they were decimated!"

Colonel—Chairman—Jose dela Cruz was less than pleased as he stormed around the one-story, former municipal building of Población I. As he screamed, he threw whatever he could around the room—papers from the previous local government, staples, a chair or two. His top lieutenants, Ernesto and Bitin, just watched him explode like a Tasmanian devil. Ernesto had been with Cruz the longest and had seen it all before. It didn't matter as much when they were on Mindanao. Back then he was just another second-rate guerilla leader whose penchant for childish tirades were witnessed by so few people that they could be ignored. Now the NPA was together as a force and with their families in a sovereign territory that had been recognized by the Philippine government and the Chinese.

Hu Tao and Makarov had told Ernesto that, in the first few days after the declaration, at least three dozen more countries aligned with China, and some, so heavily in debt to them, would also recognize their right as an independent island nation.

"Chairman dela Cruz," Ernesto began, "we have three more battalions. You saw the live video. Several of our people made it into the base. With three battalions, we will take it. Its defenders have nowhere to go. Their ships are too far to help them and they don't have more people. The Philippine government has renounced ownership of the base. The multinational armada that was supposed to sail past Balabac has broken apart, with only the United States Navy continuing. And our Chinese allies are sending forty-eight ships."

"Ernesto, everything has a price," dela Cruz said, calming down in speaking with his old friend. Old was relative since Ernesto Fuentes was only in his late thirties. He had been dela Cruz's organizer, his public relations officer, his logistics officer, his most trusted deputy, and his closest friend.

"Yes, it does, Jose," Ernesto said, chancing the familiarity.

Dela Cruz didn't seem to mind. "The price was that the Chinese would have basing rights at our naval base and they would expand it. It was a good price, Chairman. China, the world's largest navy, will now protect us. We aren't just struggling in the jungles of Cebu, or Mindanao, or Luzon, or a dozen other islands. And we aren't just some Pacific Island nation. We are going to be central to global diplomacy and strategic considerations. This is only the first step, Ernesto. Our next target is Palawan. We will grow in a way none of us or our fathers before us ever considered possible."

As dela Cruz continued to settle down, Bitin cleaned the top of her leader's desk from what he had thrashed about. It had to look like the seat of power and not the victim of some tropical storm. She straightened the flag behind the desk that would serve as the background for any recorded or live address by the chairman. Bitin dismissed the two guards by the door. She had known both of them before on Cebu Island. They were courageous, loyal, and trusted fighters for the cause, the right cause, and the right person.

"Ernesto, are Makarov's ships still going where they need to?" Bitin asked as she rolled the chair so that it was flush with the desk and symmetrically aligned with each side.

"Yes, he was waiting for the Chinese warships to be closer before he began his final run," he told her as dela Cruz walked over to a mirror to preen in his forest green uniform that was clean from never having been in battle.

"Do we need to worry about the US Navy?" she asked as she took her place to the right of the desk.

Ernesto walked across the room to dela Cruz's side and tugged on his blouse. "Here, Jose. There are a few creases that don't look appropriate."

"Thank you, my friend," the chairman said, closing his eyes and reveling in the moment at the cusp of power.

"Once the ships we took are back at the naval base, we can issue a statement declaring victory for the people. I would not parade the bodies we kill. It's a new era and we need to show something more refined for the world's media," Ernesto said as he turned dela Cruz toward him to fix his lapels.

"Why, Ernesto? We have legitimacy. We have our nation, and we have the Chinese. We should hang every mercenary body around the basin. It will strike fear in people elsewhere. It will show them what we can do if we wish."

"I don't agree. We need to be savvier," Fuentes said, looking his leader in his now open eyes. "And we need a speech after the statement. It must be like nothing in the past. We must be diplomatic."

"I don't think so, Ernesto. But you write something for me. You always know what to say."

"Yes, yes I do, Jose," Ernesto said, grabbing dela Cruz firmly by the lapels.

A pirah was a large, convex knife smaller than a sword indigenous to the Philippines, especially on Cebu and other nearby islands. At this moment, a pirah had been firmly planted in Jose dela Cruz's back. He still wasn't sure what had just happened as he was practically lifted off his feet momentarily. Ernesto released his hold as dela Cruz fell on his back, driving the blade even further through, nearly piercing the front of his uniform. He looked up helplessly at Ernesto, his loyal lieutenant, as he struggled to find his breath.

Ernesto just looked down on the colonel, the chairman, the madman, as Bitin sidestepped dela Cruz's body and stood closer to Ernesto than she ever had to the NPA's leader. She pressed her body against his as Ernesto wrapped his arm around her and kissed her. The kiss of betrayal was the last thing dela Cruz ever saw.

CHAPTER 23

The media was in a pandemonium trying to get more information from the press secretary about the president's condition. All she could tell them was that Marine One had transported him to Bethesda Naval Hospital (some naval stalwarts still refused to call it by its new name, Walter Reed National Military Medical Center). And, she admitted, he was in surgery, so the vice president had returned to the White House from his home at the Naval Observatory. Constitutional experts and medical professionals immediately appeared on the cable news networks to discuss what happens when a president is incapacitated. Only two vice presidents since the ratification of the Twenty-Fifth Amendment in 1967—George H. W. Bush and Dick Cheney—had become acting president under Section 3 of the amendment, which happened when a president voluntarily transferred his authority. No one had become acting president under Section 4, where a vice president notified the Speaker of the House and the Senate president pro tempore that the president was unable to discharge the powers and duties of his office. Until now.

Vice President—Acting President—Susan Szukalski sat in the president's chair of the Cabinet Room. With her were the secretary of state, defense secretary, DoD senior judge advocate, National Security Advisor Sumner, the chairman of the Joint Chiefs, and the Chief of Naval Operations. Szukalski had neck-length red hair and wore wide-rimmed glasses. She was much taller than Sumner but stocky, tough like her father whom she'd succeeded in the Chicago congressional seat. When Dunner won election, he selected the fourteen-term House Appropriations member from Chicago to serve as his vice president. It was a good balance for the lifelong diplomat to have someone senior from the Hill to help with his domestic agenda. Now, she faced a foreign policy crisis that had come out of nowhere.

"This is new territory for all of us. I know we all wish the president well and a speedy recovery. I also know that he'd want us to carry on. Ambassador Sumner, would you please get things started?"

Sumner briefed her on the situation with a large map of the region. China was sending forty-eight ships to Balabac Island—or the People's Republic of Balabac—that included an aircraft carrier, forty-four destroyers and frigates, and the landing ship *Kunlun Shan*, able to transport up to eight hundred soldiers. Most were from the South Sea Fleet, while it was augmented by a force from the East Sea Fleet base. China had recognized the new island nation and was apparently backing it up with a show of force.

"Don't we have ships in the region?" Szukalski asked the Chief of Naval Operations. "I've seen slides about the multinational exercise."

"Yes, Madam . . ." the CNO paused, not knowing how to refer to her. Was it Madam Vice President or Madam Acting President? Szukalski was politically aware enough to understand the pause.

"Just tell me what you know, Admiral, and we'll worry about titles later," she said.

"The multinational exercise has been reduced to only US Navy ships. Since China announced their intent to support Balabac, the other countries terminated their participation in the exercise."

"Can you or anyone tell me why we have these exercises if they don't actually help in a goddamned crisis?" she said in a subdued tone. "Actually, let's debate that later. How many ships do we have?"

"Thirty-one," the CNO responded.

"So, we're outnumbered forty-eight to thirty-one without the international ships. Can we take them if we have to?"

The room was silent as she waited for an answer.

"That shouldn't be a difficult question," she said. "How many times have you testified before Appropriations and the first sentence is that we have the best military in the world. Do we?"

Again, no one across from her wanted to answer, fearing it would likely leak to the press.

"If I may," Sumner interjected, taking the heat off her colleagues as her silenced phone vibrated with a call from someone named Melanie Arden. "Even if our allies had remained with the fleet, I'm not sure they would have remained given the legal complexity. But the question is if it's worth starting a war over Balabac. Arguably, if China has recognized and supports this island nation, it could be a play to get a foothold further out from their chain of militarized islands in the South China Sea. Balabac has a new—albeit small—naval base. We could see China getting leasing rights and building it up. That would mean they'd have control of one of the major straits in the region. More importantly, having a base on that island changes the dynamics of sovereign territory."

"We can't stop them militarily. Do we have anything else in our quiver?" she asked.

"Normally we would reach out to the Philippine government," the secretary of state offered. "President Quinta would never have allowed Balabac to secede, and Reyes is apparently pro-China."

"No shit," the plain-spoken Chicagoan replied. "What about challenging the legality? I saw a clip on the news of some Philippine officer at the base saying it's the New People's Army that seceded. Didn't we declare them terrorists after 9/11?"

"That's true of the NPA, but the media is also suggesting the claim of that Philippine Navy officer was false," the secretary of state said. "Several US-based cable news stations have dismissed the video upon pressure from the Chinese government."

"That news was coming out of Hong Kong," Sumner snapped back. "That's clearly China trying to discredit what's happening there. And there are US citizens on that island."

"What?" Szukalski asked. "Are they tourists?"

"No, ma'am. A US-based private security firm had been contracted by the Philippine government to be part of a training exercise on the island when the cyberattacks occurred. They've been there at the base with the Philippine sailors they were training."

CJ's phone kept vibrating with a call from Melanie Arden.

Szukalski tossed her pen down and pushed her chair back.

"Let me understand this correctly. The people on that island declared independence, the Philippine government accepted that, China endorsed it, and they're sending a fleet that could fuck ours, our allies have abandoned us, and all that's there is passage through one of many straits in the region and the only Americans there are mercenaries? Admiral, you recall that fleet. Get them out of there and give them liberty in Hawaii. We're done."

The press secretary knocked on the door and was let in. "I'm sorry to disturb you, but there's a report from a journalist that just went up."

"Can it wait?" Szukalski asked impatiently.

"Madam Vi—Um, it's about the situation in the Philippines. The journalist said that the island's population was displaced and trafficked, a lot were killed, and the New People's Army were transported in so they could declare independence. A company in China may be involved. It's a pretty long story, but that sums it up."

"Jesus, is this one of those conspiracy stories from one of the radical media?" Szukalski replied as she removed her glasses.

"No, ma'am. This is a credible and well-respected foreign reporter. I've dealt with her before. Melanie Arden."

Sumner sat up straight and looked at her phone again, texting Arden, who said there could be more to the story and needed to talk.

"We need to push this out," Sumner said, looking up. "Both media and our partners, starting first with the countries that were part of the exercise. How far are the US ships from Balabac, Admiral?" she asked.

"Based on their current speed, about five hours," he said gruffly.

"We have time. I think we should see how the international community reacts to this. If China is behind this, then we have the moral authority we need to reject the claim and continue on to the Balabac Strait," she argued.

Szukalski thought about it for a moment as she clasped her hands.

"Any other thoughts?" she asked, looking at each person. They simply seemed to nod in agreement with the national security advisor.

"Okay. Two hours. Contact our partners from the exercise. We'll reconvene then."

PRIVATE SECURITY VESSEL *SYREN*

The three New People's Army ships remained on a direct course for Balabac, and based on Stark's latest calculation, they were headed right for the naval base. It was likely that a Chinese fleet was somewhere behind them. Stark couldn't do anything about the warships, but he could take on two stolen ships and the fishing vessel where he had seen naval base personnel, including its commanding officer, executed by the NPA. He was matching course and speed for now.

"Captain, comms."

"Go ahead," Stark said steadily on the headset.

"Sir, two inbound messages. First one from the naval base. They successfully defended against approximately a buck and a half of NPAs. They had a couple of wounded they interrogated. One of them said there were hundreds more at Población I getting ready for a second attack. But there are two hundred more on a fishing vessel that's inbound."

"Copy," Stark acknowledged. "That was why they probably got the two warships, in order to cover the ad hoc troop transport. Why have two hundred soldiers on a ship when it would be easier to have all their troops together? Why separate them?"

"Bennington," Fisk said without changing his direction so that he could focus on the information on the screens.

"Your old ship?" Stark asked quizzically.

"No, sir, your old battle—or at least your great-great-great-great grandfather's."

Bennington was a battle fought in Vermont during the American Revolution. Stark's ancestor, General John Stark, commanded the 2nd New Hampshire Regiment and defeated a force of Hessian, Canadian, British, and Indian soldiers. General Stark had a two-to-one advantage.

"I'm still not following, Bobby."

"That force was heading down to Saratoga. Because General Stark defeated them and led to a loss of supplies for the British, the Americans were able to defeat the British at the Battle of Saratoga. Maybe this is the NPA's version of bringing in a force from a different direction."

"Is there another benefit?" Stark asked, contemplating the maneuver.

"If that ship went into the basin and dumped two hundred soldiers in the middle of the base, that would be a bad day for us," Fisk stated.

"I think you're right, XO. Jay? You hearing this?"

"Oh yeah. I think Fisk is right. The tethered camera has a bead on those ships now. Whole lotta folks on the fishing vessel."

Stark was still concerned about the Chinese warships somewhere over the horizon, whose number he didn't know, or if some submarine or jet bomber was targeting them even now. *Syren*, however, had some advantages. It had the stealth paint job in addition to its low radar signature due to its hull design, much like an *Arleigh Burke*-class destroyer. The aluminum hull and the sound-dampening technology that had gone into its construction further reduced the ability of other ships to see them.

He then realized Oliver Riddle hadn't given him the second message.

"Comms, Captain. Sorry about that. What's the other message?"

"Headquarters in Maine said a CJ Sumner was trying to reach you."

First Golzari, now CJ. He hadn't heard from either in a few months.

"You got a number?" Stark asked.

"Aye, sir. Patch one through?"

"Yes, please. My headset only. Actually, standby. Jay, can you mount one of the Jewels on the Crow's Nest?"

"Um, uh, uh, uh, nope. Can't do it. Too heavy, boss. Crow's Nest can only carry twenty pounds. The camera alone is five pounds. The rocket is fifty pounds."

"What if you remove the casing for the propellant? How much is the warhead?"

"Just the warhead? About ten pounds."

"Good. Do you have something in your mad scientist lab where you could remotely detonate it?"

"Yup, yup, yup. Got stuff. And it's only a pound or so. We're good on the drone's carrying capacity," Stark's mad scientist said, almost giggling.

"One more thing, if we untether the drone, how long can it stay aloft?"

"Boss, you serious? We need Crow's Nest and it's our only one."

"I know. We need to stop those ships even more."

"There's a fail-safe battery in case the tether was broken so we wouldn't lose the drone. You'd get seven or eight minutes tops, but all you get is stationary. It won't have enough backup battery power to fly anywhere unless you want to reduce the dwell time."

"Give me a second," Stark said as he pulled a pen and pad of paper onto his lap. He had hated math questions in high school that started, "if a car went east at 60 mph and a car heading west at 20 mph . . ." but that was exactly what he'd have to calculate. He checked their speed. They were steady at twenty knots on a course south by southeast. *Syren* was eleven miles ahead of the NPA ships. If the drone was aloft and stationary for seven minutes at the current datum, the NPA ships would arrive at this spot in about thirty minutes; he hoped that the current wasn't significant enough to throw off the math too much. That meant if he detonated the EMP warhead before Crow's Nest ran out of juice, it would have no impact on the ships. The warhead only had a range of a one-kilometer radius based on his experience in Sri Lanka.

"XO, reduce speed to five knots."

"Five knots, aye." The ship jerked a bit, then slowed to the prescribed speed.

"Jay, retract the tether and bring in Crow's Nest. How much time do you need to get the warhead and remote on it?"

"Twenty to thirty minutes," Warren replied.

"Start now. XO, mark this position."

"Marking position, aye," Fisk said clearly.

Stark calculated at his new rate and theirs that he'd have a little over an hour before he could use the EMP.

"XO, I want to know if there's any change in their course and speed. You have the conn."

Stark left the pilothouse and walked onto the massive deck as he watched Crow's Nest, nearly four hundred feet above them, slowly lower on its tether as a crewman hovered over the system to ensure nothing was caught.

"Comms, Captain. Make that call directly to my headset only."

FURNAS, SÃO MIGUEL, AZORES

Damien Golzari drove by some sheet metal shacks and another farm, careful not to run into a stray cow in the middle of the road as he had once done in Ireland. Some seventy thousand cows, mostly Holsteins, lived on this 287-square-mile island. That was one cow for every two people. The place was rich agriculturally. He passed some tea plantations. If memory served him, the Portuguese were introduced to tea when they began trading with China in the sixteenth century. In the nineteenth century, the Azoreans brought in a Chinese master tea maker, Lau-a-Pan, to teach them how to produce and prepare tea. The climate in the Azores was perfect for tea. Golzari also recalled the reason he hadn't seen any fishing vessels in the harbor or anywhere offshore. The European Union had shut down the Azorean fishing fleet and then mandated what they were to grow.

He double-checked the map and the address Silva had given him. A few tourist buses were ahead of him as he entered the town of Furnas, appropriately named because of the fumaroles. Dotted around the town with another clump at one intersection surrounded by garden paths, they were popular tourist stops. Signs in Portuguese had individual names for each of these vents that emitted steam, vestiges of the island's volcanic history. Each was about six feet in diameter, surrounded by two layers of stone. As Golzari's car was behind one bus at an intersection of cobblestone streets, he read the sign of one: "Caldeira do Asmodeu." Some of the springs probably had pipes that led to the spa he'd just passed.

Furnas was on the northeast side of Lagoa das Furnas, a crater lake with a six-mile walking trail around it. According to the map, Jean-Pascal Belanger's estate was on the west side of the lake, well above the path. It was one of the highest points on São Miguel, along with the other dormant volcanoes. After Golzari passed through town, he pulled off to the side of the road when he saw another fumarole's ten-foot steam plume. Most of the traffic seemed to be on the south and eastern roads rather than this one. He got out of the car, walked over to the steaming water, and looked around to ensure no one saw him. He took out his burner phone, removed the SIM card, snapped it in two pieces, and tossed one of them in the steaming water. After confirming it would sink, he walked another thirty feet toward a grove. He used the back of his heel to dig into the dirt and placed the second half of the SIM card, buried it, and then covered it with dead brush.

Golzari returned to the vehicle and drove the last leg of his journey as he recalled the steps he had taken. The facilitator at the trafficking house in Paris, Abdou Mansouri, was dead. The lorry driver who had taken trafficked children to Paris was dead. The captain of the ship that transported all the Molbogs—at least all they didn't kill along the way—was dead. Silva, who had helped the traffickers on the island, was naked and running for his life, miles away. The Chinese company responsible for trafficking them—Zheng R&D—was reported to Robert at MI5, to Golzari's freelance reporter ex-wife, and to the US National Security Advisor, Ambassador Sumner, for whom he had worked.

In the old days, in his brief stint as a Boston police officer, he would arrest someone, bring them in, process the paperwork, and then go right back on the street. During his much longer career in the Diplomatic Security Service, he spent his days and nights protecting diplomats, beginning with then-Ambassador John Dunner, who had once spirited Golzari's family out of Iran during the Revolution. Years later he was Dunner's protective detail when Dunner served as deputy secretary of state. And then there was Ambassador Sumner. It had been a decent career upholding the law and protecting those who advanced the rule of law. His post-Diplomatic Security Service life, however, had been fraught with nighttime illegal entries and deaths, but at least no paperwork to worry about or petty bureaucracies that prevented action. Had it really just been forty-eight hours since he followed Abdou Mansouri that last time?

He reached Belanger's residence, or at least a simple guard shack fifty yards from the main road. He slowed and stopped next to it as a security guard in a black T-shirt, blue jeans, and holstered gun approached him cautiously with the universal sign to roll down his window. He was sinewy, not one of the standard muscle men hired by petty despots or despot-wannabes.

"I'm here to see Mr. Belanger about a possible job," he said to the guard, who eyed him warily.

"He not hiring," he said in broken English.

"He hasn't met me yet. I have experience and come highly recommended. Tell him Captain Antonov sent me." Golzari was rolling the dice yet again. Word might have gotten out about the *Strident Yangkou* being taken, and it was possible that Antonov was named as someone who had been killed aboard the ship. It was unlikely that Belanger would have had contact with Antonov. Belanger's role was to push cargo through to Europe. That's when he would most likely communicate with the captain unless his intermediaries did. He wouldn't have any reason to communicate with him once the cargo had been delivered.

"Stay in the car," the guard said, returning to the shack. He turned his back to Golzari. No experienced guard would have done that. The guard said something on the phone, looked back at Golzari, nodded as he instinctively looked into the phone—again, not the mark of someone who should always keep their eyes on a threat—and waved Golzari to continue on.

CHAPTER 24

PRIVATE SECURITY VESSEL *SYREN*

"It's been a while," Stark said into his headset as he kept track of any ships in the area. The three NPA ships were still well to their stern.

"I know. We've been busy. I see you have as well," CJ Sumner said, telling him about the news reports.

Stark recounted the major events of the past few days and told her he'd have Warren send video from the computer building to her. She returned the favor by filling him in as much as she could about the broader situation, including the Chinese force that was far larger than he realized.

"How's the president?" he asked.

"We just got word that he's in surgery."

"He's a good man. We need people like him. What about Golzari?"

"Nothing since he contacted his ex-wife—Melanie. I'll see what I can find out."

"What do you need me to do?" he asked his former Senate officemate and running partner. He had long since forgiven her for not defending him in his court-martial when he accepted that only he had made those choices. No one else had to be dragged into it.

"Can you and Commander Castillo hold the base for a couple of hours?"

"I don't know."

"Give it your best shot, Connor. We need time for word and the channels to work on this one. Don't get killed—just do your best."

"I got this one, CJ. Gotta go. The ships are catching up to us."

The drone was fully retracted as Warren and one of the specialists opened their toolboxes and got to work. Stark was about to return to the starboard-side pilot house, which one of his sailors referred to as the cockpit of the Millennium Falcon from Star Wars for being oddly asymmetrical, when he opted to make better use of the next few minutes by going below to the armory. He donned one of the remaining Kevlar vests and grabbed a rifle and ammo. He still had his 9mm Beretta at his side. He snagged two more vests and rifles for Fisk and the chief engineer (CHENG) and took them up.

Stark took the helm from Fisk as he and the CHENG snapped on their vests and checked their rifles as if it was all just another day at the office. The radar still showed the three ships at twenty knots and closing on *Syren*. In the next few minutes, the ships would notice their hull, or at least their unstealthy wake. A few ships appeared in the distance, but all were freighters and tankers, making the run through the South China Sea. If they were doing so, the Chinese warships weren't immediately nearby.

After fifteen minutes, Warren called up to the pilothouse.

"Crow's Nest is ready to go."

"Let her fly, Jay."

A minute later, Stark handed the helm back to Fisk and went to the aft window to watch Crow's Nest rise as its tether followed like a snake following a charmer's pungi.

"All hands, this is the captain," Stark said into the headset with his baritone. "If you don't have your vest and a weapon, get to the armory now. We have about five minutes before the show starts."

Stark was just about right in his estimate. The ships approached the initial position and would soon approach the point where he'd need to let Crow's Nest loose.

"Bobby, how far apart are those ships?"

"They're playing it tight. The fishing vessel is in the middle with the *Jacinto*s about four hundred yards abeam of each."

Stark did another mental calculation. *The further those ships are apart, the smaller the window for knocking them out. If the EMP has a radius of a kilometer, that's about eight hundred yards or about . . . three-quarters of a kilometer . . . shit, this will be close.*

"Bobby, we're going to need to get out of range really fast so we're not affected by the EMP."

"Aye. Standing by, Captain."

"All right, Jay—let her go." Nearly as soon as he said that, the tether fell away as most of it fell to the deck and began to retract, but some three hundred feet dropped in the water on the port side when Stark realized neither he nor Warren had thought about the possibility it would jeopardize the port engine by getting caught up in it.

"Bobby, cut the port side engine. Stop now!"

"Port engine stop, aye." The ship slowed another two knots. They were barely moving now.

"Jay, can you retract faster?"

"It's as fast as it'll go," he reported over comms.

Another minute went by until he was relieved to see the end of the tether snap over the port side and retract into the winch, where it continued to spin.

"Okay, helm, take—"

"Problem, sir. The ships are veering off," Fisk said. Stark grabbed his binoculars and could see it. It wasn't happening fast, but he guessed they finally realized what the ship ahead of them was and were separating to out-flank *Syren* since they didn't know her true top speed. They were only six miles astern of *Syren*.

"Jay, move Crow's Nest. Put it as close to the middle of the fishing vessel and the *Jacinto* to its port." Stark watched the drone hover and then move to their port quarter, but he realized directing it to close that gap meant it might not reach its intended target.

"Splash, splash, splash, off the starboard bow!" Fisk said loudly.

Stark saw it. The unmistakable splash of a naval round. It was a few hundred yards from them but close enough that he realized the *Jacinto*s were within maximum firing range. They had the older OTO Melara 76mm naval guns, with a max range of about sixteen thousand meters. The other two weapons aboard those ships—the .50 cal and the Oerlikon 20mm cannon had an effective range of about two thousand and one thousand meters, respectively. They'd be in max firing range soon as well. More rounds landed a quarter mile to port, while another round was close enough to reverberate off the starboard bulkhead.

"That's enough. Helm, all ahead flank. Hang on, everyone," he said to the crew on the network. *Syren* dug into the water and picked up speed. Ten, twenty, and soon fifty-eight knots. Stark kept his binoculars trained on Crow's Nest.

"How much longer until it's in range, Jay?"

"About thirty seconds, but it's running out of power."

Five hundred feet, fifty-pound drone and what it's carrying . . . About five seconds, Stark thought.

"Jay, give it what it has left. All power to elevation and mark every one hundred feet." The drone stopped, then went straight up as he had ordered. Warren marked each elevation: six hundred, seven hundred, eight hundred . . . When it reached 1,100 feet, the power cut off.

"Stand by for my order, Jay . . . Hold . . ."

Crow's Nest began a slow tumble toward the sea.

"Now!"

Stark looked away instinctively as soon as he saw the blue flash.

FURNAS, SÃO MIGUEL, AZORES

One security guard accounted for, Golzari thought as he continued on the long, winding driveway. Gates opened as the car approached. A tall stucco fence with anti-climb spikes was on both sides, probably surrounding the property. Another minute later, the road opened up to a wide-open tiered estate. Flowering trees made way for the first tier and a parking area. There were three cars outside a three-car garage with an apartment on top. That was either for the landscaper or the night guards. Golzari parked alongside one of the vehicles and was met by another guard who motioned to accompany him up the first flight of stairs to the second tier of raised beds of flowers and vegetables. A young Filipina was restringing a lattice. She was clad in a white tank top, shorts, and sandals. She only glanced momentarily in his direction and returned to her work.

The next set of stairs led to the third and final tier with the main house. Another Filipina girl was washing interior windows but never looked at them. The guard escorted Golzari around the side through a gate. To the right was a fumarole like he'd seen in the town, with the same level of steam rising from it and larger stones. There was a small guest house on the right just beyond that. Behind it were more flower and vegetable gardens tended by yet another girl in her teens. Through the trees, he saw a path that led to a single-story building that looked like a cheap no-tell motel with about a dozen doors and windows. This was probably for the staff or, more likely, for the Molbogs.

The area opened up to a large pool. A middle-aged man with more hair on his chest than on his head rested on a lounge chair beneath an umbrella. Another young woman clad in a short white tunic handed him a drink as he read a book. To his side was a third guard. This one was bigger than the other two. He worked out—a lot. Any T-shirt would have been tight on him, but he seemed to purposely wear a size smaller to accentuate his muscles even more. He was bald with a trim beard and, like the other two guards, had exposed holstered guns. That was for in-timidation—either for visitors or the girls held on the property. He took a step closer to Golzari, who carefully opened his blazer to show his own gun. The guard asked for it but Golzari shook his head.

"There are three of you, at least," he said casually. "I'm here for a job, not a fight."

The man on the lounge chair dismissed the girl, who kept her eyes down as she departed.

"Captain Antonov recommended you? How is the good captain?" Belanger asked in better English than his guards or Silva. Golzari had to remember he was a French ex-pat, not native Portuguese.

"Dead," Golzari said. "I was informed by my network that his ship was in Le Havre and he and others were killed during their last delivery."

Belanger straightened up, indicating to Golzari that he didn't know what had happened.

"Who killed him?" Belanger asked in a monotone voice.

"I don't know. All I heard was that it happened before the port au-thorities and police arrived."

"And why do you come to me for a job?"

"I needed to leave France. My employer there was killed."

"You live in a dangerous world. Who was your employer?"

"Abdou Mansouri. He and the night team in Paris were killed. When my partner and I showed up to his house in Paris for the day shift, we saw the Sûreté everywhere. I knew the truck driver who delivered the cargo." Golzari motioned with his head toward two of the girls who were sunbathing on the other side of the pool. "He introduced me to Antonov. He was the one who recommended that I see you since this is far enough from France, and there is no jurisdiction here to take me back if Mansouri left any files with my name on them."

"I see," Belanger said looking him up and down. "Do you have any credentials on you that would confirm this?"

"No. I have nothing but what I have told you because I had no time to get my belongings. I worked for Mansouri for close to a year in Paris. Before that, I was in Yemen working for a private security company for several years."

"What is your name?"

"If I work for you, you can call me whatever you want," Golzari said stoically. "All I want is a place to do my job away from everything. And the weather here is better than most places I've worked."

Belanger managed a laugh.

"*Bien sûr, mon ami*," the trafficker replied. "You want anonymity— you may have it if your story checks out. But for now, let's have a chat about your experience. Sit down." Belanger waved to the nearby table as he rose to join Golzari. He called to one of the sunbathing young women, who immediately rose and went to the house.

"She'll bring some food and drink. You prefer wine or one of the locally-made liqueurs?"

"Thank you. I don't drink when I'm on duty," Golzari said with a half-smile.

"You aren't hired—yet."

"I'm on your property and with you. I may not be getting paid yet, but I am not drinking so long as I have my gun."

"A good answer." Belanger told his closest guard to check him for wires. He found none but did catch the gun on his calf.

"Two guns? You're a man who takes precautions. As do I," he noted as he looked up to the roof where a fourth guard had a rifle looking down on them.

PRIVATE SECURITY VESSEL *SYREN*

One *Jacinto* and the fishing vessel were now dead in the water, their electronics fried from the electromagnetic pulse burst first employed by the Tamil Sea Tigers and modified by Stark's company. Before the drone began to fall, Warren had taken video of the fishing vessel's deck, chock full of New People's Army soldiers armed with rifles.

The other *Jacinto* continued to fire at *Syren* at maximum range, but the NPAs manning it had minimal expertise with it. Stark had figured the NPA must have co-opted some Philippine Navy sailors to have used the gun at all, otherwise they wouldn't have been able to operate them. One round pierced the starboard hull just forward of the engine room, exploding near the galley. Stark ordered the damage control team to the deck as he confirmed the round hadn't slowed the ship's acceleration more than a few seconds.

"Orders, Captain?" Fisk asked calmly.

Syren had more than twice the maximum speed as the remaining *Jacinto*. If the *Jacinto* went to the aid of the two other ships, they'd be delayed even longer from their intended destination. *Syren* had no long-range weapons, and it would take too long for Warren to modify . . . or would it?

"Jay, we've got another rocket, right?"

"Last one. We gave two to Abraham and Castillo."

"Can we put one in a DP-14?"

"I would but I got no more remote detonators," Warren replied apologetically.

The clock was running out. *Syren* had accomplished its primary mission. Those two hundred NPA soldiers weren't getting to the anticipated fight anywhere on time. Two of their three ships were inoperable and the third would take at least an hour and a half to get to Balabac. *Syren* wasn't a warship and couldn't take on one that had even fifty-year-old guns due to their range. And very soon, a fleet of Chinese warships would be steaming toward him.

"All hands, this is the captain. Report on damage as soon as possible. Since the NPA soldiers' ship is disabled, we are heading back to Balabac to help our shipmates. Captain, out."

Bobby looked at him, slightly disappointed.

"I wish we could have finished them off, Captain."

"Next time, Bobby. Next time. *Syren* has her strengths, but after this mission, I think you, Jay, and I need to do some hard creative thinking."

Fisk smiled approvingly. His mind was already at work on what he would do with *Syren* and *Minerva*.

"Maybe we can start with something now. Jay, if you're not busy, I could use your help reinforcing the forward bulkhead of the pilothouse and the two forward .50 cals."

FISHING VESSEL *SISON*

"We lost the connection to two of the ships, sir," Toni said dispassionately to Makarov. "The third vessel reports *Syren*'s drone started falling out of the sky when there was a flash and the other ships just lost all power."

"EMP?"

"It sounds like it. They must have gotten them from the Sea Tigers. I wonder how much hafnium they got?" she asked of the very rare earth element that Zheng R&D had helped the Sea Tigers develop.

"There were hafnium bars on the ship Stark took in Sri Lanka," Makarov said, realizing the immediate and long-term implications of dealing with the private security company. "It's good we weren't with them. We'll pull into Población I in a half hour. The reserve force just started marching toward the naval base."

"We have other problems, Sergei. The media has picked up a story about the trafficking of the Molbog population and how the NPA displaced them. It gets worse. Zheng R&D is mentioned."

"I know, Toni. The Chinese fleet is on its way. There isn't much that can stop them now. They don't have to care, just like Putin didn't care about the global reporters in Ukraine when the war started. In this case, the Philippine government has given them the green light."

"Yes, but only so long as Reyes is in power. Can they hold the naval base?" she asked.

"A few dozen men and women with small arms against eight hundred? Plus, when the NPA is in range, two hundred of them will launch a surprise to distract the Filipinos and Highland Maritime. We know where their trenches are. We know the distances. And they have nowhere to fall back to except the water."

MANILA

Felipe Reyes sat at his desk with his press secretary and chief of staff, debating the implications of the media storm erupting around them, when Lieutenant General Eduardo Fuentes, Commanding General of the Philippine Army, marched in without knocking. The short, barrel-chested general was accompanied by six soldiers, all with their weapons drawn. Reyes wasn't stupid. Another soldier held a video camera with a red light, signifying it was recording. He knew exactly what this was about.

"Felipe Reyes," he said in a measured voice. "You assumed office upon the death of President Quinta. We have learned that her plane was intentionally shot down by a traitorous Air Force officer. We have evidence that the New People's Army, working with human traffickers, eliminated the native Molbog population on Balabac Island. We have evidence that the New People's Army, working with a Chinese company, was responsible for the cyberattacks that so disrupted commerce and endangered Filipino lives. We will present this information at your trial to determine how much you were aware of the plot against our president, our government, our people, and our territory.

"You and your staff will be held in detention until that trial. On behalf of our people, I am assuming the duties of acting president until free and fair elections are held and the integrity of our people is restored."

The light went off as Reyes sank further into the chair.

CHAPTER 25

At first, they looked like bats, but most bats flew around dusk or during the night. Sivan Abraham was the first to notice them. A swarm was rising over the hill to the east. They weren't moving in a zig-zag like bats.

"Commander Castillo," she said to the Filipino officer. "It's time to get your people out of the whalers and to their stations."

Castillo concurred and began waving to his sailors to follow him as he tossed his crutches and pushed away the pain in his leg so he could move faster.

The "bats" flew over the eastern perimeter. Most flew together but about a quarter went wrong ways or heights. Abraham figured there were a couple hundred of them—then, as the buzzing grew louder, she realized it was a swarm of small drones the size of bats. A Highland Maritime security officer shot at one, causing Abraham to order all of them to hold their fire. The bats rose more as they closed in on the fence line, then started diving en masse through the trenches, never touching the shooters, just bouncing and flying like a master dangles a ball of string at a cat.

Abraham heard the shouting emerging from the outer perimeters, and she realized what was happening. These were just cheap commercial drones with no kinetic ability, but collectively, they could distract the shooter. They were designed for home use—cheap and easy to learn how to fly. That was when she ran to the Highland Jewels, depressing the launch button on one as she rolled away. One rocket shot up a hundred feet above the trenches and detonated with a light blue flash, destroying the circuitry and connections of every drone as they fell to the ground on top of and around the trenches.

"Highlanders, fall back to position Bravo," Abraham yelled into the radio. "I repeat, fall back to position Bravo." Only then did she realize all their radios were affected as well. She turned to hand-signs as effectively as they had been for thousands of years. If Jay Warren was right about the baby jewels, the impact area was only a hundred feet or so, beyond the range of the boats in the basin.

All the Highlanders jumped out of their trenches and ran at full speed toward the headquarters Quonset hut and then toward the pier behind *Townsville*. From there they took positions on the seaside of the breakwater, protected by concrete and rocks.

The first attack that day had exposed their positions in the trenches and shown they couldn't hold back a larger force from the fence line. They needed a plan B. New People's Army soldiers approached all three sides of the base; the fence would only hold them off for a couple of minutes.

Abraham signaled to Castillo as she followed the last of the Highlanders to the fallback position.

On *Townsville*'s bridge, Castillo gave a simple order to his sailors on-board: "Fire!"

The *Townsville* exploded with a hail of bullets. Some sailors manned the two M242 Bushmaster 25mm chain gun, spitting out two hundred rounds a minute that could hit anything within three thousand meters. The guns chewed up the dirt and NPA soldiers alike on the killing field to the east. The remainder of the sailors were lying prone on the deck, focusing their shots on the soldiers cutting through the north fence line. Once the Highlanders took their position along the breakwater, they added the fire support of the FNC rifles.

More than eight hundred of the NPA horde emerged from the wood line. Three-quarters of them made it to the fence line. Half were now making their way past the trenches and around the Quonset huts. The two sides had reached a slower impasse as *Townsville*'s 25mm guns tore through the aluminum huts. The NPA had nowhere to advance on *Townsville* or positions on the breakwater because of the basin between them. Their only chance was to move more soldiers to the north side and Abraham knew it.

With both sides focusing the firefight across the basin as the Boston whalers and their wooden finger piers became the latest victims of the crossfire, no one had paid attention to the ocean.

As the NPA from the south side of the base began their move to the north side, two deafening 150-decibel horns blasted for a full minute as *Syren*'s boxy bow glided into the basin. Its two forward .50 caliber mounts ripped away at the enemy soldiers. Some NPAs began firing at the monster that now filled the basin as its two massive LM2500 gas turbines reversed the movement of the ship before it hit the wall. Two others of *Syren*'s crew began firing the .50 calibers near the stern once they were clear of the breakwater.

Under the withering fire from three sources, including two ships, the NPA began to retreat. At first it was one or two in their ranks, then it was five or six. Those who remained were gunned down. If any tried to get up, they were shot again. The Filipino sailors were especially attentive to ensure their terrorist enemies would never rise up against them again.

When the fighting was over, Castillo was carried off the ship by two of his sailors as he directed them to the headquarters hut. He emerged, hobbling until he reached the metal flag pole, which had miraculously survived the firefight. He clasped his sacred cloth to the lanyard and raised the flag of the Philippines.

FURNAS, SÃO MIGUEL, AZORES

"Can we discuss salary?" Golzari asked as he feigned sipping the Azorean tea lest something had been added to it. Another Filipina girl brought a plate of fresh fruit and placed it on the table without looking at either of them, then backed away in a forced sign of submission.

"How good are you, Mr. . . ."

"Kaveh."

"Ah, Mr. Kaveh."

Golzari didn't tell him that the name came from ancient Persian mythology. When he was a child, his father sang him to sleep with the story of Kaveh, who defeated a tyrant named Zahāk. Kaveh was also Golzari's real first name. Damien had been conferred on him when his family was in England. No one but his father's SAVAK guards knew it. In the waning days of the Shah's regime, Golzari's father had seen the coming revolution led by Ayatollah Khomeini, and Golzari's father probably hoped that, like the mythological Kaveh, Damien would also lead an uprising against evil authoritarians. It wasn't to be in Iran. The Islamic Revolution had proven too powerful. Golzari had to be satisfied with taking on petty tyrants. In this case, it was the captain of a ship implicating a powerful Chinese firm. Now, it meant eliminating this malicious French ex-pat who had enslaved these girls and arranging for the transfer of perhaps thousands of other trafficked children. But Golzari needed to do it at the right time, where either the guards were out of sight, or he convinced Belanger to hire him so he'd have direct solitary access to him.

Golazari reached for a fork to eat some pineapple chunks when he noticed the second guard near the guest house call into his radio. While Golzari was out of hearing distance, he watched as the guard tried again. The look on the guard's face was one of surprise, then he glanced at the guard next to Belanger as if confused by silence. The guard on top of the house moved from the back closer to the side.

"Something's wrong," Golzari said. "Something's wrong—the gate guard isn't answering."

"What?" Belanger asked as the closest guard eyed Golzari, wondering how he knew.

They heard two brief screams from the front of the house. It was the unmistakable sound of teenage girls' voices and then silence. The guard on the roof reappeared, falling backward until his body gave in and dropped over and onto the swimming pool patio near the kitchen. Then Golzari rose and pulled out his gun. The closest guard was professional enough to know that this was no coordinated move by Golzari. Whatever was happening in the front had Golzari just as concerned as the guard.

"Get behind me," the guard said to Belanger, who cowered behind him. The second guard on the side began to raise his weapon when his skull exploded. The last guard and Golzari stood side by side, the guard focused on the side where the second guard had just been killed and Golzari to the other in case there were two or more attackers.

"I suggest we get to some cover," Golzari told the guard.

"We need to get back to the house. There's a safe room there. Cover us," he told Golzari as he took Belanger's thin, hairy arm and made his way to the other side of the pool. A shooter emerged from where the second guard had been killed. He pointed the gun at the last guard, who fired a millisecond too late. His shot went wide as the gunman took out the guard with one shot in his chest and the second in his neck. Belanger, horrified, froze in his place, not knowing what to do.

Golzari recognized the gunman. He had first seen a glimpse of him in Hadiboh on Socotra Island off of Yemen. Golzari had chased down a murdering Somali, Abdi Mohammed Asha, who had killed then-Deputy Secretary of State John Dunner's son. Golzari had been there for the college kid's autopsy in Antioch, Maine. He remembered the kid's teeth, green from chewing khat. Golzari tracked Asha from Maine to London to Yemen. He had him in his hands. He got him to admit which high US official had hired him. He was about to arrest him when Asha's brains blew onto Golzari's face and shoulders from a well-placed shot by a Chinese sniper. It was the only open case he had left behind at the Diplomatic Security Service. Golzari got Qin's name in Sri Lanka and had tried to find him since. Now Qin was standing forty feet away, about fifteen paces if they'd been dueling.

"Jianyu Qin!" Golzari shouted at the man. And then Golzari realized why the sniper was here in the Azores. Belanger was a liability and Hu Tao had sent Qin here to clean up the mess. Qin probably realized the same of Golzari as he smirked and pointed his weapon at Belanger. Golzari pivoted as he wouldn't be denied again. Belanger's small body jerked back as Qin shot him in the chest, and Golzari dead-aimed another in his left temple, though no one could tell whose shot was first. Golzari and Qin's target fell on the edge of pool, as his blood turned the water pink.

Both gunmen now turned toward each other, each paying careful attention to any non-verbal communication their body would signal. Golzari wondered how many tens of thousands of rounds Qin expended training to be one of the best shots in the business. Stark had been good, because of his training for the Olympics, but he had a bullish luck to his shots, not the refined precision of someone like Qin or Golzari. Golzari knew Qin had been a sniper in China, but today he had a handgun. Based on the three guards he took out just now, he was proficient. Snipers were precise; nevertheless, they required patience and timing to ensure the target was in the crosshairs. Golzari remembered his childhood training with his father's SAVAK personal guards. The handgun was different, they told him. It required a different type of personality. And Golzari was certain he'd fired handguns more than Qin.

Golzari pulled the trigger as Qin pulled his. Qin's head whipped back as the bullet entered the center of his forehead and took out part of the back of his skull. Golzari's finger was still on the trigger when his torso caved in and backward. He fell to his knees and dropped his gun. He heard more screams that seemed to fade away. Golzari cupped his hands and held his stomach, desperately trying to stop the bleeding. Golzari had gone for Qin's head while Qin, less precise with the handgun, went for the easier and larger target of Golzari's torso.

They were all dead. The whole network of the bastards who put children like this to serve their petty, egotistical desires or to work cheap restaurants like that in Paris.

"Kaveh," he tried to say, hoping his father would know he lived up to his name in part.

There was more he wanted to do, more books he wanted to read, more museums to explore, more concertos to play, more time to . . .

POBLACIÓN I HARBOR

A dinghy transported Makarov and Toni from the fishing vessel to the shore as the ship disappeared in the ocean, hidden among hundreds of other trawlers. A more appropriate pleasure craft awaited them on the dock along with their contact.

"We heard the news," Makarov said to Bitin. "The attack force was defeated."

"Yes, and the Chinese warships have turned back," she said stoically. "They could not afford to alienate the new Philippine government as well as the others. It was the lynchpin, as we feared."

"What about Ernesto?" Makarov asked.

Bitin shook her head. She had watched the battle unfold from the eastern hill. She watched him fall along with hundreds of others.

"We need to return to Hong Kong," Toni said.

"Are you serious? This mission failed," Makarov noted.

"It wasn't because of anything we did or failed to do," Bitin argued. "It was a Black Swan. Had the media not discovered the trafficking operation, the governments would not have been pushed to act or reverse their action. But you go. I need to remain here. The soldiers are all gone, but their families are still here in town. They have no way of returning to their island, and the Philippine government will come for them."

"They'll find you," Makarov said. "Hu would want you back in Hong Kong. There's nothing you can do with an army that no longer exists. There are other fights."

Bitin thought about it and looked around as her people scurried about after reports that the Philippine Army was coming to Balabac.

"You're right," Bitin said as she tossed her gray and black digital uniform in a nearby trash can.

THE WHITE HOUSE

"We need to find someone to administer the oath of office," the Chief of Staff told those present in the Rose Garden when they received the news from Bethesda. They were still stunned, especially CJ Sumner, whose mentor had died of a subdural hemorrhage in a freak accident. One of the associate justices of the Supreme Court was due to arrive momentarily and Vice President—Acting President—Susan Szukalski would be sworn in as president of the United States.

CJ wanted to vomit. Someone she admired, respected, and even thought of as a second father was gone from this earth. No more conversations, no more walks.

"CJ," the Acting President called as the rest of the group walked toward the cabinet room. Sumner slowed her gait even more, still deep in thought.

"Thank you for reaching out to the Philippine general and to our partners. We were lucky a few of them returned to the exercise. I understand they'll be pulling into Singapore tomorrow. Yes, we were damn lucky."

"We had help," Sumner said, trying to hold back her thoughts about President Dunner.

Szukalski did not respond to that.

"I know this is soon, so we'll wait a few days to announce it, but I would like your resignation. I'd like to bring in my own people. I understand you personally arranged for a weapons purchase from that security company a few years ago and that you also were responsible for arranging their work with President Quinta's administration. I'm not comfortable with your ties to a mercenary company. It's not a good look for my administration."

Sumner was about to rebut her, but Szukalski was about to become the president, and everyone in the cabinet served at her leisure.

"You understand, Ambassador."

"Yes, yes I do," Sumner responded. Szukalski had already turned, not caring for an answer. "I serve at the pleasure of the president," she whispered to herself.

USS *GEORGE H.W. BUSH*

"Hello, Uncle Mike," Vice Admiral Rossberg said to the face on the screen.

"I spoke to the Chief of Naval Operations. I want you to know that he'll be giving you a medal for the steadfast leadership of your ships in the face of China's aggression," the older gentleman said in his heavy Brooklyn accent.

"Thank you for letting me know. I guess we really know who our friends are."

"Yes, and we'll get you back here to Washington soon. We're going to make sure you get that fourth star. I'll tell your mother you look well."

With that, the signal dropped from the Chairman of the Senate Armed Services Committee.

HONG KONG

Tao Hu buried his head in his hands at the head of the conference table. The spacious room on the thirtieth floor had one of the finest views of Hong Kong harbor and Kowloon just a ferry ride away. He was alone when he heard the smoked glass double doors open.

"It's time, Hu," said his now-former colleague who was backed by a two-man security team. Hu stood and looked upon the view one last time from the company he had built from nothing over the past three decades. Legitimate commerce was a front for a variety of the party's activities around the globe. Hu had once controlled politicians, leaders of countries, key business executives.

"What happens now? Will my family be cared for?"

"The president recognizes your work. You've had great success here, but with the failures in Yemen, Sri Lanka, and now a very visible and embarrassing blunder in the Philippines, the president has to hold someone accountable, especially now that he's been elected unanimously for a third term. We are not going to kill you."

Hu turned to him. This was unexpected.

"Why are you letting me live?"

"You still have connections and ideas. You can still serve us and redeem yourself. You are being sent to Dalian."

"Is there a detention facility there?"

"No, there is a new building in Dalian next to our naval academy. You are going to redeem yourself. You will lead that project. It is called PLA/N C."

EPILOGUE

Syren was back in Manila Bay, where she had transported Commander Castillo and the surviving sailors. General Eduardo Fuentes, currently the head of the Philippine government, met the ship when it was pier side. In a short ceremony with the sailors in formation, he awarded Castillo the Medal of Valor for protecting the base and saving the island. Fuentes also recognized the work of Connor Stark and Highland Maritime Defense with the Philippine Legion of Honor, given to individuals from other countries for extraordinary service. In brief remarks, Fuentes noted that the security professionals stood side by side with their Philippine Navy counterparts and partners through one of the greatest tests faced by their country.

Following the ceremony, Castillo thanked Stark. "I hope we work together again, Connor. It was a pleasure and an honor."

"The honor was mine, Renaldo. I . . . I just wish we'd found Santos. She was our only loss and I think she was the best of us."

Castillo nodded in agreement.

"I understand she was personally recommended for this assignment by someone very senior in our government. I'll contact her family. All they found was her uniform in a trash can. We'll send more patrols to search for her . . ." Stark realized Renaldo was about to say "body." Castillo realized that and then dropped the matter.

"Until we meet again, Captain Stark," Castillo said, extending his hand.

"I look forward to that, Commander Castillo," he replied as he grasped the other man's hand.

Stark returned to his cabin and, since they weren't due to get underway for another day and return home to Maine, he opened his cabinet and broke out a bottle of Talisker.

He picked up the internal comms link.

"Jay, why don't you join me since we're off duty."

"On my way," Warren said, back to his jovial self.

Stark went through a mental list of everything he needed to do before the ship got underway. There were minor repairs, refueling, resupplying. And calls. He reached Jaime Johnson on the *Minerva*, which had made it safely to port. She thought it best that they return home together. Then he remembered Damien Golzari had called his firm a few days before. Stark hadn't spoken to his sparring partner and friend in months.

"Comms, Captain."

"Comms here, sir."

"A few days ago, Mr. Golzari called the headquarters. Can you connect me to his number?"

"Yes, sir. Stand by."

Stark took two whisky glasses from the cabinet and poured a healthy share of Talisker for Warren and him to enjoy and discuss how to improve the ship. He untied his boots and slowly removed them as each dropped with a light thud on the carpeted deck. He pushed aside a history book about the Dreyfus Affair that an old college friend had sent him to make room on the desk for the drinks. A stack of papers awaited him in his inbox, most requiring signatures to authorize purchases or travel orders. He sat down, closed his eyes, and took a deep breath, then another to clear his thoughts for a brief respite.

Warren knocked and entered with a bag of chips in one hand and a can of peanuts in the other.

Stark raised an index finger, asking Jay to wait a second as the bear of a man leaned against the door frame.

"Oliver, this is the captain," he called on the phone. "Any luck calling Mr. Golzari?"

"I'm sorry, Captain. I keep trying. The line's dead."

ACKNOWLEDGMENTS

This is the third published Connor Stark novel and the first in the series with Sunbury Press. I am deeply grateful to publisher Lawrence Knorr for restarting this series. The first two books, *The Aden Effect* (2012) and *Syren's Song* (2015) have been revised and will be retitled as second editions to be released in the future. For those who read the first two books and asked me why it took so long to write the third, I took time off to research and write my doctoral dissertation. My advisor strongly recommended that I stop writing novels in order to finish the dissertation which was later published as "On Wide Seas: The U.S. Navy in the Jacksonian Era" (University of Alabama Press, 2021.) Lawrence's team at Sunbury have been extraordinary to work with. I am especially indebted to Sarah Peachey for her sharp eye. I have written enough books and articles in my career to know this one truism: a writer is only as good as their editor. Thanks also to Taylor Berger-Knorr and Crystal Devine.

There were a number of people along this particular journey who contributed much, each in their own way. While I took time off from work to write this, I found solitude in several places, each of which inspired me. The journey for this novel began in a little village on the coast of Maine where I am grateful to Steve Thomas and Evy Blum, Charlie and Maureen Cragin, and Dyan Redick. In another state, I found a different body of water to inspire me. Thank you to Don and Lynn Henry for their friendship, wisdom, knowledge, humor, and hosting me at the lake. My next stop was at a three-hundred-year-old farmhouse and the hospitality, conversation, and friendship of Chris and Ashley O'Keefe.

Charles Heller, host of a radio show, first suggested the idea of a counter-drone weapon to me in 2015 when I was on his program. The name of the Bola came from his friend Eb Wilkinson. I am grateful that both permitted me to include this concept in the story years before such technology seemed more probable. "Big Al" Zalewski provided more technical support than I can recall, and I value a now decades-long friendship with this former colleague. Michael Piasecki is President and Founder of DPI in Philadelphia. He gave me a tour of his drone company to help me understand the history and capabilities of various platforms that he has developed. Mark Tempest, a blogger, co-host of the Midrats program on Blogtalkradio.com, retired captain, and continuing to practice as a maritime lawyer helped guide me through the nuances of international law and the sea. Ryan Thomas Riddle, a fellow—but far more knowledgeable—Trekkie, kindly helped with initial questions about the Philippines. There is no greater tour de force in the Navy's wargaming community than Sebastian Bae at the Center for Naval Analyses. Through his inspiration, I purchased poster boards, ship counters, and meeples to game out some of the events in this novel.

Blake Herzinger, Evy Blum, Matt Hipple, and blogger CDR Salamander read an early draft of this book and provided important feedback. Dr. Jerry Hendrix is one of the foremost naval thinkers today. His words and work continue to make me reflect on how I can apply some concepts to the Connor Stark series regarding the nation's greatest maritime challenges. John Konrad's site, gcaptain.com, is always helpful in understanding the non-naval side of the ocean through reporting on shipping companies and other kinds of maritime activity as are the comments and YouTube videos of Dr. Sal Mercagliano, another expert in shipping. I am also indebted to former co-authors Patrick Cullen and Chris Rawley. Our work years ago on non-state actors, private security companies, and environmental activists on the high seas continues to frame this fiction series. Matt Bucher also helped me understand one of the technical issues in the book. He proves again that once a shipmate, always a shipmate.

Finally, thank you to you—the readers.

ABOUT THE AUTHOR

CLAUDE BERUBE wrote his doctoral dissertation on the US Navy during Andrew Jackson's presidency. He was a 2004 Brookings Institution LEGIS Fellow and a 2010 Maritime Security Studies Fellow at The Heritage Foundation. He has worked on political campaigns, as an analyst and team leader at the Office of Naval Intelligence, as a national security fellow in the US Senate, and as a defense contractor for Naval Sea Systems Command and the Office of Naval Research.

He has taught as both a military officer and civilian at the United States Naval Academy where his courses included American Government, Terrorism, Campaigns & Elections, Intelligence & National Security, Maritime Security Challenges, Naval History, and Emergent Naval Warfare. An intelligence officer in the US Navy Reserve, he has served on active duty assignments in Europe and Guantanamo Bay and deployed to the Persian Gulf in 2004–2005 with Expeditionary Strike Group Five. He is a contributing editor at War on the Rocks. He is the host of the naval history podcast "Preble Hall."

www.ingramcontent.com/pod-product-compliance
Lightning Source LLC
Chambersburg PA
CBHW011425010726
47494CB00011B/2506